THE STONE CROWN SERIES

Dragon Connection

Dragon Quest

Dragon Freedom

Ava Richardson is a pen name created by Relay Publishing for co-authored Fantasy projects. Relay Publishing works with incredible teams of writers and editors to collaboratively create the very best stories for our readers.

Cover Design by Joemel Requeza

www.relaypub.com

AVA RICHARDSON

DRAGON
CONNECTION

THE STONE CROWN SERIES
BOOK ONE

BLURB

One crown can unite them—or destroy them all.

The three kingdoms lie splintered, their aging dragon riders content with stories of glorious battle victories. But a new evil creeps across the land. Inyene, a powerful noblewoman of the Northern Kingdom, plunders valuable resources to power mechanical dragons in her quest to gain a foothold in the Middle Kingdom. From there she will ascend the High Throne, once again uniting the realms under a single crown.

For the wearer of the Stone Crown can wield unlimited power—*if* it can be found.

Narissea has spent a quarter of her sixteen years slaving away in the mines, accused of a crime she didn't commit. When word reaches her of the horrors assailing her village, Narissea knows she must act despite the risk. Already her arm is scarred with four brands signifying previous escape attempts. If she's unsuccessful in her fifth, it will mean death.

But her life forever changes when she stumbles upon an injured dragon, discovers an ancient shrine, and learns the true purpose behind Lady Inyene's mechanical abominations.

Now, Narissea has only one choice: gain Inyene's trust and find a way to thwart her plans, even if it means sacrificing that which she desires most of all.

Her freedom.

MAILING LIST

Thank you for purchasing 'Dragon Connection'
(The Stone Crown Series Book One)

I would like to thank you for purchasing this book. If you would like to hear more about what I am up to, or continue to follow the stories set in this world with these characters—then please take a look at:

AvaRichardsonBooks.com

You can also find me on me on
www.facebook.com/AvaRichardsonBooks

Or sign up to my mailing list:
AvaRichardsonBooks.com/mailing-list

CONTENTS

CHAPTER 1
WIND & BREAD

I'm going to remember this day for the rest of my life, I thought to myself.

This was the day that I could no longer remember the gentle caress of the Soussa winds when I closed my eyes. Instead, as I blinked back the tears, all I could feel was the oppressive heat of the tunnel that I was trapped in, and the bite of the unyielding rocks.

And Dagan's latest gift to me.

My lip curled in disgust and hatred at the thick mark of the brand on my upper right forearm. The three others before it had faded from an ugly red to a darker brown. They had stopped hurting. Sorta. Four branding marks for four failed attempts at escape from my prison beneath the world. There was space for just one more at the very top of my arm – but that would also be my last, wasn't it?

Dagan Mar was the 'Chief' as he liked to call himself – which was just a fancy term for slave master. All of the others here called him much more colorful names behind his back. I didn't even think that Tozut, which was Daza for horse-dung, was a good enough term for him. He wasn't a tall man, but he was wiry and strong. Fair-skinned like the rest of those Middle Kingdomers, and he seemed to like inflicting punishments on all of us tribespeople brought here to the mines of Masaka.

And what for? I bit my bottom lip to stop myself from screaming in rage. Sometimes the overseers and the Chief waved papers and said things like 'Bonds' or 'Crimes' – although I never committed any crime or signed any bit of Torvald paper!

I had been twelve when I had been brought here. Old enough to remember my mother, Yala, her rough sense of humor that hid a gentle heart. *I wish I could hear you make jokes about the old men of the tribe again,* I thought with a sudden hunger. She was the Imanu, or wise-woman, of the Souda tribe – which meant the Daza of the Western Winds. I was old enough to come here remembering the plains. The smell of the grasses. The caress of the Soussa winds. Bright-colored bolts of cloth rippling in an endless sky.

But all of those memories were starting to fade, weren't they? I tried not to cry as I sat in the dark. The colors weren't as bright in my mind as they used to be, and the scents of the grassland flowers not so strong.

And now I couldn't even remember the Soussa winds anymore. I wondered how long it would take me to forget everything else that came before this place, as well.

"Narissea!" my name went down the line, passed from one Daza mouth to the next. Each of us were spread out along the narrow tunnel that was barely taller than we could crouch, and each of us were working at the holes we had painstakingly driven into the hard rocks.

"Nari?" My name changed, becoming smaller as it came out of the lips of my neighbor. That was broad-shouldered Oleer of the Metchoda tribe – the Daza of the Open Places. He was a few years older than me, and had been taken when he had been older, perhaps fifteen? We didn't get much time to talk given the back-breaking work, but he sometimes told me stories of the plains.

"They call them the Empty Plains, but they were never empty, were they," he would chuckle. "I've seen horses, deer, gazelle, wild lion, condors. I even saw a flight of dragons heading westwards, once!" He had been trying to cheer me up, I think. I told him he was making it up. Dragons were rare.

"Nari – the overseer wants you," Oleer was saying, and in the flickering light of the stub of our tallow candles I could see his grimace.

"What does that fat old toad want?" I muttered back. I was in a foul mood today. Hardly surprising, given that my hands were raw from trying to hack and prod at the rock in front of me with my iron bar and my arm was still oozing and sore.

"It's only the overseer," Oleer offered gently. For all his size, he had a soft voice. "At least it's not Dagan."

"Tozut," the next Daza slave up from Oleer spat just at hearing our 'chief's' name. That would be Rebec, smaller than me. She had a scar running from her temple to her jaw from when West Tunnel Two had

collapsed. She was one of the Daza who had been here the longest and was well into her twenties.

"Ore Count!" This time, I could hear the guttural bark of the overseer from somewhere beyond me in the dark. I'd never bothered to learn his name, if he had ever shared it with any of us. "Ore Count for Narissea!"

"Oh great," I muttered, as Oleer shared a sympathetic look. "What's that, third time today?"

They were picking on me of course, their next favorite past time after branding me.

"It's because you tried to escape this moon just gone," Rebec called down the line. "You get a brand and an Ore count, and *we* all get half rations!" She was like that. She didn't mean to be nasty but being down here for so long must have done something to her heart.

I can't let myself end up like her, I promised myself. *I have to remember the Soussa wind on my face.* If I could just hold on to one memory – just one – then I might be alright. I might be able to keep my heart beating in my chest.

"Narissea! Get out and get up here!" The overseer bellowed down our small tunnel, and his words echoed and repeated. "Get out. Get out. Get out."

"I'm coming!" I shouted, then, quieter, "Tell him I'm coming, will you?" I told Oleer, who passed on my message as I gave one last crack with my iron bar, slid it out of the hole, and shoved my arm in its place. My carry-basket beside me was woefully light – the seam we were working on was tough as it was, and with all of these Ore

4

Counts I'd already had this shift I'd barely managed to make any headway.

But there, at the end, was a chunk of rock that was loose in my hand. *Aha!* It wouldn't be much, but it would help avoid any further troubles. I yanked my arm backwards—

For it not to move at all.

"Oh, come on!" I hissed. I was stuck, my arm pinned down in the hole, wedged between the teeth of the protruding rocks. I pulled again, but my arm only gave a little, and I hissed as my skin scraped.

"Nari! What are you doing?" Oleer turned back to face me, and then saw the predicament I was in. "Oh, wait," he shuffled forward to my spot, reaching out to grab ahold of my branded arm.

"No! I don't want to break my arm, thank you very much!" I snarled in pain and saw Oleer's face look as though I had just slapped it. I was going to have to apologize to him for that, I berated myself.

"Narissea! Are you disobeying me!" the words of the overseer barked and echoed down the tunnel towards me. "Disobey. Disobey. Disobey." I heard a snicker from Rebec, which only made me feel worse.

"I can do it, just everyone give me a moment," I said, wedging my cloth-bound foot against the wall and pulling. "Argh!" It felt like my shoulder was going to pop out of its socket, but I was rewarded with a *shlooop* as my arm scraped backwards, before getting caught again.

Only this time it was my fist that was causing the blockage, hanging onto that big bit of ore.

"Nari!" Oleer said in alarm.

I had a choice. It would take too long to try and break it down with my iron bar, so I had to get it out by hand. But with the overseer shouting, I had to either drop the rock and leave it or try and break my fingers to get it out of the hole. *Drat.* It was no choice really. Even if I broke my fingers the overseer and Dagan Mar would still expect me to work. That was the kind of people they were, after all. *And* they would probably give me extra shifts or dock my food rations just for having the temerity to get injured.

"Fine. Whatever." I grumbled, dropping the ore and removing my shaking and battered arm back to grab my carry-basket with its tiny number of rocks sitting at the bottom. Oleer must have seen my look of misery, as he quickly dipped into his own woven carry-basket and deposited a heavy lump into the bottom of mine.

"Here. Just don't tell anyone," he said, not waiting for my thanks as he turned back to the rock face and resumed work.

"Thanks," I muttered anyway as I clambered and squeezed past the line of my fellow prisoners, back towards the waiting ire of the overseer. When I got back, I would have to give him the rock I'd left behind and hope it would repay his kindness.

"Hm," the overseer said. He was a large, older man, easily twice my size in every direction, with a balding head and a thick set of leather and glass goggles over his eyes. We stood in one of the main avenues that speared down through the mines of Masaka, where it was wide enough to stand up straight and walk three or four abreast.

I relished the moment of luxury as I stretched out my fingers and arms.

"Not bad, I suppose," he had to mutter as he hefted my haul in one hand. "But not any good, either!" he ended with a snap as he dumped my woven and frayed basket onto the cart next to several others, before pulling on the rope that extended from the iron ring of the cart up the passageway. There was an answering jangle of a distant bell, and the cart slowly started to creak forward on wooden wheels. There was a treadmill up there, where a couple of my fellow tribespeople would be endlessly walking as they pulled or lowered the carts up and down the length of this place.

And why all this effort? It was for a woman called Inyene, we had been told – although I had never met her, nor known any slave who had. No one except Dagan Mar, if he was to be believed. He said Inyene owned this patch of highlands – although I didn't understand how anyone could own a mountain at all, that was as absurd as saying that you owned the air you breathed!

Whatever. This woman Inyene wanted iron brought up and out of *her* mountain, and so here I was.

But that wasn't all that she wanted.

"You're to go Up." The overseer jerked a callused thumb after the cart. "Special orders from the Chief himself."

"What?" I said, appalled. Every one of us knew precisely what 'going Up the mountain' meant. It was possibly the most dangerous work that any of us could do. "But our shift must be ending soon, by the time I get up there." I started to protest. I could see a few meters away the large collection of cylinders that made up the Work Clock.

It had something to do with bags of sand and ticking rings of metal, but I didn't understand it. Anyway – I could clearly see under the light of the oil lamps that the large bronze pointer hand was *definitely* not far off a full circle.

That meant that the bell would ring, and the shift would change over.

"It's not ending for you though, is it?" the overseer croaked with an almost-laugh. "Special orders I said. Now go on, get!" He aimed a smack for the top of my head, but even in my exhausted state I was too quick for him and I jumped back. I didn't even bat an eyelid at his attempt to hit me – this was just another daily occurrence for those of us unlucky enough to find ourselves down here.

"But what if I collapse up there without any dinner?" I called to him as I backed away. It was true. I would miss my next scheduled meal.

"For goodness' sake!" the overseer growled, but he plucked a skin of fresh water from one of the stationary carts and threw it at me, then tore a chunk off the round of bread and lobbed it at my face. I managed to duck that one too, and when I recovered the dusty bit of loaf, I realized that he had 'given' me the bit that was dusted with white and green mold.

"Wow, thank you so much, toad," I muttered under my breath.

"What did you say to me, you little—" the overseer shouted.

"Gotta go sir, special orders!" I called back and jogged up the tunnel after the creaking cart before he could decide to throw any bits of rock at me this time.

CHAPTER 2
STONE & SCALES

"You!" The shout sent icicles down my back. I had just managed to emerge from the Main Entrance to the Masaka mine complex, and the whole dirty, dusty, smelly horror of Inyene's work-camp was spread out before me.

"Nari!" the voice bellowed, and I wondered if I could ignore it as I ducked my head a bit lower, stuffed my moldy bread into my vest, and hurried along the wide track that led past the turning treadmills and the wooden cranes. The workcamp was mostly built in the natural bowl of the canyon, but there were higher levels that had been cut into the rock, on which stood the ramshackle wood and stone houses that belched smoke, busy tanning the leather or smelting the tools we used day in, day out.

Below me in the canyon was the majority of the buildings however – from the long wooden dormitories where we slept to the tall guard huts on stilts that overlooked the fences. And out there in the distance, above us all and on the banks of one sweeping arm of the

9

canyon, was Inyene's keep – a yellowing stone structure with towers and turrets, and lush greenery terraced around it.

Ugh, I groaned, as there was the sharp *thock!* of something biting the stone path a few meters ahead of me, sending a spray of rock dust.

I'd thought I'd managed to feign ignorance from my caller, but there was no such luck

It was a crossbow bolt. That pig had *actually* fired a crossbow bolt at me! I halted and looked around with a very real sense of trepidation.

"When I call your name, I expect to be answered. You got that, you little whelp of a girl?" shouted the chief of the mines, none other than Dagan Mar himself. He was lurching towards me from the lower level cut into the rock, waving that ridiculous little crossbow thing that he carried around. It was barely the size of his hand, but he menaced us all with it as if it were as large as a battle-ax.

Dagan Mar was getting old, I considered as I dropped to my knees, head bowed in the traditional mode of supplication that all of us slaves had been taught before their Chief.

"Better," the man lurched and lunged. He wore part leather armor whose ties were pulled open at the chest to reveal his pale skin, scattered with chest hair that was wiry and long. He wasn't as old as the Elders of the Souda that my mother used to make fun of. I imagined he was somewhere north of his fourth decade, but his years of being horrible had clearly aged him.

There was something wrong with his hip, I think – and although I didn't know what it was, I hoped it was due to him being horrible to someone a lot bigger and meaner than he thought himself to be.

"The Oversee gave you my order, did he?" Dagan said, toying with the child's crossbow in his hands as if he were considering whether to reload and fire it at me again. He was actually a good shot, I had to grudgingly admit. The Daza people were deemed good with their short bows and thrown javelins – I remember regular contests and practices out by the Silver Fish Lake – but I had never seen anyone shoot the birds from the sky, one-handed, as Dagan did.

So he wasn't actually trying to kill me, I realized. Just scare me. What a surprise.

"Answer me, girl!" Dagan shouted. He was that kind of man. Why talk, when you could shout?

"Yes, Chief," I forced myself to say his title.

"Up the mountain. You know what you have to do. Where's your carry-basket? Lost it, have you? Thrown it away?" Dagan barked at me.

I cast a glance to where the last cart was slowly being wheeled to the Loading Ground, where other Daza from various tribes were busy hauling each carry-basket and emptying them into the back of another, bigger sort of cart.

Pick up rocks. Put down rocks. Move rocks. The sheer monotony of it all would be enough to kill me alone, and that wasn't even accounting for the injuries we sustained doing it, or the neglect and abuse we were subjected to.

"No, Chief, it's—" I started to explain that the overseer had taken it off me.

"I don't want to hear it!" Dagan hissed. "Get another. A good strong one. I want it full of scales by nightfall!"

"Yes, Chief," I nodded my head. Scales. That was the other thing that Inyene wanted. And not just any scales. Not the skins of the rock snakes or lizards or even the stonedogs! No. Inyene, our powerful and mighty leader, wanted *dragon* scales.

"And you're on the night shift in Western Tunnel One tonight, too," Dagan said with a leer.

What!? I had to bite my tongue to keep from exclaiming. He must have seen my look of appalled shock, as his thin-lipped smile only grew wider in his chiseled face.

"Maybe tomorrow, after three shifts in a row, you won't be so eager to try and run out on your debt!" he snapped at me. He meant my attempts to escape of course. The only thing was – I didn't remember owing him or Inyene anything.

"What do you say?" He leaned a little lower to make sure that I couldn't avoid his glaring, stupid little eyes.

"Yes, Chief, sir." I bobbed my head. "Can I go now?"

Our Chief straightened up, satisfaction and pride pouring from every line of his ugly body. "No. One last thing." He gave a shrill whistle, and there was the pound of booted feet coming up from the Loading Area. More of Inyene's guards, no doubt – what were they going to do? My stomach turned over. Give me a couple of black eyes for daring to exist?

But this time there were no punches, kicks, or nasty little shoves from the burly men and women that Inyene employed. Instead, a set of shackles were clamped to my feet, and, even as I protested, they were hammered shut with a small metal bar. I had about a meter of heavy chain between my ankles – which was going to make clambering the Masaka mountain an absolute *joy.* My heart plummeted.

"And just in case you get any bright ideas about wandering off into the wilds alone, you won't get very far like that now, will you?" Dagan laughed.

He's trying to kill me. He's actually trying to kill me, I thought with a sick sensation in my stomach. Only I'd never seen him outright kill any of the Daza slaves before. Perhaps Inyene wouldn't let him. Probably only because she needed us carting bits of rock and finding scales.

But it was clear as the skies overhead that I would be lucky indeed if I managed to make it up the mountain and back again.

Past the outer palisade wall and a long trudge up the unforgiving rocks, the gray reach of Masaka Mountain rose into the heavens above me like some kind of giant. The skies were high and blue, and it would have almost been a nice day were it not for the fierce sun – and the heavy drag and rattle of the chains around my ankles.

Dagan is such a—I couldn't finish the thought.

Words failed me. I hated the way he treated all of us, like his personal property. And I hated the way he made me feel, angry and resentful all the time. *Just like Rebec.* I shook my head, letting the fresh mountain winds tug at my long black hair. It was knotted and tangled, and

I reached up to tease it through my fingers as I trudged. Mother would never think of allowing me to go out without brushing and binding my hair.

Enough. I told myself, sternly. *Don't think about it. Think about what is in front of you. Think about the dragon scales that you have to collect.*

And think about where my next escape attempt was going to be.

The work camp was already just a child's toy behind me by the time that the sun had crossed the three-quarter point. I only had a few hours of afternoon left. I was already high up on the slopes of Masaka, and I could see its larger sister mountains starting to crowd on either side of me.

The north creek had been my last attempt. I turned to survey the small runnel of water that scraped up the north face of Masaka. But that had ended in a sheer waterfall. I had been tracking around it when one of the camp scouts had spotted me and hauled me back down for my latest branding.

"So, not that way then," I sighed.

I'd tried heading south across the front of Masaka on my first two attempts – the slopes were gentler that way – but they were also much more open for Dagan's eagle-eyed scouts and their telescopes. I wondered if one of them was watching my progress even now, chuckling at how I had to shuffle and stumble with these heavy shackles.

Which left... I looked up the slope I was following. It ended at the face of a cliff, with tumble-down rocks and scrubby mountain trees on either side. The mountain was wilder up there, with tall spires and stacks of ancient rocks jutting from the ground, as if this place had been torn apart a very, very long time ago.

Over the top of Masaka. That way was the Middle Kingdom of Torvald, wasn't it? It was the wrong direction to take to get back to the plains, which were due East – on the other side of Inyene's camp itself. But there was no way to hide in that direction. The land rolled gently from foothills to the long grasslands. Dagan's guards would pick up my movement from miles away.

"Ugh!" I kicked at the scree that scattered the slope. It was useless! My only hope had been to strike out westwards, into the wilds of the World's Edge Mountains (as the Torvaldites called them) and then loop back around, approach the plains of my foremothers from higher up or lower down. But every time I had tried that, I had failed.

"And what about Oleer and the others?" I said aloud. That was the next complication. My plan had been to forge a way ahead, find a route through the mountains for others to follow.

"Who am I kidding?" I stopped, reached down to pull at my shackles a little to stop them chafing my ankles so much. Just like my memories of the Soussa winds, were fading fast too.

It was then that I saw it. Something large and angular that reflected the light. Something I'd uncovered with my kick.

A dragon scale.

It was a shining black on its outer curve, while its inner was a lighter, bone-like cream. It was also large, nearly the size of my entire hand. The only imperfection I could make out was a series of small nicks and notches along one of the tear-drop edges. The dragon who had plucked it must be *very* fastidious, I thought! Or maybe it was just an old scale, like shed hair.

The black scales were rare – I had only ever heard of one girl finding a couple more than a year ago. Much more often they found the greens or the mottled ochre ones, all of which were far smaller than this. I didn't know if that made it more valuable, but it didn't feel brittle – there was still some spring to it, and when I tapped its outer edge against a rock, it felt sturdy and strong.

"What does Inyene wants with all of these, anyway?" I murmured as I hurriedly dropped it behind my head into the woven carry-basket on my back. It would take a long while to fill the basket, but I had until evening, didn't I?

Which isn't too far off, Nari, I told myself. The sun had sunk lower between the mountains – it went down early up here.

"Oh, tozut! " I swore as I picked up my pace and tried to remember what Mother had told me.

"The other animals are just like you and me. They have friends. Favorite places. Spots they go when they are tired, hungry, or injured," she had said. This had been on the night before my Testing – three days out in the wilderness with nothing but my wits to keep me alive. Every Daza went through it, and not every Daza came back.

"You find the signs and follow them. Where there is one, there will be another."

"Right," I turned my attention to the rocks and scrubby grasses around me and tried to remember the lessons my mother had taught me.

"Close your eyes." I did.

"Relax." That was much harder to do, especially as the wind was growing colder and was starting to make me shiver. And the fact that I had a heavy set of shackles attached to my feet. And that I was still hungry. And exhausted. And a slave for no reason whatsoever.

"Just breathe, Nari," I muttered to myself, allowing my lungs to fill with the biting-cold mountain air, and then letting it out slowly. In, out, in, out.

Right. *What do I hear?* The high whine of the winds. The rustle of the grasses and scrubby trees. *What do I smell?* The metal-like tang of rock, all around me.

And then something else. Right there, right on the edge of my abilities. It was something fragrant but also heavy, like the scent from one of the rarer bushes of the plains. I could still remember the squat, heavy bush had sap that almost smelled like a Trader's Frankincense. We children of the Western Wind had tapped and harvested it. But this scent was mixed with something acrid, like the charcoal from a day-old fire.

But there shouldn't be any of those bushes up here, should there? I opened my eyes for the final test. What do I see? There were the slopes of the Masaka mountain around me, now picked out in fresh detail after I had calmed and focused my mind. There was the flatter patch of rock and scree that I thought of as a 'path' that led up to the cliff.

And there was the claw-print.

It was obvious now that I had stopped to *really* look at my surroundings. The scree of small gray and yellowing rock chips had scattered across the 'path' in front of me in a natural spreading pattern. Apart from one place, where there was a slight depression in the gravel chips, and three deeper 'cuts' down into the softer brown earth below.

And it was big. The depression of the foot must have been almost the entire length of my hand and forearm together, and the three scrapes at the end – from the talons – were about one hand's breadth apart. There wasn't much of anything that could make that large of a print.

Well, anything other than a dragon that was.

So I had found a scale, and there was the print. The dragon with the black scales had definitely come this way. I picked up my feet and moved a little further towards the cliff, hoping that it was long gone.

Another one! Right there between two tumbled boulders, where it must have been scraped off, was another large black scale. Now that I really looked, I could even see the slight striations of scratch marks across the boulders. *A good scratching spot in the full sun,* I thought with a small smile. That would have been midday, wouldn't it? Hours and hours ago now.

I grabbed the next scale and continued my search in the wide bowl of broken rocks underneath the cliff, finding two more scales, and then a further few here and there. It looked as though the great beast had stopped to preen itself!

I was so overjoyed with my lucky find that it was only when a tumble of smaller rocks spilled from the slopes nearby that I realized that I wasn't alone – and in fact, I was being hunted.

Stonedogs!

Fear tore through me. Gone was my exhaustion and tiredness, to be replaced by the sudden need to *get away from here as fast as possible.*

The first of the creatures known to us as stonedogs was already padding slowly, warily, down the slope towards me. It was about half my size, about as large as one of the small mountain ponies that occasionally picked their way around Inyene's keep.

But that was where the resemblance ended. The stonedogs had skin like plates of rock that sighed as they moved. *How had I not heard it coming?* I cursed myself for being so enamored of the six black dragon scales that were even now sitting in the carry-basket on my back.

Stonedogs were the most fearsome predators of the World's Edge mountains – or at least, that was what the gossiping guards always claimed. They had squashed muzzles, and a set of four eyes, two large oval ones in the front like a wolf's, as well as two smaller ones that never closed on their temples. This was one of ways that made them so deadly – they could see all around themselves.

The first stonedog was the biggest. I heard a rasp of breath and the hiss of rocks as the 'plates' behind its ear-holes rose and flared, like a mane.

"N-nuh… *nice doggy?"* I took a step backward, my chain clanking between my feet.

The thing growled, a deep echoing rumble of a sound in the back of its throat – to be joined by the growls of two more, slightly smaller stonedogs padding down the slope, flanking it.

They were between me and the path down the slope. I couldn't go back that way. There was a cliff at my back, and the rise of the slope on the other side.

But a low growl told me another stonedog was approaching from *that* way, too.

"Predators exist to hunt. That was the story whispered into their blood at the Beginning." My mother's words fluttered up to me. Not comforting.

But they did help. Hunting things chase smaller things. That's what they do. As soon as I ran, that would trigger their hunting instinct, and I would be doomed.

"Easy, easy now," I heard myself say, my voice quavering as I slid my foot back across the rocky ground, and then the next foot.

No sudden movements. Don't give them an excuse.

With a thump, my ankle hit the rocky wall behind me. Oh no. I hadn't thought that I was that close. What was I going to do? I risked flicking a glance up to the cliffs around me – maybe there was a handhold, a ledge.

With a guttural bark, the bigger 'lead' stonedog jumped forward as soon as my head turned. Panic filled me.

I slammed one of my feet on one of the tumbled boulders at the base of the wall and jumped, my hands slapping the rock, sliding.

"Ach!" I had caught a handhold and was swinging my legs up just as there was a furious scrabbling beneath me, right from where my legs had been.

Oh no oh no oh no-

My heart beat in time with my panic as I hooked a foot onto a rock and exchanged hands for a higher hold, and then another. There was a deep, grating bark from beneath me and the snap of air against one of my calves. The lead stonedog was trying to leap up at me, and it was very close indeed.

With a growl of pain and frustration I pushed myself up on shaking legs, my fingers finding cracks and crevices in the cliff wall before my eyes did. *Just keep climbing, Nari. Don't stop climbing.*

But it was agony. The initial burst of energy had now given way to the limb-deadening sort of panic. I hadn't eaten enough. I hadn't slept enough.

"Pull, Nari – do you want to end up as dog food? Pull!" I could hear my mother berating me as I forced myself up higher, and higher still.

My efforts were rewarded by another of those deep guttural growls, only it didn't come from below me – it came from the side. *Huh?*

I looked over to see that one of the stonedogs had abandoned scrabbling at the base of the cliff to run back up the slope to my right, and this time it was pouncing and bounding through the broken rocks at the top.

"Oh, come on!" I hissed as I hung there, two thirds of the way up the cliff and now as stuck as a fly in a web. Or a girl on the face of a cliff.

"No point in wallowing. Survive first. Be sad later." That was another of my mother's favorite sayings. She had been using it to stop me thinking too much about a failure when hunting. If I had failed to make my shot, or the animal had run away too fast then there was no point in getting downhearted. What I had to do instead was to survive. To take another shot. To find another source of food.

Which in this case, translated as climbing in the *other* direction. I couldn't go right, and I couldn't go up – so I reached out to grab the next handhold that would swing me towards the left-hand slope.

Except a waiting, growling stonedog had just appeared there, too. I froze. What was I going to do?

Then the creature on my right gave a short, strange sort of sound. Almost like a whimper. Why was it making that noise – like it was uncertain or afraid?

Looking up, I saw that the stonedog was trotting nervously back down the slope, and the one on my left was doing the same. *What?* With a short, gruff bark, the heaviest one at the base of the cliff, along with its smaller companion turned tail and loped back down the slope, looking back over their shoulder at me.

Okay, I thought, confused. I thought predators lived for the hunt? Why would they stop before the chase was completed, the kill made? But then I noticed how the sky was taking on a pink and purple sort of hue. The sun was starting to set, and nightfall wouldn't be far off. Maybe that was why. Maybe the stonedogs were afraid of the dark? I had no idea, and it was hard to think of such strange and fearsome creatures being afraid of anything. But I wasn't about to turn down any good fortune.

My arms were shaking, and it was too far to go back down again to the floor. Instead, it would be wiser to finish my climb. Either way, I didn't want to go back down there just yet, where the Stonedogs had so recently tried to eat me.

With grunts and groans, I hauled my shaking and exhausted body up and over the top ledge of the cliff, to see that there was *another* rise beyond this one. It was crowned with outcroppings of rocks, creating a wide ledge on the top of the cliff, and with a large cave entrance right here.

And a whole heap of black dragon scales, looking like droplets of night on the floor.

"Ten, twelve, fourteen-fifteen-sixteen…" I couldn't believe my luck as I gathered the scales and added them into my total. It almost made up for the fact that the light had become a dull crimson burn, glowing through the mountain valleys like fire.

No, it definitely made up for it. I didn't care if I would be walking home in the dark. The stonedogs were scared of the dark, right? (At least, that is the only explanation I had). And even Dagan couldn't get mad with me when he got a look at all of these scales that I had managed to collect, could he?

But there were still a couple more, right in the mouth of the cave. I could see the last of the daylight glinting on them in the dark. I started walking over to gather them and then paused, as a strange feeling washed over me. My heart thumped, and the hairs stood up on the backs of my arms.

It was nothing. I was just spooked from my recent encounter with the stonedogs.

"It's only a cave," I muttered to myself. There are lots of caves in these mountains. I spent most of every day crawling through them, didn't I? I stepped forward into the dark.

Just as two large bronze eyes opened, and they were shot through with flecks of burning red.

CHAPTER 3
HOW TO TALK TO DRAGONS

"*S* *ssss…*" The dragon made a deep sighing sort of sound in its throat. Despite the fact that I was gazing into the eyes of a dragon – nothing else was that big – my first thought was:

It sounds like the Soussa winds in the long grasses…

But then with a snap, my senses came back to me. I was a sixteen-year-old standing in front of a dragon. And I had just been stealing its scales. I wasn't sure – but did dragons care if humans took their scales? Or was it like discarded clothes? Either way, I didn't want to insult a dragon.

"Don't eat me?" I whispered into the dark, dropping the two black scales that I had been holding and starting to step backwards very, *very* slowly.

The creature blinked, just as slowly. And when it opened its eyes again there seemed to be fewer flecks of crimson red this time, and more bronze-gold. I didn't know dragons could do that.

But then again, how much do I really know about dragons anyway? Only that there had been loads of them once upon a time, and that my mother had repeated the tales passed down by *her* Imanu of flights that had covered the sky, once.

But the dragons had faded, hadn't they? They said that even Torvald – once the greatest city in the world – had lost its dragons, leaving only these wild ones. The ones that didn't like humans. The ones that sometimes *ate* humans.

"Please, I'm only a slave. I don't even want to be here," I mumbled as I stepped back. I didn't think that the dragon could understand a word I said, but my mother had once told me that you should always talk in a low, calm voice to a wild beast.

Apparently, my voice wasn't very low and calming, as there was another sighing rattle of scales as the dragon moved.

"Aii!" I yelped in shock, springing back out of the way to the ledge – but in my fright I forgot my shackles, which pulled tight and made me trip, tumbling to the floor and spilling half the contents of my carry-basket all around me. Every fiber in my being told me to jump up and run – but I didn't, because there was now a very large, solid black dragon crouching on the ledge over my prone body.

I scrunched my eyes, unable to believe what was happening. Not to me. I had *plans.* I was going to escape. I knew how to survive in the wilderness. I was going to use those skills to get out of Masaka, to get help, to return and save—

But it didn't look like that was my fate right now, was it? Especially as there was a deep, resounding *huff* of hot air, laced with soot and something fragrant – that Frankincense scent again – that washed over me. The dragon had lowered its snout towards me, and I was sure at any moment it was going to pick me up between its massive teeth, toss me into the air, and gulp me down like a fish.

How could my life end like this? Suddenly, something catalyzed in my heart. It was the same spark of resentment and pride that made me remember who I was, and where I had come from. Maybe it was all of the pokes and prods and kicks from Dagan and his overseers that made me finally snap. It all just seemed so unfair.

"You are *NOT* going to eat me so easily!" I rolled over and screamed up at the beast, raising my finger and pointing at its snout. "I am a Child of the Western Wind! My mother is an Imanu of the Daza! And if you're going to gobble me up, you can at least do it with me looking straight at you!" I screamed at it, not really knowing what I was saying but at least wanting the creature to *know* who I was.

For someone to know who I was, in my final moments.

But then, the massive black dragon did something I did not expect. It drew back its mighty head on its long neck and chirruped at me. "Skree-ip?" It blinked several times, as if confused at what I was doing and why I wasn't screaming in terror. It looked at my pointing finger, and then looked at my face as if it was saying 'What?'

In the four years of being here at the Masaka mines, I had never once seen a dragon. I had never known that they were this big. This one had a long snout with nostrils at the end that flared like a horse's, over a maw that was filled with teeth as long as my arms. Its eyes were large, and, if I wasn't lying here underneath it I would have called them beautiful. They were intricate and patterned like lichen on a plain's boulder. From just in front of two large, ragged and torn ears swept back two brackets of horns.

If dragons are anything like deer, then that means it's a male. And a fully grown one at that.

And then came the bulk of its body. Large scales as big as the guards' shields, far larger than the hand-sized ones I had been picking up, spread out from its shoulders and down its arms, each one precisely overlapping the next. Its spine was marked by bony ridges, none of them as sharp as the horns on its head.

I couldn't take my eyes off of it as I marveled at the way that the scales grew smaller and seemingly more delicate as they swept down around the creature's belly. I saw the way that the fading light caught them and turned them indigo and viridian, like a crow's feathers.

But then, my eyes had to take in the thing's paws, which were huge and ended in gigantic talons like a bird of prey. The dragon was making absolutely no move to eat me, but it easily could have, any moment it wanted.

It was then that I saw how the great beast was holding its wings. One side was concertina folded up along its side like a bat, while the other was spread out awkwardly to one side and dragging on the floor.

It was wounded! Maybe that was why it hadn't eaten me. Maybe, just like me, it had more important things to think about than a human woman. Now that I had a chance to breathe and *really* look at it, I saw that its eyes were returning to a slightly covered, almost pained expression. It was leaning on the leg on the other side of its body, as if its entire left-hand side was tender.

How are you supposed to talk to a dragon? "Uh, sorry for shouting," I whispered, and gulped nervously, slowly moving to a crouch.

The black dragon pulled back a little more, leaning more heavily on one leg as it tried to fold its injured wing – and suddenly growled in pain.

"Woah!" The sound of an adult male dragon growling was like rattling shields and the roar of the mines' furnace works. It was terrifying. I froze, but I knew that it wasn't directed at me.

What can I do? I looked at the creature's awkwardly held wing, and then up at its half-lidded eyes. It regarded me steadily, and I felt my heart lurch in my chest with sympathy for the poor thing.

"Maybe you and me aren't so different." I muttered sadly. "You're injured, stuck up here in that cave when all you want to do is to feel the wind under your wings."

And there was me, stuck down in the mines, trying to remember the feel of the Soussa on my cheeks. It was a sort of freedom, wasn't it? Feeling the wind, knowing that you could follow it anywhere.

"But neither of us are free right now, are we?" I said sadly as I slowly shuffled to my feet. "Not yet, anyway," I murmured as I backed away from the dragon. "But we will. You'll see, you'll heal, and I'll escape."

I found a large rock with a scooped-out sort of depression in the middle. I very slowly took my water skin (with the dragon's eyes following my every movement as I did so) and poured its entire contents into the bowl. If the thing couldn't fly, then I don't know where it would get its water from, unless it was licking condensation from the walls of its cavern. I then put the hunk of bread beside it, doing my best to dust off the mold.

"I'm sorry, it's all I have. It's not very nice, but it's all they'll give me," I said sadly, as I gave the dragon one last look and looked to the spilled carry-basket on the floor. I could leave it – but that would only mean more beatings. I was already on my fourth brand, and manacled – what worse torture would Dagan do to me if I came back empty-handed? "I hope that you get better," I said awkwardly, slowly reaching down to snatch the handle of the carry-basket and drag it towards me. *Don't get mad, don't get mad.* I fervently prayed as I stepped back down to the slope, and back to the trail that led down to the mines.

I could feel the dragon's eyes watching me on my long, shuffling journey down – but strangely, I no longer felt frightened. I wasn't even scared of the stonedogs that were still somewhere out there in the night. If I had managed to survive encountering a dragon, then there really wasn't much else that would dare harm me in the mountainous night.

CHAPTER 4
TAMIN

"What time do you call this?" barked the very rotund figure of Toadie, my overseer. By the time that I had managed to hobble and shuffle back down the track to the edge of the great wooden wall, it was fully dark and there was already a team of people with torches standing by the open door.

"We were just debating whether to come out and find you!" Toadie swiped his hand towards my head – but I managed to duck it, as usual.

"Or whether to search for your body in the morning," chuckled one of the guards, leaning against the open gate with his big fur cloak wrapped around him, and smoking something that smelled foul out of a small clay pipe.

Yeah, they probably thought I'd been eaten by stonedogs or fallen down a gully or something, I thought. Not that any of them would care, would they?

Apparently, however – I realized that they would care, as the over-seer continued to shout at me. "You know if I lose one of you, *I'm* the one who gets my wages docked? Do you know how selfish you're being!?" he snapped, pointing back into the camp, where even the dull firelights of the dormitories in the canvas windows looked inviting right about now.

Not that I was going to see them close-up, was I? I was still supposed to go straight to a night shift down the mines after this. Despite everything that I'd been through. Maybe it was standing next to a dragon this evening that gave me the courage to turn to overseer Toadie and say, "Look, can I just get some sleep? I'll work double-shifts tomorrow."

"You what?" Toadie was having none of it as he angrily pointed at my feet, made me sit down as he knocked out the metal pins holding my shackles in place. It felt good not to be lugging them around.

"Special orders," the overseer continued. "You remember that? Are you not hearing a word I've been saying? *I'm* getting it in the neck thanks to you – you're going back down to Western Tunnel One right NOW!" He ended on a yell, but I was too tired to flinch or cower away from him this time.

I had shouted at a dragon. Don't forget that, I told myself.

"Here." I said, unslinging my carry-basket from my aching shoulders and dropping it on the ground in front of him, before turning on my heel and making for the mine entrance. Suddenly, all the rules and orders of Inyene's camp didn't seem as important as they had this afternoon. I was sure that I could pick up another empty carry-basket from the Loading Area.

"Hey, wait!" Toadie shouted behind me, but I kept walking. I heard his grumble and then a gasp as he must have looked at what I had collected. Maybe about eight or ten good and strong, large and shiny black dragon scales. Maybe other slaves had collected more scales than that on a work shift – but none of them had found the rarity or the quality that I had.

The overseer didn't shout at me again as I trudged the distance to the tunnels, grabbed a basket and a stub of tallow candle, and made my way down under the earth.

The mines felt different in the night. They always did, I knew – there were usually fewer of us working down here, and the overseers generally left us to our work as they didn't want to be running around in the dark when they could be slumbering in their guard posts.

With fewer workers, it meant that there was less noise. None of the big machines were being used – we didn't have the treadmill up top pumping water down the gutters to be used to heat up new schisms of rock. We didn't have the two-person stepping-machines that drove bellows or lifted and released the pounding iron weights.

But strangely, with the less sound *we* made, the more we could hear of the sounds that the mountains themselves made. As I trudged down the Main Avenue on my way to Western Tunnel One, I could hear the deep, resonant booming from somewhere far below.

Like the sea, one of the guards had called it – although I wouldn't know, never having seen a sea.

And then there was the smaller ticks, taps, and knocks that washed upwards through the tunnels in little bursts. The overseers claimed it was when one of our own echoes – a steel pole hitting a rockface – got lost, and then came back hours later.

But we slaves thought differently. I had been taught by my mother that sometimes the spirits of the Daza still walked the Plains. If the poor soul had gotten lost, or had died in battle, or their tribe had moved – or maybe these souls returned just to smell the plains' winds again. The knocks and sounds down below, to we Daza at least, were our brave lost kinsmen who must have died in the Mines, and could not find their way back out.

"What are you thinking about, Nari?" I shook my head and took a glug of the fresh water pouch I had been given at the guard station up top, along with my steel pole.

It had to be meeting the dragon, hadn't it? I thought. I was thinking about my life and the stories of the Plains. And about being trapped down here in the tunnels. And that there was a whole lot more to life than this.

I am going to get out of here, I promised myself as I found the stone-cut stairs that led up the side of a chasm to the entrance to Western Tunnel One. I thought about shouting at the dragon again, and it put a fire in my belly as I walked next to the Drop. Just a little way in was a larger cavern before Western Tunnel One began proper, with tonight's overseer – a woman with an eye patch – and a guard sitting around a metal burner and a table, playing a game of cards.

"I see you got here at last, girl!" the woman snapped. "Go on and get down there. We've had a new batch of workers arrive while you've been off frolicking in the meadows, and so I'm going to need you to show them how to do it properly, you got that?"

"I wasn't frolicking in any meadows, ma'am," I muttered resentfully but nodded all the same. "Yeah, I'll show 'em how to chip rock." *For what good it'll do them.*

Western Tunnel One was in a state, with very little chipping going on and lots of muttered talking. It was always like this when they brought in a new team. Usually, I would let myself fade into the background, offer a bit of advice if I thought it could help, or a shoulder if someone was crying.

And there was always someone crying.

"But *why?*" an older woman was saying. I didn't recognize her, but from her black hair tinged with a touch of auburn she had to be Daza. From one of the northern villages perhaps, I thought.

"They say that we owe them – but I was making my payments!" the woman was sobbing – but one of the older slaves, a man who had been here longer than I had, and whose eyes were starting to mist with unseeing white, was already at her side, comforting her.

"Water," I called out, passing my water skin down the line. When you're new, you don't understand how to ration it yet. I remembered being parched and thirsty and having all of my skin peeling from my fingers for days. "Take a sip and pass it on. If you need more, just ask," I said, nodding at the muttered thanks as I edged my way past the knot of people.

I hefted my steel pole in my hand – it was short, just a few hand lengths long, and it had a rounded end. The overseers wouldn't even let us have sharpened tools. In my heart I wanted to wait before I started to instruct them about what they had to do – but I knew that would only lead them into more trouble. By the time that morning came around, the overseers would be demanding to see how much of the reddish rocks they had gathered and would already be targeting the ones they deemed 'work-shy'.

"Welcome to Masaka," I muttered miserably, moving to the largest of the holes that the teams before had punctured into the rock. My mind wasn't on the task however; it was still up there in the mountains, far above me. The contrast between up there, standing before the great dragon, and down here couldn't be more stark.

"Narissea? Is that really you?" a man's voice said.

What? It was a voice that I recognized. But it couldn't be. How could he be here?

"Tamin?" I looked up to see the larger, older man emerging from the crowd. "Uncle," I said, as feelings that were too strong for me to name threatened to drop me to my knees.

Silver-haired Tamin wasn't really my uncle at all. But I had known him for so long that he had earned the nickname. He was spirit-brother to my mother, meaning that the two were almost inseparable, laughing and joking and sharing everything together. When he was in the village, that was. Tamin had grown up as my mothers' closest friend – maybe there had even been a childhood crush, I considered – before he had traveled to the Middle Kingdom to learn how to become a Magistrate.

'What does a fool like him need with Torvald books and papers?' I remember my mother grumbling on more than one occasion – but he had always returned to the village every summer, and always at the head of a caravan of Traders. Tamin had done okay for himself, he had said. He was a Senior Clerk in some Middle Kingdom Border Town, and he had been trying for years to cement the relationships between the Torvaldites and the Daza on the Eastern Plains.

Not that his efforts were that welcomed by mother and the others, I recalled. We Daza people – apart from Tamin, apparently – prided ourselves on our self-reliance. The bolts of cloth and the triple-forged tools that he had brought back with him were useful, it had to be said. But every time Tamin brought up the topic of a Middle Kingdom Outpost, or a Trader's Station or something similar, it had been rejected by the Daza council. *We don't need their laws,* as my mother had always said. *And every time you deal with the Westerners, it comes with a price.*

I didn't know it at the time, but she had been correct.

"Fierce little Nari," the large, silver-haired man sighed as he folded me into his bear-like hug. I forgot all about Tamin's past, and for a moment I only remembered what it had been like on the long and hot Plain's evenings, in our hut, eating fresh-cooked tagine around a fire and listening to stories.

I had to pull away though, for fear that I might cry. "What are you doing here?" I sniffed and looked up at his wizened face. The flickering candlelight of the mines only cast deeper shadows around his eyes, making him look older. It was clear from his mortified expression that the light didn't do any good for me, either, as his mouth dropped.

"What happened to you?" he gently held my hands up to the light, turning them over so that he could see the scrapes and wounds on my arms.

And my four brands, there dark and one still puckered and livid.

"Dear Stars!" he gasped.

But I didn't feel ashamed. If anything, I was proud of them. "These mark the times I've tried to escape," I held my forearms out of his grasp and held them up higher, defiantly. "I've been here four years, and every year..." I nodded to my arms.

"But, they look so painful, Little Nari!" a tear welled in the corner of Tamin's eye.

"Don't be sad, Uncle! Be happy, that the daughter of your spirit-friend was raised so well that I can *still* remember what it means to be free!" I said loudly, letting the other new slaves hear me.

Tamin held my gaze for a moment as a small, crooked smile quirked one side of his face. "You were always trouble, Little Nari," he said. It was almost his old humor, but then his look darkened, and all trace of mirth vanished from his features.

"Nari, I have something to tell you. Something about your village," Tamin said heavily.

Around us, the rest of the Daza slaves, both the new and the old, fell to silence at the serious tone in Tamin's voice.

"Inyene's men came to your village this last Winter gone. Your mother Yala sent word of it to me through the Traders, and I returned as soon as I could," Tamin said.

"What did they do?" My voice was hard and cold. There were always people coming and going from Inyene's keep on the mountain side. I would often see groups of riders or sometimes whole caravans snaking down the slopes.

And I didn't think that any good would ever come wherever our 'masters' went.

"They have been offering goods, loans, services," Tamin said. "I didn't realize that was what Inyene was up to, but I had been seeing reports come across my desk at Fairwater – that was the Middle Kingdom village where he worked – for the last few years or two. People trying to fight debt claims."

"Debt claims?" I echoed. I didn't understand. The Daza people had no 'debts.' If one of us owed another tribesperson for a service or an object, we would help them with what we could and that was that. It wasn't a 'debt' – it was an act of gratitude, of thanks.

But wasn't that what Dagan Mar and the overseers have been saying to us? That we owed them somehow? Just for merely existing, it seemed to me.

"I know. It's a new thing – or a very *old* type of thing, actually. Inyene has been using some very ancient Torvald laws about property and debt, allowing that if you owe somebody something, they have a right to come and take it from you." Tamin's eyes swept around the cramped tunnel. "Or, if you have nothing, they can force you to work off what you owe."

"That's insane," I spat.

"Yes. But not illegal," Tamin said carefully. *Illegal.* That was another of those words that the Three Kingdom people used. Some things were against the rule of the King, or the Princes, or the Chiefs, and if you broke the rules, they would punish you for it. Again, it was a strange concept for us Daza – but it was one that I had quickly gotten used to here in the mines.

"Anyway, Inyene has been sending her emissaries across the borderlands, picking on small villages and the Plains villages as they don't understand Three Kingdom law," he said.

Mother had been right. We didn't need Torvald paper!

"She offers loans of good solid gold coins for the people to do whatever they want with, and she expects payment when her Collectors come back," Tamin explained. "Or else, she will do something like drive into a plains village with a cart stacked with tools and weapons and expensive wines, and just leave it there and ride off. Then, the next season, a Collector will turn up at the head of a guard outfit, and they will demand that the goods be paid for, along with *interest.*"

"Interest?" I asked. "What does that mean?"

"It's a fine, a punishment for taking out a loan or borrowing something from Inyene," Tamin explained.

"Then why does she offer anything in the first place, if she feels she has to punish people for accepting it?" It made no sense to me. These Middle Kingdom people were crazy.

"She's dressed it up in all sorts of fancy language – something about the cost to employ clerks and repair cart wheels and feed her horses." Tamin endeavored to explain the unexplainable. "But yes, essentially you are right. It is all a lie. But it is sadly a *legal* lie at the moment."

The great man shook his head. Around him, the pale faces of the other Daza were already stern and angry, as they nodded and agreed at this description of Inyene's injustice.

"What happened at my village?" I sighed heavily in disgust.

"What your mother told me is that Inyene came, and she offered the loans and the wine and the swords and bows – but a few of your tribespeople took out the loans for the items, but your mother was strong in resisting her," Tamin explained. "I think Inyene had not bargained in finding a woman as determined as your mother!"

"No, I bet she wasn't." I grinned in the dark. *Good on you, Mother!*

"But Inyene wouldn't leave. She had a horrible man with a limp—"

"Dagan Mar," I said. "He's her head slave master," I explained.

"And a whole contingent of guards. Mercenaries, I think. Inyene then told your people that she had already loaned the use of cattle guards to all of the neighboring villages – which she had – and that these guards were busy rounding up and protecting the herds so that no other village could hunt them."

"What? But the herds move freely!" I burst out. It was true that we Daza people hunted the gigantic herds of cattle or the flights of birds that moved over the plains. We would send out seasonal hunting parties to follow them, always leaving if they wandered too deep into another tribes' territory. It had been the way of the Daza for a long, long time – and together we had made it work.

"Well, not anymore," Tamin said sadly. "So, your village had to take out loans to hire their own guards, and lawyers to negotiate with the other villages, and better bows to hunt quicker…"

I could see where this was heading. Inyene was setting the villages against each other and forcing them to take out her loans with 'interest' just so that my people would get into debt.

"And then, when we can't pay her back, she sends her guards in to drag us to the mines," I growled. It was wrong. I don't know much about whether it was legal or not, but it was just plain *wrong*. "What about my mother?" I asked. If anyone could make the other tribes see sense, it would be my mother, an Imanu.

"She owes the most out of anyone from your village," Tamin said.

"What!" I couldn't believe it. I shook my head and clutched my stomach as I suddenly felt sick. How could my mother fall for such a cheap trick?

"She took money out to hire lawyers, to help fight for your freedom," Tamin said softly.

"No," I moaned, and felt even worse. I didn't know why I was here. I didn't know what I was supposed to have done to deserve to be here – all I knew was that when I encountered Inyene's guards out on the trails one day, they said that they had been searching for me, and that I was to come with them. I had shouted and tried to run away – but they had been on horses and had nets.

"Inyene's people have testimonials. Saying that you stole. And trespassed, and that you owe her many years of service." Tamin was trying to break the news to me gently, but I was only getting angrier and angrier. I heard the gasps of outrage from the other Daza around me.

"*Tozuts!*" I shouted and banged a fist against the stone wall. It didn't make me feel any better. On the other side of the tunnel, Tamin was silent for a long time, as he wisely let me catch my breath and calm down. A little.

"I'm sorry, Little Nari, I thought that we could fight these cases with lawyers and laws. That is why I came back to your village. I brought Middle Kingdom Law Books with me, and I was searching for a way to help your mother fight for a way out." He looked traumatized.

"When I realized that Inyene was only getting richer from everything we were doing, hiring the Middle Kingdom lawyers and borrowing money to do so. That was when I realized that there was only one way out of this mess."

"We fight back," I snarled. Even the small metal bar in my hand looked pretty good right now.

"That is what I tried to do. I tried to raise the warriors of the village, to drive the Collectors out – but Inyene's men were too strong, and too many." Tamin looked ashamed. He was in his middling years, and I think it had been many, many years since he had lifted anything heavier than a book or a quill.

"When they caught me, that smaller one with the limp – Dagan Mar – produced a piece of contract with a signature on it that was supposed to be mine. They had forged it, claiming that I had agreed to work off my crimes here in Masaka, in return for daring to attack Inyene's guards." Tamin glowered, looking down at his hands. "I, I just fear that I have made everything worse for your village."

"No, Uncle." I crossed to him, laying a hand on his copper-skinned arm. "You were trying to help. Always remember that. We will find a way out of here, I promise," I said. "How long did they give you?" I asked gently.

"Fifteen years," Tamin muttered sorrowfully.

Fifteen years! His hair was already streaked with silver, and he had spent most of his life in libraries and sitting down, I think. How was he going to fare with fifteen years of hard physical labor?

My surrogate uncle must have seen the thoughts in my face, as he nodded sadly. "I know," he whispered.

No, not him, I thought, turning to pace the tunnel as much as I was able. We had to do something. We had to stop this madness. I stopped when my way was blocked by the press of other, watchful Daza slaves – many of them new, and many of them in their middling years. Their eyes had that same pained expression that the dragon had. Of being trapped and desperate to be elsewhere – to go where you wanted to be.

How many other Daza had I seen work themselves to death down here? I thought as my eyes flickered to the floor. I couldn't hold their gaze with so much fright and pain. *How many souls of my people are now forever knocking on the walls below, unable to ever find their way out again, back to the plains?*

I thought about that wounded black dragon up there in his cave, trapped in the same way the spirits of the dead Daza were – as the bodies of us *living* Daza were! The memory of his pain tasted bitter in my mind. *There's nothing worse than tasting freedom and then having it denied,* I thought.

I took a deep breath. I simply *had* to escape. But it wasn't just *me* who had to escape – it was all of us, wasn't it? My heart lifted a little at the wild fantasy, of leaving here with my people. *All* of my people. *And then I would return,* I thought, *at the head of a troop of Daza warriors, and tear down each and every work hut here and block of Inyene's keep.* I slowly raised my head, and at the same time raised both my forearms, just as I had done to Tamin, only this time I held up my wounds and my scars and my brands proudly before the rest of the Daza.

"Take a good look," I said out loud. "I'm not going to stop trying to escape, and these are not the marks of shame, but badges of pride. I'm going to get out of here, and I'm going to find a way to bring the rest of you with me."

Stamp. It was the sobbing woman who was the first to wipe her eyes and stamp her cloth-bound foot on the rocks. It was a traditional Daza way of agreeing or celebrating at our festivals. As I stood there with my forearms up, the next Daza and then the next stamped with one foot, until we made our own drumming noise on the tunnel. We may be forced down here, but we weren't lost. And we were very much alive and kicking.

"Oi! What's going on down there! Get back to work!" came the snarl of the overseer from further up the tunnel, and I slowly lowered my forearms. Not tonight – the word had to spread to the other Daza first. And I had to find a way to get everyone out. It would mean lots of preparation. Lots of watching, and lots of planning.

But I knew that I simply had to do it. I had to get out of here and save Mother – if I didn't want to see her shackled and chained up down here beside me, that is.

CHAPTER 5
WESTERN TUNNEL TWO

"I s it true?" broad-shouldered Oleer whispered to me the next morning. His eyes were not filled with the same sort of determined, fervent light that I had seen in the eyes of the Daza last night.

We were standing in a line that snaked out of the wooden-shack dormitory, about to be given our bowl of gruel, a hunk of bread, and our work assignments for the day. It was a few hours after sun-up, and I was exhausted. *How much sleep did I manage to get last night?* I didn't recall. Our shift had ended as it always did, in the small dark hours of the morning, with the overseer and guard kicking and shoving us back to the dormitory.

It would probably be a lot easier to ask how much sleep I *didn't* get last night, I thought miserably. Somewhere ahead of me was Tamin and the other newcomers, already with their gruel, sitting down in small groups in the main open area in the center of the camp.

"Is what true?" I asked noncommittally. I was already receiving far too many loaded glances from the other Daza prisoners. It made me feel uncomfortable; if the overseer caught wind of our newfound resolve to escape, they would probably beat us to within an inch of our lives – or beyond.

"What you told the new people last night," Oleer muttered as we shuffled forward. "That you were going to find a way out…"

I could hear the resignation in his voice. He had heard me talk like this before, and over four years I had so far failed in every attempt I had made to escape.

But it was different now, wasn't it? I told myself. None of the others knew that I was the girl who had stood up to a dragon and walked away. It was a secret that I hadn't meant to keep, but one that was precious to me anyway. A memory that had nothing to do with the overseers or the mines. Something for me alone.

"I can do it," I said hotly, thinking, *I have to do it.* "Inyene's not going to stop," I hissed back at Oleer. "She's not going to stop until all of our people are down here, working as her slaves."

Oleer gave a heavy cough. This wasn't like him to be so pessimistic, I thought. What had changed?

"Nari." He turned around to face me, and I saw that on one side of his face was a shining purple and red bruise of a black eye.

"Oleer!" I gasped. "What happened to you?" I said before he could open his mouth to prove to me just how wrong I was being. No wonder he was in bad spirits today. "Which one was it? Toadie? One-Eye? Rat-catcher?" I rattled off the nicknames of the overseers that I knew.

"Not an overseer, not a guard," the older youth said.

"Dagan?" I said in alarm.

"Not Dagan. It was them." He nodded to the other side of the open area, where there was an entirely new collection of prisoners being brought out from Hut Number 3. They were, for the most part, men, and none of them appeared to be as young or as old as the prisoners of the Daza did.

Working-age men, I realized. They were mostly lighter-skinned Middle Kingdomers, but there was also a fair number of the darker and richer skin tones of the wider world as well. "Who are they?" I whispered. They were being treated just the same as us Daza, forced to wait in line for their bowl of gruel, bread, and water before directed to sit down somewhere in the open space.

The only difference was that each and every one of them wore the ankle shackles that I had the misfortune of wearing yesterday.

"They came in yesterday afternoon, while you were up the mountain," Oleer said miserably. "They're criminals. *Actual* criminals. The overseers don't like working with them."

I could see why. Several of the criminals were loudly complaining about the state of the food, and it looked as though a fight was about to break out at any moment between another two. They were a noisier bunch than the Daza, and they took to the floor in ones, twos, or threes, and didn't seem to want to mingle.

"So, we'll just stay out of their way and we'll be fine," I said, although my heart fluttered a little. *What would this mean for my plans to escape?* It was a factor I couldn't have guessed. But maybe it was even a good thing. If these people had been in prisons and work camps before – maybe they knew ways to escape from one?

"I just don't think it's a wise idea, Nari," Oleer whispered to me as he turned back. It was clear that he wasn't talking about the prisoners, but about my plan. "We should keep our heads down for a bit, wait until the overseers relax."

"Relax?" I burst out, just as there was a sharp rap of a stick on the ground in front of us. It was Overseer Toadie, handing out the clay pots.

"You don't get paid to chat," he growled in a tired and grumpy sort of way.

"We don't get paid at all," I muttered under my breath, earning a growl from Toadie, but he gave me my gruel, bread, and water all the same.

"Get out of my sight, the pair of you!" Toadie snapped, turning to dish out the next ladleful of gruel to the Daza behind me.

Oleer came with me as I made a beeline for Tamin and some of the others, both of us silent until we had sat down.

"Nari! What is up with you?" Oleer whispered, alarm pitching his voice higher. "Talking back to the overseers? Planning what you're planning…"

"Young man." Tamin turned to look at my friend. "Narissea's mother is the Imanu of the *Souda*; it is right that she is thinking of her people." His words made me feel embarrassed and proud at the same time, but Oleer's look darkened to one of shame and resentment as he lowered his head and started eating. I would have to apologize to him for that later, too, I thought.

So many things to do. I sighed, as I turned to my surrogate uncle, hoping to start making plans. He knew the recent Daza arrivals better than me and could spread the word. We needed to work out numbers of Daza in the entire camp – and how many could manage a long-distance journey over difficult terrain. Probably at night, and with stonedogs and wolves and Inyene's guards around.

But before I could even get out more than a few words, we were interrupted by the recognizable screech of Dagan Mar as he limped and lurched into the center of the space, flanked by Inyene's guards.

"Workers!" He greeted us.

I rolled my eyes. "*Slaves,* I think he means," I whispered to Tamin.

"There's going to be a change to your shifts. And a chance for you to cut what you owe Inyene in half!" he called out dramatically.

Really? It was hard to hide my disbelief. When I looked around, my feelings seemed to be shared by a lot of the Daza who had been here the longest.

"First, we've had a lot of new intake here, from the recent troop from the Plains"—a slight sneer in his voice as he said that—"to a comple-ment of workers from the Middle Kingdom."

"Ha! He called us workers!" one of the criminals called out. Dagan shot him a dark look, but the man was still chuckling as he ducked his head. *Interesting,* I thought. If the new intakes are going to prove a problem for Dagan and the rest of the guards – then that might be something I could take advantage of.

"*So,* we will be switching your work teams around. Every Daza group will be mixed with some Middle Kingdomers."

Oh no. I glanced over at Oleer, who was glaring into his empty gruel bowl.

"Hopefully, you will learn from each other. I fully expect there to be no problems. And those of you who have been here the longest will already know what will happen if you fail me."

I knew precisely what he meant: more 'debt' added onto our sentence.

"He probably doesn't want to have all of those together," Tamin whispered at my side, casting his gaze up to the larger, noisier, and rougher crowd. I nodded my agreement – it made sense for Dagan to split up the troublemakers. But would his attempt at control be my gain? Maybe if I got to work with a Middle Kingdomer who knew a thing or two about prisons.

"But now, for an opportunity. Inyene needs Earth lights. You must all have seen them," Dagan said.

I had. But only the once. They were small outcrops of crystal that glowed green or blue when exposed to any kind of light and would hold onto that radiance for long periods of time. I had no idea how they did it, but they were a natural feature in the roots of the world.

"For every Earth light you find, Lady Inyene, in her generosity, has decided to cut an entire *week* from the debt you owe. The more you get, the more time comes off! And for the person who collects the most – there will be an extra *month* taken off their debt! For some of you, that means that you might even be out of here and returning home by Midsummer!"

Yeah, right. I'd heard things like this before in the last four years: promises to cut our sentences if we managed to bring the biggest load of iron ore in, or the most scales. I'd once had a whole month taken off my sentence for something – I can't remember what – but somehow it never seemed to make a difference to who was here. Whatever time was taken off would only be added on again for minor misdemeanors – talking back to an overseer, whispering, not walking fast enough – even looking funny at one of the guards!

I'd never seen anyone released early, I thought grimly. Tamin beside me raised an eyebrow, but I only shook my head to let him know it was all a trick to get us to work harder. "I'll tell the others," Tamin murmured under his breath.

"That's it! Wait here while your overseers assign you to your new work teams!" Dagan shouted, as the guards stepped closer towards him and they stalked back out of the open area, to the small wooden tower-hut that was Dagan's 'office.'

"Stay by me," I said quickly to Tamin, before looking over to Oleer, who was still looking sullen and angry. I beckoned him to shuffle closer. "We stick together," I told him. Oleer only shrugged, but he did move nearer to me all the same.

"You, you, and you." Overseer Toadie was busy walking through the seated Daza, while on the other side of the assembled throng Overseer Rat-Catcher and a couple of guards were busy pushing apart the criminals from the Middle Kingdom.

"You lot, join them," Toadie said, gesturing. He didn't seem to care too much how he separated us, just so long as there were some of the new Daza intake mixed in with the old. I saw that he was picking the nearest people in groups until they added up to the twenty-five on each shift, before adding the 'new' Daza. It took a while, but eventually he got to us.

"Nari," he greeted me – I was one of the few Daza that Toadie apparently knew by name, given our history.

"Sir," I said meekly, not wanting to give him any chance to take out his ire on me.

"Stand up, you and you," Toadie started to say, and then stopped when he saw the new collection of Daza I was sitting with. "Already made friends, have you?" he said heavily.

Oh no, don't do this.

"One-Eye told me to show them how to chip rocks last night, sir," I said, keeping my head bowed as I stood.

"One-Eye? Who's… Oh yeah, you mean Maribet." Toadie's scowl for once broke into a cheerful grin at the nickname that we had given the other overseer. "Go on, the lot of you before I change my mind." He waved a hand to encompass our entire small group, which was pretty evenly mixed between the newer Daza and the longer-serving slaves like me and Oleer.

Phew.

"Oh *tozut*-cakes," I heard Oleer growl as I saw the small gaggle of Middle Kingdomers who were to join us. Five in all, bringing each work team up to a shift of thirty. There was only one reason why Oleer would be so disheartened by our new mine-colleagues.

"Chubby!" called out one of the lighter-skinned men. He was taller than Oleer, but not as tall as Tamin, who stiffened at my side at the insult. This Middle Kingdom man was thin, with a very short, brown fuzz of hair and a sharp face. He looked a little like a weasel, I thought.

Beside him, the other four criminals appeared to be an even mixture of those who laughed at Weasel's comment to Oleer, and those who sidled away. The two larger men were chuckling, while one blonde-haired woman and one much smaller, black-haired and black-bearded man who was as thin as a rake just appeared to want to keep to themselves.

"There is no need for this," I heard Tamin say heavily, in his sonorous tone. I got a picture of how he must have been as a Senior Clerk in that village of Fairwater – dignified, restrained, authoritative.

It did not go down well with Weasel, apparently.

"Say what, grandpa?" the sharp-faced man laughed, rocking back and forth on his heels. He appeared agitated, excited even. I would have wondered if he was drunk, apart from I knew that there was no way any of us prisoners could get our hands on any wine or beer in here.

"We are all slaves for Inyene, we might as well do what we have to do," Tamin said in measured tones.

Measured, apparently, was not what this little man understood. He bounced forward suddenly, right up against Tamin's chin as he glared up at him. "You sound like you want to be some kind of boss, old man," he growled, his earlier enthusiasm gone, and replaced with a terrifying, cold snarl.

"Oi! Fankin!" I heard a sharp snarl, as Overseer One-Eye was marching forward, with a trio of guards at her side. Each of them had their crossbows slung at their hips – but held their stout hardwood batons in their hands. "What did I tell you earlier about no trouble?"

"Sorry, ma'am," the Weasel Fankin said immediately, stepping back from Tamin. All this time, my heart was in my throat, and I cursed myself for not acting quicker. I should have stepped in the way. I should have protected my surrogate uncle and my friend, Oleer – but how? How could I, alone, stand against all of these?

And just how am I going to be able to lead these people out of the mines, if I can't even stand up for the people closest to me? I thought, moving to Tamin's side as One-Eye pointed at the Mine Entrance.

"Western Tunnel Two," she snapped, and my heart sank. It was the most unstable of all of the mine workings under Masaka. Maribet One-Eye must be hoping that it would collapse on us troublemakers. Never mind how I was going to lead the Daza out of this prison – right now I had to make sure that they all survived the mines!

"Careful," I said, pointing to the narrow rift in the rock underfoot running parallel to the wide ledge that we were traversing.

On our left was the Drop – our name for the chasm that opened up in the middle of Masaka and seemed bottomless. We had several ledges that ran along the face of the Drop that we used to get to the various tunnels.

And of all of them, Western Tunnel Two had claimed the most lives of the Daza in the time I had been here. At least three or four times that of any other part of the mines.

I held my candle stub lower, making sure that everyone could see the crack that I was referring to. "When they get larger, they fall away into the Drop, sometimes taking whole ledges with them," I told Tamin, who was behind me. He nodded that he understood and gave an owlish look at the expanse of subterranean dark on the other side.

"You get used to it," I said. I remembered the stomach-grab of fear and anxiety I used to feel every time I even stepped out from the overhanging wall. That had dominated year one of my incarceration down here but had completely gone in year two.

"Hm." Tamin and the other new Daza did not sound so convinced at my assertion, which was natural. We were plains people, used to looking up at the wide expanse of sky far above us. For most of us, the world was a landscape we traveled *across* – not *above.* Heights were a new thing for us. I wondered, if – no, *when* – I ever got out of here, whether this would mean that I would be much better at climbing trees. Now in my fourth year here, neither the heights of the mountains nor the depths of the Drop bothered me in the slightest.

"And here is where we'll be working," I said as we came to where the ledge stopped and a large tunnel shot down into the right-hand overhanging wall. Its entrance was propped by a mess of wooden beams, and I held my candle inside to illuminate the repeated supports like wooden gates, every few meters or so. The floor of

Western Tunnel Two was still littered with boulders and rock chips from the last cave-in. We had cleared out all of the larger blocks, tumbling them over the edge of the Drop, but a host of smaller material was still shaking itself loose from the walls and the ceilings.

"It's *very* important to be careful as you chip," I said, miming the action we would be making with the steel pole. I showed them how to twist their wrists at the last moment and explained how multiple smaller jabs – like using a hammer – would be better down here than powerful lunges.

"Great," Fankin snarled from his place a few people behind me. He had been more subdued on our long journey into the bones of Masaka, but now it appeared his 'sunny nature' was starting to perk up again.

Just what I need. But behind him was Overseer Maribet One-Eye and two of Inyene's guards. They would be acting as our chaperones for this shift, and I was pretty certain they would spend most of their time observing the Middle Kingdomers rather than the rest of us.

Which was good, I thought. It might give me time to talk with Tamin, and Oleer, and do some thinking.

"Get a move on! It took you long enough to get down here!" Maribet snapped, and I nodded. Nothing much changed.

"Everyone got water? Your bread?" I said as I led the way down into Western Tunnel Two. There was a muttered chorus of affirmatives – and if no one sounded enthusiastic, then I didn't blame them.

"We split up, three at each hole," I said, indicating the small apertures in the rock that appeared every five or six meters or so. All of the Daza here had already had some experience – even if it was only last night, where I had shown them how to take turns, each one of three tapping and chiseling at the rocks before the next person took over. It was a technique that we slaves had devised a long time ago, and although it earned some mockery from the overseers, it meant that none of us tired ourselves out completely – which was good for Inyene in the long run, as well as good for us.

Not that it mattered. When Inyene announced a 'rush' then we all had to work three times as hard anyway!

Whatever. I carried on walking as the group behind me peeled off into their trios. It would be warmer at the far end of Western Tunnel Two – but there was another reason why I chose to venture down there, too. It was also the most unstable. I didn't want any of the first-timers working there, and although I wouldn't have minded asking Fankin and his goons, it seemed as though Maribet One-Eye had already earmarked them for the nearest hole to the tunnel entrance, where they would be easier –and safer – for her to watch.

"At least it'll be quiet," I muttered as I carried on walking, with Tamin and Oleer behind me.

The tunnel narrowed a little, dropped a few feet, and turned. We had to edge ourselves around a place where a large boulder had burst from the walls and splintered the support beam. The sounds of tapping from the work team behind us grew fainter and fainter. I slowed my pace and started to breathe again.

"Your plan?" Oleer's voice swam forward to me. It was clear what he was talking about.

But I hadn't had time to think about it yet. I sucked the air through my teeth.

"You always did that when you were thinking. Even as a child," Tamin said. It was strange to have someone here who remembered me from before all of this. I didn't know if that made me feel more vulnerable, or less.

"Well, the plains are East," I thought out loud. "But so are Inyene's watch towers. And her horse guards can cover the ground easily."

"We can't walk out of here. That would be impossible," Oleer said. He seemed more despondent since his encounter with Fankin. I wanted the old Oleer back.

"That was why I was heading West, into the mountains, to loop back around," I explained my previous attempts. The gulley that led to a waterfall, or the more open slopes on the southern face of Masaka.

"But neither of those routes worked!" Oleer said. "What does that leave us?"

"Well, there's only one option left, isn't there?" Tamin was saying. "Due West. Up and over the Masaka. Get to Middle Kingdom land proper, and then take one of the northern passes. I know Traders who might be able to smuggle us back," he said.

I was surprised at his pragmatism. He thought like a senior clerk, I imagined, cutting away all of the mistakes until only one option was left.

"*Over* the mountain?" Oleer sounded incredulous behind us. "Do you know how difficult that will be? There's lynx and wolves, snakes."

"Stonedogs," I muttered. I still hadn't told anyone about my encounter with the stonedogs – or the wounded black dragon. I knew that it had been a personal experience, like my three-day Testing in the wilderness – but something in me told me to keep quiet about my experience, as well. If the newer prisoners like Fankin found out there was a wounded dragon up there, and that Inyene was after scales – then I was sure he would sell it out for any advantage he could get!

"What about dragons?" Tamin asked warily. The World's Edge were one of the last refuges of the wild dragons, after all.

"Rare." I thought of the way that the gigantic black had looked at me. It hadn't challenged me. It had been hurt. "But I don't think they'll want anything to do with humans anyway," I mused. *Not in my experience, anyway.*

"How many Daza are there down here?" Tamin asked. "I saw members of Souda and Metchoda, Uoda and Jinda tribes."

"Almost three hundred, I think," Oleer said. It was hard to argue with the pessimism in his voice. No one asked the obvious question in the dark, and none of us had to.

How, under the stars, were we going to smuggle three hundred people up the mountain? *And* keep them hidden in the Middle Kingdom, and then find a Trader friendly enough to bring all three hundred back to the Eastern Plains?

Oleer had been right. It was impossible. I was so caught up in my morose spirits that I didn't notice the tremor until Tamin suddenly gasped, "What's that?"

A trembling rose through my legs, and in the light of the candle I could see the shake of dust and rock chips on the floor. "Back. Everyone back," I said, already turning, a spike of fear going straight through me.

Oleer was now in front of our group. Over Tamin's shoulder I could see him start to jog with that awkward, hunched gait that came from working for years down the mines. The trick wasn't to sprint. If you sprinted, then you would trip and smack your head on the rocks. I had learned that the hard way, many times.

"Not too fast!" I hissed at Tamin. No time to explain why as now the walls were visibly shaking, and from all around us there came a growling, groaning noise. It was louder than all of the previous times that I had heard it before. It was almost as loud as I imagined what a dragon roar would be.

Maybe we SHOULD sprint.

Before I could even open my mouth to shout, there was an almighty crack as if someone had broken the mountain in half, and a blast of cold air hit me from behind. It was laden with dust and grit, making me cough and choke.

And then I ran smack into the back of Tamin, who had paused, his hands clutching at the walls.

"What? Run!" I coughed.

But he couldn't. As I raised my eyes, I saw that the shaking tunnel ahead of us was now filled with gray smoke. A shadow moved across my eyes as one of the wooden supports gave way with an almighty roar, releasing a torrent of rocks from the walls and ceilings--

"Oleer!" I screamed. I couldn't see him. Had he managed to get to the other side of the cave-in? Was there even another side?

"Agh!" Tamin threw his arm across me, clutching me to his side as another billowing cloud of dust tore at our hair and clothes. Sharp fragments of rock bit into my cheeks and arms, even though I was sure that Tamin must have taken the brunt of the blast. The tunnel around us shook and roared, and I thought that this was it. There would be no escape for us. There would be no feeling the Soussa winds ever again, I would never be free, and neither would my people.

CHAPTER 6
THE SHRINE

"Nari? Narissea – are you hurt?" Tamin's choked voice came from beside me. I opened my eyes and realized that I was not dead. Neither of us were.

The roar of the rocks had stopped, leaving instead just the rain-like tapping as bits of gravel and splinters of stone dislodged around us. But that didn't mean that we were safe. "The tunnel might still collapse on us," I whispered. "We have to be very careful." I blinked and rubbed my face – my hands came away gritty and dry from the dust.

And I could see, I realized. Which I shouldn't be able to, as both myself and Tamin had dropped our candles, and which had gone out in the rock blasts.

"What is that?" Tamin whispered warily.

There was a soft, hazy bluish glow coming from behind us. It wasn't bright. All I could see was the shadowed form of my surrogate uncle and the tumbled rocks around us. But it would be enough.

"That's an Earth Light," I said. I had never been so glad to find one in all my life. Not for Inyene, but for us. "Come on." I patted him on the shoulder and started to carefully crawl back down Western Tunnel Two to the source of the blue glow.

The tunnel where we had previously been was now completely different. Rocks almost as large as I was were jammed and jumbled across our path, so that we had to squirm and shimmy past them to get to our destination.

"The rock fall must have opened up an underground fissure," I said.

"A what?" Tamin asked.

"A crack," I explained. Masaka mountain was full of them, and none of the slaves or overseers seemed to know why. Lots and lots of cracks just like the Drop, but some only a few meters tall and a finger's breadth wide, while others might be much larger.

There had been two rock falls, I now saw, and recalled the blast of cold air that hit my back first, before the one in front of us had cut off our escape. The first rock fall had blocked off the rest of Western Tunnel Two, but it had dislodged a huge plate of rock, revealing…

"That's not a fissure," I corrected.

"Oh." Tamin sounded bemused.

It was a tunnel. An almost perfectly rounded tunnel, fairly short, and leading to a larger cave, which was where the eerie blue glow was coming from. "This has been worked," I explained, pointing to where the tunnel walls did not have the smoothed, organic flows of natural rock – and neither did it have the sharp edges and jags of fractured rock. Instead, the walls were pocked and bubbled, as if they had been carved out of the stone by chisels.

The blue glow was growing slightly, not becoming dazzling, but bright enough to see that the cave on the far side was small, and that it had—

"Columns?" I said in wonder. I pushed on through the tunnel as my curiosity was piqued.

The cavern wasn't large; it was roughly circular with rough-hewn columns seeming to grow out of the rock walls, from floor to ceiling. And there, in the center, was a carved stone pedestal with some sort of design on it, like birds, that I couldn't quite make out. It was from four little alcoves in this pedestal that the glow was emanating, where four roses of blue Earth lights sat.

But I was far more intrigued by what was sitting on *top* of the pedestal: a large chest, made of dark metal.

"It's not rusted one bit," Tamin said in hushed tones as he joined me beside the chest.

"It wouldn't be. It's so dry down here," I whispered, creeping towards the chest, and hesitantly reaching up a hand.

"Nari," Tamin whispered cautiously. But, without any sign of danger, I pressed my fingertips to the chest. The metal felt cold. When I tapped it with my nails, it rang like a bell.

"We have to look," I said. The chest didn't appear to have any locks on it at all, just the lid that met the opposing edge. A little nervously,

I prodded my steel bar, which I'd still managed to have with me, under one edge and lifted it open. It gave out one long, singing creak of metal, before the lid overbalanced and banged down to the far side, making both me and Tamin jump.

And there, looking up at me from the inside was the face of a woman.

"Uh?" I made a questioning sound in my throat as I looked. It appeared to be a roll of canvas, flexible and soft, and smelled strongly of resins and oils. The uppermost side had the pale face of a Middle Kingdom woman with large stylized curls of yellow-gold hair, swept away from her face, against a red backdrop. She was staring off to one side, although I couldn't see at what.

I looked at Tamin, who made a 'I have no idea' gesture with his open palms, and so I reached in, carefully grabbing the topmost edge of the canvas and pulling it upwards.

It rolled out underneath its weight, dislodging just the slightest clouds of dust. There were heavy crease lines like tide marks across the length of the picture, but they did nothing to hide the image that was revealed.

A woman, wearing armor and holding a short spear in a defensive posture – and behind her, with its head curling low in front and wings outstretched, was a large red dragon.

"She must have been a Dragon Rider," Tamin whispered in awe as he looked at the unrolled picture. He meant one of the many such warriors and heroes who had roamed the world in centuries past. Their natural home had been the Training Academy at Torvald – capital of the Middle Kingdom – but I had once heard that every kingdom had their bands of Dragon Riders.

Back when there were more dragons in the sky, I thought. Before they vanished. And when the dragons had been a lot friendlier to humans than they were now. *Or at least, that is what everyone had always told me,* I thought. The dragon I had met had been wounded – and even though it had a right to be upset and angry – it hadn't been unfriendly at all!

The image on the roll of canvas was striking. The woman's expression was captured as one of fierce defiance and dignity as she stared off at some distant horizon or enemy. Her red dragon, too, was well-captured (I could say that because now I knew what a dragon looked like up close). A female, I assumed – as it had no pronounced horns. It was snarling in the same direction as the woman was.

I wish I was as brave as she was, I thought.

"Look, there's more!" Tamin pointed to what had lain under the canvas: another fold of canvas – much lighter this time – as well as a bundle of dark cloth. I hesitantly laid the painting off to one side and reached for the cloth bundle while Tamin reached for the fold of canvas.

"It's heavy," I announced, unwrapping the cloth to find it tearing easily in my hands. This wasn't the sort of oiled and waxed cloth that the others were. It appeared to be just someone's old cloak.

And inside was a leather-bound book, and something else.

"A dagger!" I said in surprise, almost dropping both book and dagger at once.

The dagger had a small scabbard made of stiffened leather, but its crosspiece gleamed of a bronze-colored metal, and its handle was wrapped in cord. It ended in a small pommel with a green gem at the end. Tamin watched me as I pulled the dagger from its sheath, revealing a fat blade that gleamed like a mirror, and had been engraved with the curling shape of a dragon.

"It's still sharp," I whispered in awe. Was this that woman's very own dagger? Had this woman once fought alongside a dragon? I thought, as Tamin unfurled the paper.

"This is a map," Tamin breathed, carefully kneeling on the floor so he could lay it out. "Look, there is the Midmost Lands." He pointed to a fat shape in the middle like a jagged tear drop. Several lines of mountains scored up through its middle and along its outer edge.

And a little off to the left, near the outer mountain range someone had painted an over-large golden crown over a 'T'.

"That's the citadel of Torvald. Once home to the Dragon Riders." Tamin's voice was excited.

"I know that, Uncle," I said in annoyance. Just because I couldn't read, he had always treated me like I didn't know anything!

But Tamin either hadn't heard me or wasn't worried about upsetting me at the moment, as his hands moved across the map, pointing at various settlements and places. "Scorched Lands. Vala. Queen's Keep..." He looked up at me, his eyes bright. "This map dates back to the early Kingdom of Torvald. Perhaps even before it was Torvald!"

"What do you mean?" I asked.

Tamin could see I had no idea what he was talking about. "Before there were Three Kingdoms in the Midmost Lands, the North, Middle, and South, there was an Empire. Torvald," he tapped the air over the golden crown, "had expanded to conquer all three, ruled over by an evil wizard-king."

Children's stories. I'd heard fragments of this from Mother – but always told as something that happened far away, and not important to us in the Eastern Plains.

"But before *that* it was Three Kingdoms again, ruled over by three brothers. Each one wanted to control all of the Midmost Lands, just as *their* mother, the original queen, had done. She was the one who first became friends with dragons!" Tamin said excitedly. "Because there aren't the large coastal towns of Redport, and Roskilde the island nation isn't mentioned here, then we can assume that this map is before the people who made it knew much about them!" my surrogate uncle said excitedly. "That makes it *very* ancient indeed!"

"Wonderful," I said. I was less impressed with the map than I was with the dagger and the painting. What good was a map that was out of date, anyway?

But in my hands, I still held the heavy book. I flicked it open casually, hearing the pages sigh and crack a little – but they were still good. It revealed lots and lots of cramped text that was completely gibberish to me.

And pictures. These, I paused over each one I found.

They appeared to be sketches, made by whomever had written this book perhaps, of the things that they had seen. There were drawings of mountains as well as different kinds of trees, strange shells with lots of holes in them, bugs and beetles, and the pommel and handle designs of different weapons.

Interesting, I thought, and wished that I could read.

But then my thumb flicked the pages right to the back, where there were still some blank pages, as well as a lot more sketches. No, doodles, really. I made out a large eye, surrounded by the smallest, most delicate of scales. A talon, as well as intricate drawings of a scale from different angles.

"A dragon!" I said out loud, knowing them from what I had seen myself. And something else, too – it was clear that whomever had made these pictures had spent a lot of time on them. The sketches of the dragon were far more detailed and sophisticated than any other drawing in the journal, as if it was something that fascinated and captivated the author.

"May I?" Tamin was at my side, smiling broadly in the weird blue light. I let him take the book from my hands, where he went through the pages just as I had done, gasping and making awed noises, until he came to the start, and stopped.

"What? What is it?" I asked excitedly.

Tamin cleared his throat, and then read from the first few leaves of the book. "This being the journal of Lady Artifex, detailing my attempts to chart and plot the confines of the World, under the rule of High Queen Delia the First, with my faithful companion Maliax."

"Maliax," I said out loud, turning to look at the canvas picture on the floor as Tamin flipped the pages and continued to read silently. My eyes sought out the fierce red dragon. "Is that your name?" I asked its frozen form. *Maliax.*

I thought about the black dragon, far above us. I wondered if he had a name too. Did *all* dragons have a name? How did they get one? 'Maliax' sounded like a dragon's name to me. It didn't sound like any sort of Daza or Three Kingdom name that I had ever heard of.

Who named you? I asked the picture. Did they get named by their Riders, or did all dragons already have their own names? I wondered.

And just what did it take to learn one?

"What is going on here!" bellowed a sudden voice. It was Maribet One-Eye, emerging from the small tunnel with a torch in one hand and a stout metal quarterstaff in the other. And coming right up behind her were her two heavyset, frowning guards.

CHAPTER 7
ABIOYE

"W hat are you doing?" One-Eye snarled at the pair of us. And then her eye fell on the knife in my hand. For the briefest moment I could *feel* the thought rise in me: I was holding a weapon. I could use it—

Tamin moved first, slapping my hand down with a hard smack.

"Ow!" I dropped the knife and it clattered on the floor, as the two guards behind One-Eye converged on us. One kicked the dagger across the floor and pushed me roughly up against the stone wall with a heavy thump, as the other grabbed Tamin by the shoulders.

"Nobody move!" One-Eye was shouting. "This is your little game, is it? Sneak down here and start your own little mutiny?" She was stalking into the room, with her staff waving in the air between us.

"Maribet, that is ridiculous," I gasped under the guard's rough hold. *Even though that is exactly what I had wanted to do.* "Look. How could *we* make this place? We just found it after the rockfall."

"This room is hundreds of years old. These documents are antiques!" Tamin said from the other.

"Hmph," One-Eye growled, kicking the corner of the canvas painting of the Lady Artifex.

"Don't!" I said instinctively. It seemed a dishonor somehow to have someone like her even touch it.

"What's it to you?" the overseer said, and I saw the gleam of cruelty in her eyes when she realized how important this was to me. "Maybe you thought you could make some money, huh? Find a guard to sell this to?" She rounded on me. "Well, I have something to tell you, my girl – *everything* under this mountain belongs to the Lady Inyene. *Everything.* Every bit of rock, every slave, every forgotten scrap," she aimed another kick at the painting, and the cloth was thrown to the side of the room, hiding the Lady Artifex's face.

"Does that mean you, too?" I muttered under my breath. It was loud enough for One-Eye to hear me, as she hissed in anger.

"Right. We're taking all of this rubbish up to Dagan. He'll be the one to decide what your punishment will be!" she crowed, seizing every-thing that was on the floor and jamming it back into the metal chest. Tamin made a noise of horror as there was a ripping sound from the journal as some of the binding came apart, but that only made One-Eye shove the contents all the more roughly into the box.

I saw the overseer pause as her hands snatched up the Lady Artifex's dagger, then cast an irritated look in our direction "What are you two looking at?" she snarled, and I lowered my head.

"Right. Pick up the chest, and follow me," Maribet One-Eye ordered as she straightened up, and now I saw that her hands were empty.

Did she just steal the dagger!? I thought, almost about to say something – before I realized how useless it would be. Who would believe me, after all?

"You heard what I said! Get moving!" Maribet bawled once more, and Tamin and I grabbed the heavy metal rings at either end of the chest. "And don't think for a minute that either of you are getting the reward for these," she said, and grabbed the four blue Earth lights, stuffing them into her jerkin pocket before leading the way back out of the shrine, with us lugging the heavy chest behind her, and the guards following.

The entirety of Western Tunnel Two had been shut down by the rockfall, I saw as we clambered our way back out. There were also a whole lot more guards now than there had been before. And torches.

"We spent almost two hours excavating the collapse!" One-Eye hissed from in front. And when she said 'we' she meant the slaves, who were still passing rocks hand to hand up from the tunnel and heaving them over the edge of the Drop, as the Daza who had been here the longest were knicking into place new support beams.

"Your carelessness almost closed down this tunnel for good! Do you know what that would mean for the mines?"

Careless! I gritted my teeth. I had been the one who was being careful! Not shouting down the tunnels and barging about! And did I care what it would mean to the mines? I thought to myself. *Not at all.* My arms were aching when we reached the ledge, to find the slaves and guards filing down into the tunnel one at a time. They had to halt their work all over again to let us past.

"Up to the Main Avenue," Maribet hissed, and even though there were many more hands and ore carts around us, she wouldn't allow us to let go of our heavy burden.

It was a long walk.

But even though my shoulders were screaming by the time we climbed up the length of the Main Avenue to Dagan Mar's platform at the very top of the mines, my thoughts kept turning to what we had found.

The Lady Artifex had looked fierce and proud, I thought. She didn't look like the sort of person who would have stood for the sort of treatment that we received on a daily basis. Even though I could never have known or met the woman, seeing her practice sketches at the back of her journal gave me some sort of connection to her. I had seen the care with which she had tried to trace the lines of her dragon, Maliax, again and again, always trying to get it right.

It meant that she cared about her dragon, I thought. Just as I cared for Tamin and even Oleer and the Daza. It was her trust and friendship that had kept her going, pushing forward into all of those new places.

"You found them, I see!" Dagan Mar's harsh tones broke into my fantasy, and the pain leaped into my arms, shoulders, and back with renewed vengeance as reality hit home. Here at Dagan Mar's office, the inside of the Mine entrance was large and open. There were the deep gutters running down the floor where water would be pumped, as well as the runnels for the cart tracks on their ropes, powered by the treadmills outside. One side of the wide semi-circle was given over to crates and barrels and spare beams, while the other side had been built into a wooden platform with a high stool, where Dagan Mar could sit with the fresh air and the sunlight of the outside hitting his face as he watched us slaves come and go.

"Both alive, sir," One-Eye called, stopping at the bottom of the stairs. "We haven't lost their debt," she said proudly, and I scowled. "And they found something down there. A cave, with this." She gestured for us to haul the metal box up the stairs to the platform, as Dagan descending from his high stool.

Nice while it lasted. I thought of the wondrous pictures and glimpse into another life we had found inside that chest as I thumped the metal box on the wooden boards, stepping back next to Tamin as Dagan's eyes gleamed with greed as he flipped it open, only for that eagerness to be replaced by a look of deep disappointment when all he found there was old paper and canvas.

The inscribed dagger was gone, I saw, and realized that One-Eye must have stolen it, just as I'd thought. I cast a glare down at her, but she remained focused on Dagan Mar, a tight little smile on her face.

"Worthless." Dagan slammed the lid down again on the junk, not even bothering to fold the canvas painting back inside. "These mountains are full of old tat as one army or bunch of crazies moved through here." He shook his head. "I don't know why you bothered to show this to me; you should have heaved it over the Drop!" Dagan said irritably to One-Eye, and I saw her flinch at the rebuke.

"No, you can't!" Tamin, beside me, took a step forward before I knew what he was going to do. *You can't interrupt Dagan Mar!* I thought, reaching for his shoulder.

But it was already too late.

Dagan's hand shot out in lightning-fast speed, backhanding my surrogate uncle around the back of the face with a loud slap, sending him to his knees.

"No!" I growled as I took a step forward, half-covering Tamin's hunkered form with my own.

"Oh, you want some punishment too, do you?" Dagan turned on me.

For a moment I almost *wanted* Dagan to hit me. Or try to hit me, anyway. Four years was a long time to put up with the abuse, and meeting the black dragon and hearing about Lady Artifex had changed something in me.

But I won't be any good to the rest of my people if I'm dead. The thought flashed through my mind as I lowered my eyes and my chin, appearing submissive before him. "No sir, it's just that he's new. He's still getting used to – how this place works," I said awkwardly.

How not to get yourself a beating, I was thinking.

Our head overseer snorted in disgust, and the boards creaked as he stepped back. "You're both docked one days' wages for wasting my time. Another day for disturbing the work of the mines, and for the insolence?" I dared to look up, just in time to see his cruel grin. "Ten lashes and three days solitary confinement, only water rations! That will teach either of you to speak back to me, or to slack off work with this nonsense!" He nudged the metal box with his foot.

The guards stepped forward and seized my shoulders and I looked in alarm at Tamin, also being seized. He was an older man – how would he survive ten lashes and no food for three days?

"Wait," an unfamiliar, polished voice said behind us all, and even though it was a quiet voice, the guards froze instantly. Who could have this much effect?

The owner of the voice was a young man, maybe a year or two older than me, with strong blue eyes and messy reddish-brown hair. The chop and snarl of his hair contrasted strongly with what he was wearing, which was a finely tooled leather jerkin, inlaid with green dyes, over a cream shirt, open at the throat. A pair of heavy leather trews finished the ensemble, and at his side hung a sabre.

A sabre! This man had a weapon – but he didn't look to be a guard or an overseer. If anything, the way that he casually climbed the platform, and then ignored the pair of guards and me and Tamin seemed to suggest that he didn't have a care in the world.

But the effect that he had on Dagan Mar was like the older slave master had spotted a rattlesnake in his path. Our 'Chief' straightened up as if to attention, though he didn't bow or salute. Instead, Dagan raised his chin high, in defiance.

"Your *lordship,*" Dagan said, and the way that he dripped venom over the second word made me think that there was nothing in Dagan's heart that meant it at all.

"Dagan." There was a flicker of something in the young man's eyes as he paused, making it clear that the dislike flowed both ways between these two.

"Might I ask just what brings you to my mines?" Dagan said.

The young lord ignored him, walking between us to stoop down to the metal box and pry it open. Beside us, Maribet One-Eye suddenly stiffened, and her face went pale.

Thief! I thought, and wondered if there was a way to make this noble angry with her.

This Western lord took his time carefully unfolding the roll of canvas as One-Eye shifted from foot to foot.

"Permission to get back to work, Chief Mar," One-Eye suddenly blurted out, earning a sharp look from both Dagan and whomever this important young man was.

"Wait a minute." The young lordling frowned. "This is... *interesting,*" he said as he picked up Lady Artifex's journal gingerly between his long fingers. Eventually, he made a considering noise in the back of his throat and looked up at the chief. I had never seen anyone be so unafraid of our slave master before!

"I came down here because my sister wanted to check on the progress of the collection," he said. "And so, naturally..." He raised a hand to indicate that here he was. Then he turned his head to look back at the journal once again. "But *this* is something new."

Maribet One-Eye beside me made a small, nervous cough. She must have realized how badly she had messed up, I thought in glee.

"We've uncovered eighteen Earth lights for her ladyship!" Dagan said with a note of pride.

Not for your *lordship*, I noted. And he said that his sister had sent him. That would make him Abioye, wouldn't it? I had heard of the brother to the Lady Inyene, but I had never before seen him down in the mines.

"Not enough," the young man said in an offhanded way. "Where did you find this?" he raised the journal to ask Dagan Mar.

"That's nothing, Abioye, just some trash that these two wasted their time dragging up," Dagan said. "You can tell her ladyship that I'm resuming work right away, and I am sure that I will find more Earth lights before evening!"

"On the contrary, Chief Mar – this certainly isn't trash," the young man said, frowning as he looked up at me and Tamin. "Is this all that there was in the chest?" the Lord Abioye said seriously.

I froze. Now was my chance to open my mouth and say something – but the fact that I was a slave closed my throat. Even if I *did* tell on One-Eye, she would only get her revenge after this Lord Abioye had gone – or she could get any of the other overseers and mine guards to push me and Tamin over the Drop at any time they wanted.

And then, Lord Abioye did something strange. He looked past my shoulder, straight at Maribet One-Eye and said, while apparently still talking to me, "You know, my sister will be *very* displeased if anything is stolen from her mines."

One-Eye didn't say anything, but from the corner of my eye I saw her flinch.

The Lord Abioye sighed and returned to page carefully through the book. He paused to glance up at a picture of comparative types of animals and gave a slow exhalation of breath.

Why was he doing that? I wondered. Was it because he thought the pictures were worth something? The very thought that he might sell these rare finds I found disgusting. He set the journal to one side and flicked the corner of the canvas painting, revealing the creased features of Lady Artifex.

"No punishment for these two." The young man frowned deeply as he studied the painting before he looked up at me again. "Where did you find these?"

He was gazing at me directly with those Middle Kingdom blue eyes. They were piercing, the color of the high Plain's sky at noon.

And he was the brother of my captor. I glared back and said nothing.

"Can you take me to the site?" Abioye said, a little slower, a look of confusion creasing his eyebrows. I guess he must be wondering if I understood common tongue, which of course I did.

"Abioye," Dagan growled. "It is not your place to make decisions about the running of the mine. If *I* say that these two are to be lashed, then that is precisely what will happen to them!"

Abioye stood up slowly and scratched his chin. "I know that you have been an indispensable servant to my sister, Dagan," he began, and the chief slave master noticeably bristled at the very mention of 'servant'. "However, I have to insist. *I* am my sister's heir and representative. That should be enough to heed my orders. But in case it is not, I must tell you that my sister does not solely want mere rocks and metal. There is a *reason* why my sister wants these Earth lights. And I think that what we have discovered here," he nodded towards the box, "is also important."

It was the first time I had ever seen Dagan flustered. He made small chewing movements with his jaw, as if the words he wanted to spit were too difficult or too hot to even get past his tongue. In the end however, he settled for snarling. "Fine. If her ladyship wills it, then of course I wholeheartedly agree."

"Of course," Abioye said, looking away from the man, but there was a small, cynical smile on his face. These two had some kind of history of these encounters, I thought, and it looked as though this one was a win for 'Lord' Abioye.

"Shall we go?" he turned to say to me.

It was my turn to stammer and feel confused however, as none of the superiors or masters here had ever asked my opinion on anything.

"Of – of course," I said, nodding. It was with a weird, surreal feeling that I saw and felt the guards release Tamin and me, before stepping back out of our path as I led the way.

Shame it was back down the mines, it had to be said.

CHAPTER 8
OPPORTUNITIES

"Have you ever seen anything like this before in the mines?" my captor's brother asked as he walked behind me. Ahead of me walked one of the mine guards with a torch and a long metal rod, next came myself, Abioye, another guard, Tamin, and then another guard. If I had believed that I might have free rein of the mines at last, then I was sadly mistaken. But of course, Inyene's brother would require protection from such riff-raff as inhabited the mines.

"No," I answered truthfully. I had never come across any pieces or areas of worked stone that we had not carved ourselves – and even then, anything that we slaves had carved had only ever been functional, never elegant or decorative like the worked pillars.

"Careful, sir," the guard ahead mumbled – not caring for mine and Tamin's safety, obviously – as he used the metal rod to tap and prod at the ledge as we stepped down onto it.

"I see!" Abioye gasped behind me as we waited for the mine guard to complete his initial inspection. We had space for me to look across at him, and I could tell that he was trying to appear nonchalant, but really the Drop was terrifying him.

"I'd better not ruin my clothes down here," he said in a slightly too-loud voice, tugging on the large white cuffs of his shirt and pressing them back into the sleeves of his jerkin. I wanted to point out that perhaps a crisp white linen shirt wasn't the best attire to go jaunting in a mine – but decided against it. For all of his strangeness, and his apparent difference from the cruel overseers and Dagan Mar, he was still the brother of Inyene. He was probably going to sell any artifacts he found and didn't care how many of us Daza fell over the edge of the Drop in the process.

"Safe," the guard announced, casting a dark look back at me which told me silently just to 'get moving!'

I did.

The ledge that led to Western Tunnel Two was wide, and really it should have presented no problem to even three people walking abreast, but Abioye kept firmly behind me, and reached out to touch the reassuringly solid overhang of the wall to his right.

He's probably never even been down here before, I thought with contempt.

Eventually, we came to the reinforced entrance to Western Tunnel Two, whose entrance was pale with the bare gleam of fresh wooden supports. There were already two guards stationed outside, and I could hear the gentle murmur of tapping from the work team they had sent back to excavating.

"Idiots!" I couldn't help but cough in the back of my throat. Not three or four hours after a rockfall, and they send people back down there!

"Everyone out," Abioye said behind me. "I can't do my thinking with that racket," he said, and when I looked up at him, I saw a pained expression on his face.

If he thinks that is a racket, then he should spend some time in Eastern Tunnel Three! I thought. The mountain there was much more stable, and the rocks much harder. Sometimes we were even allowed to use slag lumps of metal that had been cast-off from the foundry as hammers.

"Whatever you say, sir." The guards gave a variety of haphazard salutes before turning to bellow down the already fragile tunnel. "*STOPPAGE!* Everyone out!"

Is this guy a total idiot!? I gasped, turning to look past Abioye's shoulder, past the guard, to Tamin. His eyes were wary and owlish, but I had no idea if he understood my meaning of 'if everything starts shaking again, run!'

"Nari!?" someone said in front of me, and I turned around to see that one of the first to lay down his tools and leave the tunnel was Oleer.

"Oleer! Thank the stars you are alive!" I said, stepping forward to raise a hand towards him.

"I am," he said, and pulled away before I could touch his arm. His face darkened as he saw the guards around me, Tamin, and the finely dressed Abioye. He'd been here longer than me, and it was clear that he recognized Abioye for who he was.

"Get moving!" one of the mine guards said, raising his metal staff in the air, and Oleer ducked his head and shuffled back.

"Oleer!" I whispered back at him, but he didn't turn. Instead, he was quickly replaced by the other assorted Daza slaves and criminals, all of their eyes on me as they filed past. At least some must have been glad to have their work shift stopped, but suddenly I felt very uncomfortable indeed standing next to the 'representative' of our captor.

"All clear?" the guard ahead of us asked the mine's guard, who nodded.

"Then, lead the way… uh…" Abioye stumbled over what he should even call me, as if the word 'slave' was somehow distasteful to him. As if the truth of it was too ugly to befoul his mouth.

"Narissea," I murmured. "My name is Narissea, of the Souda." I made sure that I met his eyes as I said these words. I didn't think that the Lady Artifex would hide who she was.

And neither would Mother, either – and so neither would I.

The shrine looked empty now that we had removed the chest, and One-Eye had taken the Earth lights. It had lost that wondrous, magical quality that it first had when Tamin and I had found it. I wondered if it was due to the fact that the place was now lit by the glow and sputter of yellow oil torches and not the soft blues of the crystals.

But it wasn't just that, was it? The sense of reverence had gone now, I thought in dismay. Bits of gravel had been tracked through the little room and dust yet swirled in the air, while the presence of the guards at our sides, whispering and muttering to each other, destroyed any momentary peace this place had held.

I had to admit that it didn't look like much under the glare of the torches.

"Interesting." Abioye had already moved ahead of me to examine the small column on which the chest had rested. He tapped at the stone experimentally, and I winced when he gave two ringing taps on the carved dragons.

"Torvald First Age, for sure," he said, looking back up at us with a smile.

"Oh," I said. For some reason, Abioye's historical details didn't make the place seem more magical, but less.

"And there was just the journal, the map, and the picture?" Abioye frowned a little.

And the dagger, I almost said – but something told me not to. If I did, then I would have to suggest that One-Eye had stolen it. Which might get her into trouble (good!) but would also mean that she would take it out on me or the other slaves later (bad).

"Just those three," I nodded, hating myself for becoming an accomplice in an overseer's deception. *But how can I say anything!* I seethed inside. *Maribet could take her revenge out on Tamin, or Oleer, or anyone else down here!*

"Oh." Abioye's voice was low for a moment, as he held my gaze with those blue eyes of his. "I see." For a moment I could see a look of weariness pass over his face, as if he had been hoping for something else. But what?

"Well, never mind." Abioye shrugged and stretched his arms out to yawn as if none of this bothered him in the slightest. *It's his way of hiding his disappointment,* I thought. It was like he didn't want the rest of us to know how much he cared. Why?

"I would say that it's a classic example of a primitive Rider Shrine." The young lord stood up and brushed some of the dust from his trews. "I've read about them, of course. The first Dragon Riders were regarded in such high esteem by the Torvaldites at the time that they were treated like prophets." I watched as the young man shook his head, apparently at the gullibility of those 'primitive' early Torvaldites.

Just like you Midmost Landers think we Daza are primitive? I could have growled.

This man's casual disregard for an entire culture irked me. Yeah, I knew that there had once been a whole history of Dragon Riders all over the Midmost Lands, and at one time they were even used to attack other kingdoms, I think. But this Abioye was acting as if they were nothing special at all.

He's probably never even seen a dragon, has he? I thought. I had. Anyone who could ride a beast like that had to have something about them, hadn't they?

"But I have never read reference to Lady Artifex; I will have to do some research," the young man said, casting an eye around the rest of the small grotto. "You never know, maybe her followers left something more valuable down here!" he said, and weirdly grinned at us as if we were the ones to agree with him.

It wouldn't matter if she or they had, I thought sullenly to myself. It's not like any of us slaves were ever going to keep anything we found, was it? I was so busy scowling at my cloth sandals that I didn't realize that Abioye had walked in front of me until his shadow cut across the torchlight.

"You seem upset… Narissea." He said my name awkwardly. Probably because he'd never talked to a slave before.

"Upset, sir?" I said, looking up at him. *I was furious.* Behind Abioye I could see Tamin's eyes widen as he looked at me in alarm. Despite our time apart, he still knew me well enough to know that I could have a temper.

"You… *like* this place?" Abioye said, sounding a little surprised. He was probably wondering how an uneducated slave like me could ever appreciate why this place was built. *I don't need to know the numbers and the history,* I thought. I don't need to know which queen or king did what. But the thought of people – perhaps like me, using the same sorts of tools that I did, had painstakingly crept down here into the dark to carve this place out; probably months of back-breaking work, just to keep alive the memory of a woman who was so brave, and so inspiring that it would stay alive down here until the world ended.

Yeah, that I could appreciate. That passion and that dedication to what they loved.

But what would be the point of sharing all of this with the brother of my oppressor? I would never be able to make him see me as anything other than an ignorant 'savage' could I? So instead, I just nodded. "I do. It's – it was, something special," I managed to say.

There was a snigger from behind me from one of the mine guards. I felt myself blush and looked at the floor. It shamed me to be treated like this.

Abioye was silent in front of me for a second, before he abruptly cleared his throat. "Right! I think I've seen enough here, you may go." He nodded to the mine guards. The two looked a little surprised but didn't waste any time pushing Tamin first back through the tunnel, one of them turning to point his metal club at me.

"Oh, my man will see that she doesn't get up to mischief," Abioye said in a loud voice, flipping a hand towards his personal guard standing in quiet reserve to one side. The personal guard looked older than anyone else in our little group, save for Tamin, and had been completely expressionless throughout our entire descent into the mines.

"As you wish," the guards muttered, leading the way ahead, before Abioye gestured for me to go first, to be followed by himself, and finally his man. We had barely walked a couple of meters into the small tunnel that joined the shrine to the rest of Western Tunnel Two, when one of the mine guards called back down the tunnel to Abioye.

"She not giving you trouble, is she, sir? Chief Dagan warned us this one likes to cause trouble! She's a little rat, alright!"

I clenched my jaw so hard it hurt and had to steady myself against the wall for a moment until the wave of hatred had washed over me. As I hissed out a sigh, Abioye said in careful tones behind me.

"You know that Dagan Mar will never let you go free, don't you? He will kill any of you before he lets you leave," the lord said. "He doesn't care about any of your lives at all."

My foot caught on the uneven rock and I stumbled. I wasn't surprised at the idea – it was something that I had pretty much realized myself. But I was surprised to hear it from Lord Abioye, of all people.

"None of your people care about us Daza," I couldn't stop myself from saying.

Abioye cleared his throat. "No – no, that's not true," he said, and his voice sounded hesitant.

What!? I shot a glance at him, to see that he had paused, and was fiddling with the laces of his shirt at his throat.

"Not all Three Kingdomers are like Chief Mar, you know," he muttered.

Maybe, I thought sullenly. My face felt hot with anger, but I knew what this lordling said was technically true – there had been Western traders and merchants who had passed through our village who weren't cruel. But from where I stood underground, with brands on my arm and the chafe marks of the heavy collars still on my ankles, it was easy to be angry.

"And yet you still provoke him," Abioye continued. "I've heard Chief Mar complain to my sister about 'the escaping Daza girl' before. Why infuriate a man like that?"

Why do I try to escape? Are you kidding me? I could have bitten the tongue from my own mouth as I glared at Abioye – to see that his eyes were wide. He looked momentarily fearful for a moment. *Of me?* I thought. *Maybe he should be,* I grumbled inside my head.

"Dagan is," Abioye whispered the words, his voice so low that I knew he meant them only for me. *Why?* "...volatile." It was clear that the young lordling had chosen the word very carefully indeed.

"I know that, *sir,*" I muttered back.

We reached the entrance to Western Tunnel Two, and the guards and Tamin were waiting for us with their torches, the heavy look of prejudice and suspicion on the faces of the mine guards ahead of me. There was never any mercy or understanding in any of those faces. It made me think about my answer.

Why provoke Dagan Mar, and Toadie and the rest? One of these days one of them would lose their temper and do more than try to slap me or have me lashed. They might even throw me over the Drop.

But just what was the alternative? To give up? To bow my head like Rebec and become something smaller, lesser than what I was, even now?

To do that would be an insult to everything that had come before. A betrayal of my mother's faith in me. A betrayal of the memory of what my life had used to be like – out there on the plains, riding ponies or hunting in the long grasses.

And it would be a betrayal of myself, most importantly. Of the four previous attempts that I had made to get out of here.

"I need to feel free, even if I am not," I hissed under my breath.

"One day, I hope we can all be free," Abioye murmured behind me, and it surprised me so much that I almost stumbled again. *How are you not free?* I would have asked him, but then his guard had rejoined us, glaring. We made our slow way back up the Western Tunnel. I felt worse now than I had before going down. My conversation with Abioye had just made me see what my situation was like from someone else's eyes. *Hopeless,* I thought miserably.

We reached the mouth of the tunnel, where the rest of the work shift were still waiting in line. And, much to my dismay, Abioye chose to once again address me, this time in front of everyone else.

"Narissea, there is a position as a house servant in the keep. I think that you might be a good fit for the role," Abioye said, already turning around as if that was that. I found myself staring at his back, and at the assembled queue of my fellow Daza people, all glaring at me. I could see in their eyes the questions: What had I done to deserve such a position? How had I wheedled and wooed my way to three meals a day, a fire, and maybe even a linen bed?

"No." I said abruptly. *I couldn't abandon my people down here!* How could Abioye ever believe that I would do that?

"I beg your pardon?" Abioye stopped and turned back around. He didn't look angry, just puzzled.

It would have been easier if he was angry, I thought.

"I won't do it. Sir." I said, and even managed to hold my chin high as the first mine guard made a snarl of indignation and raised his metal club.

"Wait." Abioye held up a long, fine-fingered hand. "It's fine." He straightened his jacket and shrugged. "She can stay down in the mines for all I care," he said, before appearing to forget that I even existed as he started talking animatedly to One-Eye about where the possible 'seams' of more Earth lights might be found.

Whatever. I threw the thought back at him. *As if I wanted to present food and wash laundry for that jerk anyway.*

"Come on, princess," chuckled a voice. It was Fankin, looking about as happy as a dog with its dinner. He and the rest of my work shift had been watching the whole exchange, but clearly he had found it all hilarious. "Work shift's over anyway. Maybe you can catch up to lover-boy if you hurry!" the man nodded back in the direction of the retreating Abioye.

I hissed at him, but as the mine guards started to corral us back up the Western Tunnel to the Main Avenue above I realized that the damage had been done. Just yesterday these Daza had stamped their feet at what I had to say, and now they acted as if I were some kind of traitor and could barely look at me.

CHAPTER 9
THE PLAN

"Halt right there! Don't move!" bellowed Toadie, racing towards our work team as we emerged from the mine. The man looked flustered, with red blotches blooming in his cheeks as he waved a cane menacingly at us.

"What did we do now?" I groaned. It was late in the afternoon, with the sky turning the golden yellow that it always did as the sun lowered itself over the plains. Below us, the work camp seemed in a state of turmoil, with what looked like every slave and prisoner already gathered in the central yard.

"None of you lazy sluggards move, you got that?" Toadie harangued, whipping his cane back and forth in the air as if daring us to disobey him.

"Well, we're not in a hurry to run back down the mines!" sniped one of the prisoners from our crowd, earning a shout of indignation from

Toadie – but he was too slow to identify who it was. And anyway, something *else* was happening down in the workcamp.

"You lot! You! Work team 3, 4 – get over here!" There was a commotion as the thin and high shriek of Dagan Mar carved up the assembled workers as sharp as any blade. I could hear grumbles and worried voices, as each of them must be thinking exactly what I was; *What new torment have they devised for us?*

Roughly half of the assembled slaves were being marched up to one of the terraces in the cliffs, where the lines of stone sheds rattled and belched smoke, day and night. Except they weren't. I hadn't noticed before in the confusion that the smelting sheds were quiet.

Dagan Mar had sent lines of guards up with overseers to manage the slaves, and I watched as heavy ropes – the same sort that we used to pull the carts loaded with mining ore – were passed down the line. They snaked back to the double iron doors of the largest of the sheds.

Whatever it is, it can't be good. That was my first thought. Whatever was in that shed had to be some new sort of mining machine that Inyene (*and Abioye, no doubt!*) had dreamed up.

My second thought, however, was that just about everyone was busy.

The guards were out, and I'd never seen so many of them, all concentrating on the shed.

If ever there was going to be a good time for a breakout, then now would be it. From my previous attempts, I knew that the guard changeovers were the easiest of times. I would be a fool to not take this opportunity.

I looked behind us to where the main entrance to the mines stood. If I could run past that and get to the far end of the terrace, that was where the tumbled boulders led up the side of the Masaka mountain to an old creekbed. Even as tired as I was, I could make that scramble.

But I couldn't. I couldn't make my legs move at all. How could I run away, and leave the rest of my people here? *The people who thought I was making friends with Abioye? Who wouldn't even look at me now?* The thought flashed through my mind.

No. I stood firm. I had turned down Abioye's offer of more comfortable employment because of these people around me – *my* people. I couldn't just run away and leave them here, could I?

"Heave!" the small and faraway form of Dagan Mar had climbed the terrace to better bawl at the slaves. The iron doors of the largest of the smelting sheds had been swung open, but whatever their ropes were now attached to inside was dark. The backs of Daza and the western criminals alike strained and stretched in the last of the burning sunset.

"Not enough!" one of the overseers shouted, and there was another commotion as more of the available work teams below were sent up the terraces to be given ropes, and to heave.

"She's moving!" someone called, and, to my dismay I realized that it was none other than Abioye, marching out of the smelting shed with his hands raised up in victory.

So. It looks like you were just trying to fool me with all that pretending to be nice, I thought bitterly. For some reason, I felt more deeply hurt and betrayed than from any of Toadies' slaps or Dagan Mar's nasty little whips. *But why should I care what that man –*

Inyene's own brother – did? Maybe it was because he had seemed to want to be nice. Maybe it was because he had actually talked *to* me rather than *at* me.

"Clear the space!" Abioye called, gesturing down the main ramp of the terrace to the main yard. It was Dagan Mar however, who instructed the remaining slaves to form a circle, with a thinner line of guards behind them.

And what of us? I thought. My work shift was still here by the mine entrance, with Toadie, our overseer, pacing back and forth in front of us nervously. It looked like we were being held in reserve, but why? And for how long? I was painfully aware of the boulders behind me.

"Heave!" Dagan shouted again, and this time the mine guards set upon the pulling slaves with jabs and prods from their clubs. I had never understood that. Why on earth did they think that hitting us would help us work better or faster?

But then, all my irritable thoughts were washed away as I saw what was being pulled out of the smelting shed. It was a dragon.

"That thing is no dragon," I said urgently. Although it had *almost* the outward appearance of one, everything about it looked wrong.

The main reason being for this – was that it was made out of metal. I could see the ruddy gleam of golden-bronze struts and supports that jutted from its spine, shoulders and hips like bones. Where the creature's elbows, wrists, or knees might be were pairs of giant bronze cogwheels. Gray-silver glinted all across it in drops, until I realized that they had to be steel bolts, each as big as my clenched fist.

But the very worst thing was what it was covered in. An eye-boggling, multi-colored array of scales. They were the same scales that we had been collecting, I was sure of it. Someone had tried to match the gradient of a real living and fire-breathing dragon's skin, with the largest of scales occupying the most area, gradually getting smaller and more closely knit as they met limbs, joints, and underside.

They've done a poor job of it though. I could remember the glossy sheen of the Black Dragon's scales, and how his entire suit had sighed gently as he had moved, and there was no seeming complication. On the mechanical monstrosity below however, there were several places where the wrong sizes and shapes of scales had been used, creating weird patches that stood out like the way that scar tissue or my old branding marks forever pulled oddly on my arms.

The creature lay on its haunches, its metal head resting on giant talons of curved swords. It had no ears, I realized. Its eyes weren't closed, they were just black almond-shaped holes. Its muzzle was too blocky and exact. It looked dead in a way that I couldn't describe.

"Heave, stars damn you!" Dagan Mar was lurching at a running limp, snapping his whip over the backs of the nearest slaves. There was a cry of pain and I saw one slave stumble, only for Dagan Mar to redouble his attacks.

"Stop it," I hissed under my breath, taking a step forward. But before my temper could get the better of me, a hand on my shoulder pulled me back. It was Oleer.

"Oleer?" I whispered, surprised that it would be him to want to help me. Last I had seen, he had been glaring at me along with all the other Daza in our work team. I looked up at his face to find that it was still troubled, his brow scrunched as he frowned back at me.

"No point in getting yourself beaten," he whispered, before nodding at the scene ahead of us. "That's bad news. For all of us."

I nodded. I couldn't begin to imagine what Inyene had been thinking.

The slave had gotten back to his feet by the time I turned back to look at the strange sight below us, and the dragon had been pulled forward to the main yard, where Dagan Mar had yelled for them to halt. Around it was the circle of my fellow slaves and prisoners, and then the circle of guards behind them. I was starting to get a bad feeling about this.

Clang-clang-clang! It was the harsh, ringing sound of a bell, but it wasn't one that I had ever heard before. The overseers and the mine guards routinely used high-pitched, screaming whistles to signal the end of shifts or alert each other to problems.

All eyes looked up to where this sound was coming from – the towers of Inyene's keep.

"What does it mean?" I heard a whisper on the other side of me. It was Tamin.

"I don't know." I shook my head, just as – *something* – swept over us all.

It felt like an icy blast of winter wind, although no hair on my head was moved. There was nothing to hear apart from the ringing of that deranged bell, but I could feel the ache of something in my ears all the same. And the backs of my teeth. And now, in the pit of my stomach, making me feel nauseous.

"*Urgh.*" I wasn't the only one who could feel it apparently, as Oleer on my left suddenly stumbled, one hand clutching his belly.

And then, the metal dragon below us started to move.

I gasped in shock and took an instinctive step backwards at this unnaturalness. There was a grinding, clacking noise as the dragon pushed itself up from its front haunches, the cogwheels at its elbows spinning in a blur. Its head and neck were still bowed, pointing down at the ground – but then blue light flared from its eye cavities, and the thing started to raise its snout.

Blue light like the Earth lights, I recognized. That had to be why Inyene wanted them so badly.

"Stoke the engines! Get her lit, quickly!" a voice shouted – Abioye, down below and running the length of the dragon. The creature was starting to shift and totter on its legs, the blue radiance spilling from its face in an unholy river. Abioye was hurriedly directing the teams of smelting workers to run towards the thing's belly with long poles, at the end of which appeared to be metal scoops filled with coals, which they were ramming *into* pre-designed vents in the thing. The sight made me feel sicker even than the eerie non-sound did. *These things are machines.* I grimaced. *Uncaring. Unfeeling. Unthinking machines – just like any of the mine equipment that Inyene was constantly cooking up.*

There was a *whump* as whatever internal fires that the thing had ignited, and thick black smoke started to steam from the creature's nostril holes, and with it came more life. The metal dragon raised on its rear legs and, with a grating snarl that sounded like metal-on-metal, opened its wings.

Hisses of alarm spread through the crowd of slaves and prisoners below us, as they convulsed backwards. Even the guards appeared terrified by this thing. The creature's wings spread out in segmented jerks, revealing bat-like fans made of some kind of thickened leather on bronze ribs.

"She's done it!" A victorious shout cut through the sounds of anguish. It was Dagan Mar, waving his fist in the air back at the keep. His celebration was short-lived however, as the thick clouds of the dragon's black smoke suddenly increased. There was something wrong and Abioye raced back to the team of smelting workers.

The dragon opened its metal maw, and for a moment I could see rows and rows of steel teeth like swords.

And with a grunt of thunder, a jet of thick coppery flame burst from the thing's mouth.

"Aiii!" The dragon's head had been raised, so the jet shot out into the air above the mining camp, but that didn't stop everyone in front of it – all of us, to tell the truth – from shouting in terror. The Daza started to run, pushing against the guards and each other ahead of this monster. Knots of prisoners – pale in the burning light – elbowed and shoved both Daza and guards out of the way.

Pheet! Pheeet! came the overseers' whistles, while still another shouted, "Breakout! Contain them!" and the guards started to push back. But they were using their metal clubs, shields, gauntlets, and boots–

"Nari," it was Oleer, pulling at my elbow, wrenching me from the sight below us as screams rose. "Now is your chance. Go," he said.

"What?" I looked at him in confusion. "No, our people…"

"Our people are going to get beaten by the guards or eaten by Inyene's dragon," Oleer hissed quickly. He was already pulling me through the crowd of our work team, pushing me in front of the mine entrance, towards the far end of the terrace where the boulders were – the same spot I'd scoped out earlier. "Now is your best chance. Get back home. Raise the alarm!" he said as we broke through the back of the team, and I could hear Toadie blowing his whistle again, calling for more guards to come help him. Some of the other slaves were clearly having the same idea I had – a knot of prisoners was already scaling the near slopes beside us. *But they won't get far,* I knew. *Up there it's open slopes, no cover. You have to use the old creek bed.*

"Tell the others. We'll travel as a group – I know the mountain trails," I was saying hurriedly to Oleer, who responded by pushing me, not too lightly, towards the boulders.

"Hey!"

"You're being stupid. And you don't get to be stupid. You're the daughter of the Imanu," Oleer said. "There's too many of us here. And now that Inyene's got the dragon, she'll only hunt us down. Thirty people will leave tracks, but one person might get through!"

I was stunned at Oleer's insight. He was using hunting logic. Daza logic. I was ashamed that I hadn't thought about this before. *He was right.* This was suddenly much more important than even I had thought before. Inyene had a dragon. If she had already captured or blackmailed half the Daza tribes just with her thuggish guards – imagine what she could do with a dragon?

Someone had to warn the rest of the Plains people what was coming. *And I was the Imanu's daughter.* That someone had to be me.

Thirty people couldn't get through – but a handful might. And of that handful, if only a few managed to get back to the Plains it would be worth it. "Come on," I said, pausing only to shout for Tamin. "Uncle! Follow me!" I said, running past the mine entrance to the far end of our terrace and the boulder wall, scrambling past the first few monoliths of stone and turning back to reach down to help Oleer,

who wasn't there!

It was Tamin who was behind me, looking wide-eyed and spooked. "It'll be alright, Uncle," I said to him urgently. "Up there to the creek. Turn left at the top. Quickly!"

Oleer still stood at the foot of the rocks, looking up at me. He had that flat, stubborn expression on his face that I had seen him use against a particularly hard bit of ore many times.

"Oleer? What in the name of the wind and the sun are you doing? Get up here!"

"You'll be quicker with two people," Oleer said resolutely.

"Oleer! Don't be an idiot. Grab my hand, now!" I said, reaching out to him.

Pheet! Pheet! The sounds of the guard's whistles were loud, and a gang of them was already racing towards us all, crossbows in hand.

"Tamin's smart. You're tough," Oleer was saying to me. He was already walking backwards, back across the mine entrance to where the rest of our work team was trying to scale that easier slope of the mountain. "We'll draw them off. Now go!" he turned and started climbing up the slope nearer the guards and the overseer. There were already about ten or fifteen people ahead of him, but they were all way too exposed. Way too easy to get shot.

"Oleer!" I shouted desperately.

"Little Nari – he's right." It was Tamin, who was only a few meters above me. "Most of the others have gone that way. We can sneak through, and take the message to the Plains."

I looked from Tamin's solemn face back to Oleer's climbing back and knew that they were both right. I hated it – but that didn't make them wrong. With a snarl of frustration, I turned and clambered up the side of the mountain, my heart burning in my chest.

CHAPTER 10
THE CHASE

P*heet! Pheet!* The sounds of the mine guards' whistles seemed to be everywhere as we clambered up the dried-up creek bed.

"I can't see them," Tamin whispered in the dark. He was just a shadow against the starry sky, and for a moment I wondered if this had been such a good idea – to go mountain climbing at night. But what other choice did I have?

Oleer. The others. My heart still ached, but the frustrated rage had subsided now to the ache of useless impotence. I could have done something to save him, couldn't I? I could have led more out.

"He's brave, that one," Tamin seemed to read my thoughts as I crouched beside him.

"He's stupid," I muttered, but I knew it to be a lie. Oleer had been brave. Braver than me. I wondered if he was still—

No. I wouldn't let myself think that thought. Oleer was no fool. He knew when to hold his hands up to the mine guards. He might get a beating, but that didn't mean that they would.

There was a sudden skitter of rocks from over on our right. It could have been anything of course, but it was matched by a smell that was out of place. The haze of acrid and bitter smoke, the same as came from the small pipe of one of the wall guards. I hunkered down a little lower, and I saw Tamin ahead of me do the same. If I had wondered if Tamin, with all of his time apart from the community, still knew how to hide – then I was clearly wrong.

Neither of us held our breath. That only makes you gasp and gulp for air when you can no longer take it. Instead I breathed shallowly through my mouth and did my best to remain calm as the skittering turned into the thud of footsteps and the flare of light.

There were two of the mine guards all right, each carrying a lantern in one hand and their metal poles in the other. It was too dark to recognize them, but I was sure one of them was Pipe-Smoker. "I'm telling you, this is too far – they all went that way!" said Pipe-Smoker.

"You want to be the one to explain that to Dagan?" muttered the other one. I wasn't surprised that Mar had a bad reputation with the guards as well.

"Nah, maybe not," huffed Pipe-Smoker. "But still, my legs are killing me. The bleeding stonedogs will get them, or the dragons, I say—"

"Ha! Dragons pass by here as often as fish, mate," said the second, proving just how stupid he was. For one thing, all of these mountain streams held silver fish, and there was at least one lake past the saddle of the Masaka which was teeming with them.

"Ugh," Pipe-Smoker groaned. "Look," he held his lantern high. "Out from here is the crags, and then it's just leagues of bare rock before you get to the Middle Kingdom. D'you reckon that anyone is really going to—"

And then there was a sharp, wet thud as Pipe-Smoker fell to the ground.

"Alar!" the second guard managed to say, racing forward as another dark figure rose from the rocks, armed with another boulder. It was one of the runaways, it had to be – but I couldn't see who it was.

The silhouette threw his rock, missed – but the second guard had stumbled to get out of the way – straight into Tamin.

"Ach!" Tamin burst to his feet, and the second guard screamed in shock. Our cover blown, I rose from my crouch, one hand already clutching a rock just as our mysterious interloper did.

Just as he sprang forward into the middle of us, bringing his rock down on the second guard. There was a strangled cry of pain, and silence, but both I and Tamin had clearly seen who our 'saviour' was.

It was Fankin, worst of the criminals.

"Get behind me, Uncle," I said, holding my rock high to my shoulder. Fankin just sniggered at my display. He was too busy ransacking the body of the second guard.

"Don't move," I said. I was a good throw. But I probably wasn't as strong as this criminal was. And it was dark.

"Calm yourself, princess," Fankin snapped back at me. "I'm not here to kill you or grandpa. I'm only here to get what I need to get out of here." He stood up slowly, and now in one hand he had the metal pole, as well as the guard's pouch-belt slung across his chest. He raised the pole slowly between us, pointing it straight at me.

"Now, I figure that you *might* be able to brain me with that lump of rock just like I did poor Alar over there," the horrid man said with obvious pride in his voice. "But I reckon I can dodge it. And then you and grandpa will just be standing there with stupid looks on your faces, won't you?" He waggled the metal club again.

"So, here's my plan. You're a pair of these 'wild people' right? You gotta know how to find the nearest road, settlement, inn – whatever. You two are going to help me out. And then you can wander off back to your bushes or wherever it is that you lot liv—"

"Plains," Tamin growled. I had never heard so much vehemence in my god-uncles voice before. "It's called the Plains."

"I don't care," Fankin sighed. "Now – I want princess here to grab that one's belt, and tie grandpa's hands behind his back. You got that? And then I'll tie your hands and we'll be getting on our way, right?"

"Get out of here," I said instantly. There were two of us, after all, we could—

"Ah!" Fankin waved the metal club menacingly. "You speak to me like that again, and I'll knock his head straight off his shoulders – or don't you think I'd do it?"

I did think that he would do it. I'd never met a man like Fankin. Even Dagan Mar and Toadie and One-Eye I could kind of understand. They did what they did for money, or because they believed in Inyene. But this man was like one of those crazed wolves that had lost their packs. They grow strange and cruel.

But there are still two of us, I told myself. *Even Fankin has to sleep some time,* I was thinking as I started to turn to Pipe-Smoker – just as there was yet another shout and the sound of approaching feet over the side of the mountain.

Pheeet! There were three lights appearing over the dark slopes, accompanied by the sound of the screeching, high-pitched whistles. But then more appeared. And then some more.

At least seven mine guards, I thought. *And they were making such a noise that there were bound to be more following behind them.* "Run," I said to Tamin, seizing the old man's hand as I picked the direction in the dark.

"Move it! They're coming!" Fankin shouted from behind us, already gaining. There was no way I was going to let him escape with us.

"This way," I said, recognizing the way that the dark shape of the mountain cut across the night sky. I knew what that place was. I had been there before.

"Ach." Tamin grunted in pain as he scrambled, but I wouldn't let up. I hauled and pulled as behind us Fankin cursed and abruptly changed course to follow me. But I had chosen one of the hardest routes. It was a boulder field, and it stretched around this entire saddle of the mountain.

Bang. "Ah!" But even after my four previous attempts to escape across the Masaka, and all of my scale-collecting shifts, it seemed that I was not immune to scraped shins either. It was less of a run than it was a fast crawl, as I pushed Tamin between two larger boulders, and then jumped atop another to pull him up behind me, only to repeat the process all over again. And again.

"Scale-collecting missions?" a small voice in the back of my head said.

Pheet! Pheet! The sounds of the whistles echoed over the mountains behind us, but they were fading. I heard at least two startled shouts of pain as various mine guards must have fallen and sprained ankles or even broken bones.

Fankin however, was still coming. I couldn't see him clearly in the dark, but I could hear his grunts and gasps of pain as he pushed and pulled himself over the rocks below. He'd given up talking or threatening us, but that didn't mean that he wasn't still there.

"Nari? How much farther?" Tamin panted as our ascent had slowed considerably. I raised my head briefly (a little afraid that Fankin would knock it off with one of his thrown rocks). The boulder field continued above us, but we had rounded the slope and were looking back down on the high crags.

And not too far from us was a midnight-black void like a pit. If I had done my reckoning right, then that would be the gorge and the cliff, which meant—

Yes! There. I could see the ledge and the cave. The same cave where I had met a dragon.

The sounds of the guards had become just a distant murmur behind us now, and far less agitated or angry. They must have lost us in the dark and were now wondering whether or not to abandon the search and come back the next day.

But Fankin was still there, grunting and growling, his breath ragged. He wasn't far behind us.

Well, let's just see how his charm works on a dragon, shall we? I thought as I helped Tamin down onto the ledge and put one hand under his shoulder. He was now limping from our wild escape. The cave was only a little way ahead, and I sidled him towards it.

"What's that smell?" Tamin whispered. It was that fragrant scent like frankincense again, mixed with charcoal.

"Don't panic, god-Uncle," I breathed, listening for Fankin's loud gasps as he rounded the edge of the boulder field. *With any luck he'll slip and fall down the cliff,* I thought – before quickly deciding that would be a terrible outcome. Not out of mercy, but I really didn't want to have to clean up his body after the fact.

"That smell is dragon,"

"*Dragon!*" Tamin said in alarm, but I pushed him ahead of me, into the dark.

"A dragon!" Tamin repeated. "I used to see them as a child, but that was a long time ago now."

"*Shhh!*" I pointed back at the entrance to the cave, knowing that Fankin would be on this ledge at any moment.

And then I realized that Tamin probably couldn't see me, so I tugged on the hand I was still holding, and hissed "*Fankin,*" instead.

"Oh," Tamin said in the gloom.

But of the dragon, there was no sign. The problem with the cave was, that it was black and the dragon, well... But I could still smell the aroma of charcoal and incense. Just how far back did this cave go? With a sudden sense of loss, I wondered if it had healed and flown away already. Maybe my plan had been to no avail.

But surely not even Fankin would creep into a dark cave on a dragon mountain in the middle of the night, right? I thought.

I was wrong.

"Here, princess." The man's footsteps crunched on the loose chips of stone outside. Right outside. Suddenly, there he was, silhouetted against the night sky, holding up his metal club. "You think you can hide from me, huh? Well, better men than you have tried," he said and smacked the side of the mine with a dull thump.

He took a step inside, another thump on the walls. "Sooner or later, I gotta hit something soft, right?" I could smell his sweat wafting in the air.

"Do yourselves a favor and come out now, all peaceful." Thump. He hit the other side of the cave.

"Maybe I won't even bash you about too much." Thump.

There was a rattle of stone as something moved in the darkness, near the floor. "Aha!" Fankin leaped forward, bringing his metal club down on it.

Clang! Only this time it didn't make a dull thudding noise as the metal hit rock. Instead, the bar rang like a bell as if it had hit metal. Or something just as hard as metal.

"Sssss…" The sound behind us grew like the coming hurricane winds in early autumn, the ones that brought with them towering thunderheads and threw lightning across the Plains. The hissing grew louder, turning into a fierce storm of noise.

And two familiar, baleful gold-red eyes opened further back in the cave.

"Duck!" I pulled on Tamin's hand as the dragon surged forward. It was like the mine collapse all over again –a blast of hot air and dust pulled at me, in the same moment as something very large and very angry passed overhead. I heard a startled gulp, and a scream.

The black dragon roared, and it was a sound worse than the collapse of Western Tunnel Two. I think I shrieked, but if I did then I couldn't hear my own voice in my ears. The echo of the dragon's anger rolled back into the cave as it must have rolled down the mountain outside, too. I held onto Tamin as he had one arm around me, too, waiting for the noise to fade. As it did, I heard something scrabbling and running on the rocks outside – it had to be Fankin, fleeing.

The dragon stood awkwardly in the mouth of his cave, and there was a dim orange glow illuminating gigantic fangs as he swept his mighty head back to regard us.

"It's me!" I said desperately. "Narissea of the Souda. I brought you bread. It was terrible bread I know, but I brought it. We weren't the ones to hit you, I promise. That was Fankin, he was the one we were running away from." I was panicked and speaking fast, praying that the black would remember me. I had only decided to come here at the last minute. It had seemed like a good idea at the time, to hide near a dragon when a murderer was chasing us.

Huff. There was another blast of hot air, as the dragon had moved his head closer to us, his great nostrils flaring against the starlight, just like a horse as it took in our scent. That simple gesture gave me hope.

"I'm sorry to disturb your rest," I managed to catch my breath and say in a more even tone.

The black dragon slowly turned its head back to look out of the cave, and for a moment held the posture. I could see the light of the distant stars catching its muzzle and side, and I saw just how noble – handsome – it was. And also how hurt.

The dragon was leaning against the cave opening strangely, with one wing squashed up behind it and one front paw held up in front of its chest. It was breathing shallowly. I didn't know much about dragons – okay, I didn't know anything at all – but to me it looked in a worse state than before. Like it was weakened by hunger, or feverish.

"You're still hurt," I said, and it was only when Tamin reached up to grab my elbow did I realize that I had risen from my crouch to move towards it. How could I not?

"It's going to be okay, Uncle," I said to Tamin, and somehow I knew that it would be. Creeping forward, I reached out a hand towards the dragon's side. I don't know what I was expecting to do, but Mother always said that half the battle with illness is knowing that there is someone else there.

"Please, if we can stay here tonight, then tomorrow I'll find a way to get you food. I promise. There are fish in the streams," I was saying, and the dragon spun its head around to regard me with wider eyes this time. Softer eyes. They weren't as crimson red this time either, but a rich golden-amber color.

"Fish? You like fish?" I said, and the dragon cocked its head to one side at me, like a cat. "Just one night, and I promise I'll get you some fish," I said, and stretched my hand towards its snout.

The mighty creature moved its head ever so slightly, and ignoring everything I'd ever been told about keeping a safe distance from dragons, for the first time in my life I touched a living, fire-breathing dragon. Its scales were warm to the touch. Very warm, in fact – and they were also softer than I was expecting, near what I guess would be the creature's lips.

You're hurt, but you're not alone, I thought, and something passed through me. It was like the opposite of whatever had powered that mechanical dragon. It wasn't a painful, uncomfortable feeling that made me think of ice – but a rush of warmth that made me remember warm evenings in front of our hut's fire, listening to Mother singing songs as she cooked dinner.

With a sudden blast of warm air, the dragon moved and very carefully turned around to stretch itself back down the tunnel. It had to daintily step around me and Tamin as it did so, and when it settled itself down with a heavy sigh, there was its large belly right in front of us, radiating warmth. It didn't seem bothered that we were here, and it felt as natural as breathing to beckon Tamin over and lean against it.

As I drifted into a deep and dreamless sleep, my last thought was, *Have I just made friends with a dragon?*

CHAPTER 11
OF FISH AND FRIENDSHIPS

O w. A pain in my arm woke me up. For a moment I didn't
realize where I was – but then I remembered the events of
last night. The chase. Fankin. The dragon.

There was a high-afternoon light filling the cavern, making me
realize that I had slept all the way through the dawn and the morning.
Beside me, Tamin was still hunched against the warm belly of the
black dragon, snoring like a goat.

And there was the black dragon, who was already awake and looking
at me. "Oh, hi," I said, feeling suddenly a little self-conscious. Just
like last night, all trace of crimson red had fled the dragon's eyes, and
instead they were a deep gold. He blinked slowly at me.

Ow! My left elbow throbbed in pain, but when I hesitantly stretched
it out, I could see no injuries or marks, and there was no pulling or
clicking from my elbow.

There was a rustling noise, and the dragon shifted in his stretched-out position, carefully extending his wing as open as he could in the tight space. In the late afternoon light, I could clearly see the rent that stretched up one of the middle ribs of his leathery wings. Its edges looked puckered and swollen, and I bet it was painful.

"That's why you haven't been eating, isn't it?" I said, reaching up a hand gingerly to the wing. As soon as I touched its edge, the black dragon opened his maw and gave out a breathy sort off hiss. Not a growl or a snarl, but enough to let me know that it hurt.

"Okay, I get it." I nodded. I tried to remember what I had been taught as a child around our ponies, goats, hunting dogs. "You need to build up your strength first," I remembered. That was the key to fighting any ailment. "Let the body heal itself."

"Snghr! What – huh?" Tamin's shoulders slid from the dragon's belly with a thump and he snorted awake. "Nari! Ah…" He looked up to see the black dragon regarding us with half-lidded eyes and froze.

"He's hungry," I said, before quickly adding, "not for humans, though. He wants fish." *He would have eaten Fankin if he wanted to, right?* I thought. But then again, I really wouldn't have blamed him if he couldn't bring himself to digest that horrible man.

Tamin was still looking between me and the dragon with a certain amount of worry. He shuffled slowly away from the black, even though he had been happy to use its warmth through the night.

"He's in pain, Uncle," I said.

"You did make a promise to feed it," Tamin agreed, and he was looking at me oddly, his brow heavy as he bit his lip.

Whatever. I shook my head. Tamin, as much as I loved him, had been gone from the Plains for a long time. Perhaps he had forgotten how to be around animals. "I'm going to find him and us some fish. You're welcome to stay here with the dragon or come help me," I said, standing up with a stretch and walking back out of the cave.

A few moments later, I heard Tamin's footsteps following me.

Even though the sun was burning bright in the cloudless sky, it was still chilly up here on the Masaka as the winds howled and played over the rocks. As soon as we had left the ledge and scrambled up the boulder field, a sense of danger possessed us. We decided that we would travel relay-style, with me going first (as I knew these places best) as Tamin hung back, acting as lookout – and then our positions would reverse as Tamin scrambled up to join me and I would watch the slopes from my hiding place.

It was slow going, but eventually we had worked our way around the nearest ridge (I didn't want either of us to be silhouetted against the skies up there) and down the far side to where the Masaka split into ravines. We passed by scrubby trees and woody shrubs with small, deep purple berries that, after a careful tasting, proved edible.

"They look related to Bilberries," Tamin said. "They grow on the foothills on the other side of the mountains." We filled our pockets with them.

This side of the Masaka was less battered by the wind and less exposed to the high glare of the sun, and it wasn't long before we started hearing bees and seeing sprouts of rough grasses and fragile-looking mountain heathers.

"Here," I pointed to a spray of water that fell down the side of one of the ravines to fill a long, thin lake. We didn't even have to wait before we heard the fat *plop* of a fish jumping for insects.

If I had wondered about all that Tamin had forgotten, I was proved wrong as we made fishing spears out of the straightest branches of the trees, sharpening their points with the chips of flint that we had to knap against other granite boulders. "My grandfather used to hunt this way," Tamin said with a smile, and for a while, there in the sun, it seemed as though a weight had fallen from his shoulders.

It was hard to not feel at least a little optimistic as we rolled up our canvas trews and waded out to the edges of the lake. The water was freezing, but it still felt good. We threw handfuls of the Bilberries in wide arcs around us, knowing that the fish would be attracted to their bobbing forms – and that there would be plenty more to harvest on our way back to the cave.

Splash! With sharp smacks into the water, we threw our spears, Tamin getting the first fat silver fish with one, and me missing. After which, we had to wade a bit further, throw our Bilberries again, and wait. The afternoon went like this for a little while, until the shadow of the Masaka behind us started to stretch long.

"The sun drops quickly up here," I told Tamin, who nodded. I remembered how it was different out on the Plains – where the land seemed to stretch out in every direction forever, and the days lasted longer.

Or so it had seemed, anyway, I thought with a pang of doubt. A finger of cold wind reached the back of my neck and brought with it my doubts as I shivered. I had been a child back then. Only just passing my Testing before I was captured. My memories felt like a fairytale, and I wondered if it really had been the way that I remembered it.

With my change of mood, came my questions. *Had Oleer made it? Was he out on the mountain somewhere, like us? Or had he been recaptured?* And, just as worryingly; *how many of our people had survived the escape attempt? How many had been beaten or punished?*

"Out of the water." Tamin seemed to sense my unease as he helped me up, back to where a rise still held the last of the sun. On the top of a wide, flat rock was our collection of six large silver fish. Even one would probably be more than enough for me and Tamin, I guessed – but who knew how many a dragon could eat?

"You know that Torvald still trains dragons, don't you?" Tamin asked me as we gutted and skewered our catch. It was messy, smelly work, but anything that wasn't chipping rock felt like such a relief.

Which is what Oleer and the others are probably doing right now. I faltered. "Really?" I said, not exactly paying attention.

"Yes. Although their number is far smaller than they ever were before." The wistful note in my friend's voice made me look up at him. He was looking out to the west, and even though the mountains were in the way and the sky was darkening out there, I wondered if Tamin could still feel the pull of that almost-mythical place.

'Torvald'. The Citadel-on-the-Mountain. Shining white walls. The place where anything could be bought and sold. Once an empire, and now just another kingdom like all the others. Home to the Dragon Academy. I'd heard stories about wars and great magical battles

happening out there on the other side of the mountains all through my childhood – but they had always seemed so distant and far away. Not real. I had never even *seen* a dragon before the black.

"I would go there, as a part of the Scribes and Magistrates Guild," Tamin said, explaining a way of life to me that sounded strange and foreign.

"We would be trained every few years, kept up to date with recent rulings and changes in the law," he explained.

"The law changes?" I frowned. "That seems… *messy.*"

Tamin chuckled, but it was a sad laugh. "Yes, it is. For the Middle Kingdom it is, anyway." He nodded back west. "New kings and queens come and go, they make new decrees, and different magistrates and judges decide different things. It's the reason why Inyene can do what she does." His voice faltered, and I understood why.

The mines. Her slaves. The mechanical dragon. From our vantage point, standing in the fading afternoon light with fish guts all over our hands, it seemed too nightmarish to be true. But it had been, hadn't it? Which brought back the urgency of our mission: We had to find a way out to the Plains, and to warn the rest of our people of what was coming.

And then raise them to form warbands, encourage them to attack Inyene's camp and free the others, I thought.

But then I remembered that mechanical dragon once again, how it had stood tall and breathed an inferno of fire into the sky. It had been smaller than the black – but not by much. I remembered the clang as Fankin's bar had hit the black's tail – how useless would the very best weapons that the Daza had be against the scales of Inyene's metal monsters?

I looked over to Tamin to see that his eyes were shadowed and serious. He must have been thinking the same thing. "What are we going to do?" he said.

I looked at our fish, and at the ridiculously simple wooden spears we had fashioned. *Inyene has a dragon, Inyene has a dragon,* I kept thinking. My elbow throbbed with a dull ache again, and I remembered the far greater pain that the black dragon was in, right now. "I don't know," I answered truthfully. "But that dragon is in pain and needs our help too," I said seriously. I wouldn't be a Daza if I just abandoned it. "After we have helped the dragon and built up our provisions for the journey ahead, then we'll be in a better position." I tried to sound as confident as Mother had been when she dispensed wisdom.

But – be in a better position to do what? I couldn't help but think as we made our way back to the cave.

"You know, Narissea?" Tamin said as we climbed, once again looking at me with that odd, serious look, "It is a very serious thing to make friends with a dragon. It's not like you train a pony, a hawk, or a hunting dog, it's…" He shook his head as he tried to explain it, and settled for just, "There is an old word for that type of friendship: A bond."

"I know that it's serious, Uncle," I threw off his concern with a laugh, all the while as I was thinking, *every friendship is important, isn't it?*

The sun was getting low, but it still wasn't true evening as we rounded the ridge and onto the boulder field, loaded down with our catch. Again, we practiced the tandem creeping and look-out that we had used before. It was on our second such leap-frog scurry through the boulders that I reached Tamin's crouch by a large boulder and wondered when he remained frozen where he was.

"Uncle?" I whispered.

"Nari – out there, look." He nodded down the slopes, to where the two near arms of the Masaka held the work camp between them. I could see Inyene's keep clearly at the end of one of the Masaka's 'arms' just as I could see the work sheds and the terraces, but the entrance to the mines itself was obscured below our height.

Not that it mattered, as it was clear what Uncle wanted me to look at.

They were pulling out a wide cart from the smelting sheds, and on it was another mechanical dragon. I knew that it was a different one because the first dragon was sitting up with long forelegs straight like a cat on one of the higher terraces, looking down at the work camp below it like it was going to pounce.

But there was no smoke coming from it, I could see. No movement, no hint nor sign of life.

"How is she building so many, so fast?" Tamin whispered. We could see the lines of slaves pulling on the ropes, and the circle of slaves in the main yard again, just like before.

They're using us as shields, I remembered the previous night when the first metal dragon had been raised. It seemed that Abioye or Dagan – perhaps even Inyene herself – could barely control them. The first had looked as though it had malfunctioned when it threw out its fire.

I shook my head at the horror of the sight and tried to focus on Tamin's question. "We've been collecting scales for a long time," I said. "I've been here for four years, and in all that time, they'd send us up the mountain to hunt for scales." Not that we'd ever managed to gather many, but over four years that had to be a lot, right? And how long had Inyene been gathering them before that?

But it wasn't just the dragons below that was making me feel queasy. It was the number of slaves and prisoners that I could see. They were too far away for me to work out how many there were, but it still looked like a lot.

"Not that many managed to escape last night," I whispered, realizing what must have happened. And if that was true, then that probably meant that a lot of people had been hit by the guards' metal clubs. Or worse. *My friends and my people were down there, and they were in pain.* I clenched my jaw.

"Come on," I said, moving past Tamin. It was even more important, now more than ever, that we come up with a plan.

We had just rounded on the final part of the boulder field that led to the cave when I felt that surge of cold, sickening nausea that I had felt before. I heard a small noise and turned to see that Tamin was leaning against the nearest boulder, looking aghast. "You feel that too?" I said.

He nodded. "It must be Inyene. Whatever she is doing. Whatever powers she is using…" He didn't need to finish the thought. It was clear to both of us that whatever it was she was doing, was wrong.

"*SKRECH!*" And then, ahead of us, there was a loud cough of rage, and the gravel trembled around my feet. I could see the cave ledge, and there was a pillar of thin black smoke rising from it, clearly from the dragon inside. It was as if he had sensed whatever it was that Inyene had done, too – and he liked it about as much as we did. I broke into a scramble to the ledge with my five speared 'dragon' fish, hurrying to calm the black down before he drew attention to our position on the mountain.

"Hey now, here now," I said in low, coaxing tones as I rounded the cave at a slow, sidling walk. Despite what Tamin seemed to think about my actions, I wasn't so brash as to run at a wounded and distressed animal with a stick!

A hissing sound came from ahead, and there was the dragon's head, with the evening light glinting along its scales. Its eyes had flushed that angry, crimson red – but they immediately started to lighten to amber gold as they saw me.

"Here now, it's only me," I said. "Look, I brought you something." I edged closer with the fish.

"Skree-ip?" The dragon made a new noise. A chirrup as its eyes widened and moved forward.

"You like fish, huh?" I said, walking backwards slowly to the ledge and levering the fish off of the stick, leaving them in front of the cave's entrance. Tamin had joined me on the ledge, but was hanging back, watching me.

"I don't know how you're supposed to feed a dragon—" I was saying, just as there was a sudden burst of flame from the cave.

"Nari!" Tamin moved towards me, but the flame was yards ahead of me, and it was nothing like the flame that the metal dragon had produced. Instead of that fireball, it was just a direct and thin needle of fire, hitting the five fish and roasting them in an instant.

"Look, it's fine," I laughed. As the dragon moved forward and greedily started picking each roasted fish up between the tips of its teeth, I noted just how different it was from Inyene's macabre creations. Of course, it was different, it was made of flesh and bone, right? But the black could seemingly use its flame like a tool, entirely unlike the metal dragon.

The black dragon seized the second fish and crunched it down, and then a third disappeared the same way. He started to make a deep, rattling noise in his chest as he paused and took his time with the last two. "Look, he's purring!" I said happily, crouching down. I waited until he had finished, and then gestured for Tamin to bring our final, fat silver lake fish to the hot stones to roast.

"Nari, how do you know the dragon is a he?" Tamin said to me in a low voice as we watched our dinner sizzle.

I could feel the dragon's eyes on our dinner and could sense his excitement, but he had also pulled back, as if he wasn't ravenously hungry, just interested.

"How do I know?" I hadn't considered it. I just did. I shrugged. "It's his antlers. It's a he," I said with certainty, and to my surprise, the dragon made another chirruping sound across from us.

"Hm." Tamin was looking at me funny, before he stooped to flip the fish over.

"What?" I asked. "Look, I know he's not a pet. He's a dragon. A full-grown bull dragon," I said confidently.

"A bull dragon?" Tamin repeated my words. *What was up with him?* I was hungry anyway, and used the fishing spear to hook our fat friend from the hot rocks and start to scrape away the skin. Even Tamin's hunger seemed to overcome his suspicions, as he stopped his weird questioning and concentrated on not burning his fingers as we both ate.

There was more than enough food for the pair of us, and when we finished I flipped the carcass to the dragon, whose head darted forward with a *snap!* – to catch it expertly, crunch the bones, and swallow in one fluid motion. Another rattling purr came from the dragon as I poured out the water skin that I had filled at the lake for him to sip – luckily the skin was one of the few things we'd had with us when we fled the camp. As the dragon lay back down on the ledge, half his body in the cave and the rest half out, me and Tamin finished our dinner with our picked Bilberries, and soon my fingers were stained a sticky blue.

"Better," I said with a pleased yawn as the sky started to burn with the sunset – before, in the very next heartbeat, I felt guilty. *Why was I allowed to have this feeling when Oleer and the others were still down there, struggling in the dark?*

With this heavy thought, I looked out back northwest to where the mining camp would be, and wondered just what it was that we were going to do.

CHAPTER 12
CHILDREN OF THE WIND

The next day I awoke from a dream of scales and teeth and wings – but feeling strangely calm and unafraid. If anything, I remembered my dream-self feeling *excited*.

With once again no food, we decided that it would be best to go harvesting again – this time gathering enough to try and set up a small smokery, if the dragon would oblige. Which would also mean that we needed enough wood for the charcoal, and the frames.

"We'll only smoke at night," I explained to Tamin. "That way, we won't be in danger of alerting Inyene's guards." Tamin nodded, as we both knew the process was a simple one, if a little laborious. We would enclose a stack of fish on frames inside a small stone oven, before shoveling the charcoal chips at the bottom. The smoke would dry out the succulent fish meat, and, although I was sad at the loss, it would mean that the fish would keep for days, weeks if we managed to turn it into jerky. The biggest drawbacks were only being able to smoke at night, and the fact that someone had to be awake to tend it at all times, removing the stone to add more wood chips whenever the thin streams of escaping steam started to dwindle.

But I knew it would be worth it, and Tamin agreed that it would not only give us a few days to build our strength, but also to keep an eye on the work camp and try to figure out a plan.

To be honest, our resolution didn't offer me as much optimism as I had originally thought it would. I still felt powerless and shameful as I made my way back over the boulder field in the late afternoon, intending to catch the fish while Tamin stayed behind to build the stone smokery. He would use our spears as the first set of frames, meaning that I had to fashion another on the way.

I'd set myself up for a lot of work, what with all of this fishing and wood-cutting and spear-making and knapping. But it wasn't like the work of the mines. This felt good and nourishing in a way that the Mine work could never be. There was an immediate and natural rhythm to these tasks. Once again, my mind reeled at what Inyene was doing to the people unfortunate enough to fall under her thumb. *Using us has tools – just like her blasted metal dragon!*

We had found a stream not so far from the cave, and it became an extra job to keep running back and forth with Tamin's water skin, filling up the natural bowls in the available rocks for all of our drinking water.

Ow. My elbow gave me a pang of pain again, and I hesitantly stretched my arm out and around my head in the late afternoon light. Nothing tender or sore this time. I dismissed it, looking up.

And saw the tree ahead of me, to the right of the gulley that I had been about to scramble down. It was a slender and small tree with a whitish bark, but she also looked strong. Her leaves were teardrop-shaped, and they glowed with a healthy, living green.

Use those leaves to heal the dragon's wing, I thought, and then wondered how I knew that. She wasn't a tree that I could name, but I *knew* that was how I was meant to use her leaves. It was almost as if a voice had said the words in my head.

"Don't be ridiculous, Nari." I laughed at myself. What a strange notion! I clearly must have worked with trees similar to this one as a child – or maybe I was remembering some old bit of Daza lore that Mother had taught me?

Whatever. It didn't matter how I knew, just that I did. I would harvest a heavy wodge of the youngest of the green leaves, and I would mash it into a paste to spread on the dragon's wing. It wouldn't even take that long.

By the time the sun had set, I was returning back to the camp, having made a sort of pulling-frame with a mixture of woven branches, upon which I had layered my haul of wood, fish, berries, and leaves, and both Tamin and the dragon appeared pleased with what I had managed to do, all in a few watches.

As Tamin set up the smokery, I went to work on the paste, using a dribble of water and a rock to help mash and pound the leaves into a thick, sticky greenish goop. "Hey, look what I got for you!" I called out to the dragon, who surprised me by coming eagerly over, and laying out his damaged wing nearby, as if he had been expecting it.

You're a lot friendlier than I thought you'd ever be, I thought with a smile as I worked. The mash was almost like a glue, and after gingerly applying it to both sides of the dragon's wing, I realized that it could form a thick mat over the whole injury. When I had finished, the dragon chirruped once again, and laid the affected wing out over the smokery, turning the goopy mat into a sort off hardened, green scale.

"He knows more about this than I do." I turned to laugh with Tamin, only to find that he had finished his smokery and was crouching, looking between the pair of us.

"Nari," he said in a low, warning voice.

What had I done now? This was my promise. I was going to make the dragon better, in return for the safety and warmth of staying with him. What was so wrong about that?

"I didn't recognize those leaves from any tree on the Plains," Tamin said gravely. "Did someone tell you that they would help heal the dragon?"

"Tell me?" I said. Why was Tamin getting all weird again around me and the dragon? "No, no one told me. Not in the mines, at least. I think that I must have remembered something from home."

"No one told you," Tamin said more firmly. "You haven't had a dream? Or heard a voice describing to you how to care for a dragon?"

"No!" I said, and my heart fluttered in my chest as I felt like I was being attacked and I had no idea why. "I haven't had any dreams or been hearing voices – why on earth would you ask?"

Tamin was quiet for a moment, looking at the floor as he was obviously debating something. Finally he spoke. "It is written, quite plainly in the Histories of Torvald, that there were people who would hear things, be able to do things, when they were near dragons. That the dragons talked to them using their minds, and these people could talk back."

"So?" I said hotly. "It would be a great thing if I could talk to the dragon as easily as I'm talking to you, wouldn't it?" *In fact, it seemed pretty awesome, in fact!* I would be just like the Lady Artifex and her red dragon, Maliax, then, wouldn't I? For a brief second I imagined leaping on the back of the black dragon and screaming through the air, to bring a fanged and fiery justice to Inyene.

Tamin took another deep breath, interrupting my fantasies as he raised his head to look at me. Just across from us, I could sense the dragon regarding us both silently. He was waiting to hear the outcome of our conversation.

"Perhaps it would. I don't know what the best course is," Tamin said. "I have no experience of this, and it frightens me. But I have read a small fraction of the Histories of Torvald, and there is much danger, always, around these people." He struggled to look for words. "They are thrown into wars that break mountains. Some of them are able to use their minds to do amazing, terrible things. It is not so long ago that there was a Sorcerer-Emperor on the throne of Torvald, and although this 'Enric' had nothing to do with dragons apparently – he hated them – it was the magic of these ancient beasts that Enric used—"

"Sssss!" There was a sudden spurt of smoke and heat from the dragon beside us as he cocked his head to stare with one eye at Tamin. He huffed heavily into the night air and sank his head down onto his paws as if annoyed at the mere mention of the long-dead Enric.

Tamin had paused at the dragon's outburst, and in the gap I spoke instead. "Well, I am not hearing any voices, and I don't think that anyone is about to make me the Emperor of Torvald any time soon!" I kept my voice low, but I was just as fierce.

Tamin looked at me, aghast. "I didn't mean to upset either of you, I just worry. What with Inyene and those *things* and our people, our home," he said, and my anger faded away in an instant. I had always been like that: quick to anger, and just as quick to forget.

"I didn't mean to snap at you," I apologized, reaching over to grasp my uncle's hand reassuringly. "And I understand. I don't know what we're going to do either – but I know that we've got each other. I need your strength and your wisdom, Uncle."

Tamin looked at me with tears in his eyes, but a sad smile on his face. "And I fear that we are going to need your temper, too."

"Souda." I awoke with the name of our tribe clear in my mind, as if something had put it there. It was still night, but it was no longer true dark anymore. The gray light of morning was rising on the eastern horizon, making everything strange and dreamlike.

"Souda," I repeated to myself. What an odd thing to dream about! It was the name of Tamin's and my tribe of the Daza, and Mother had always told me it was a homage to the warm western winds – the Soussa – that blew best in high summer.

My body felt alert and alive, and I wasn't in the least bit tired as I got up and padded towards the mouth of the cave, to see that the dragon was sitting on the ledge, looking out over the gorge below expectantly.

Where's Tamin? I thought, before seeing that the older man was just a dark shape, snoring as was his way, next to the smokery. Thin fingers of whitish steam rose from between the rocks and I knew that the fire hadn't gone out yet. I considered waking Tamin up and taking over his shift at our food store, but something drew me to the shoulder of the black dragon instead.

"Skree-ip?" he chirruped at me softly as he turned his great snout in my direction. His large golden-amber eyes reflected the light of the sickle moon far above.

"You can't sleep either?" I murmured, reaching out with a hand towards his glossy black scales.

But then the black suddenly moved, resisting my touch as he leaped, panther-like, over the edge.

"Wait!" I called out in a gasp, as the black disappeared in a heartbeat below us. But what about his wing! It couldn't be healed yet, could it? That would be impossible! I stepped up towards the edge of the cliff.

Just as there was a great crack like the snap of our tribal banners in the winds, but much louder. With a rush, the black dragon was swooping up in front of me; a mountain of black shiny scales, claws, and cool air.

I sighed at the sheer awe of such a beast. Such power, speed, and grace all combined into one as the dragon flew over our heads, over the boulder field, and turning in an arc high over the Masaka.

"Uncle?" I said, flicking my eyes towards him. No matter his misgivings about dragon-friendships, surely even he would want to see this, wouldn't he?

But my god-uncle was still fast asleep, snoring heavily. Neither the chirrups or the beat of the black dragon's wings had woken him, amazingly.

I could *feel* the return of the black dragon in the same way that you could feel the first days of spring: a sleeping knowledge that adds excitement to your breast and a quickness to your heart, even though you might not be able to pinpoint it to any particular budding flower or turn of the wind. I turned my head to see that he was lowering himself once more into the canyon on powerful wing beats, bobbing slightly in the gray morning airs.

The black dragon was looking at me intently, his eyes narrowed but golden. Not crimson red. I had no fear as I stepped up once again to the edge of the ledge, and held out my hand.

Souda. I heard the thought once again in the back of my mind.

As if waiting for some unspoken signal, the great black dragon moved with a flick of its wings, and his shadow fell over me. For less time than it took to breathe, everything went dark, and the dragon's claws clamped around my shoulders and chest with a heavy thump. I was too shocked to cry out as the great creature lifted me up, expertly passing me back and forth between his claws to turn me around and hold me snug under his breastbones.

The wind tore at my hair and clothes, but aside from the sudden chill on my face I was actually warm from the dragon's radiating heat. I panted more in surprise than shock, looking down to see massive, slightly curving claws which were also as black as pitch folded gently over my torso and legs. Any one of those talons could have gutted me as easily as I had gutted those fish, and yet I felt no pain or discomfort at all.

We were flying! The boulder field of the Masaka was rolling underneath us, starting to blur as the dragon powered himself faster. The vibrations off his strong wing beats rippled through his body and into mine as he drove us faster and faster, quicker and quicker.

Where is he taking me? I thought, before even the thoughts in my head were blasted away by the next sight.

The boulder field fell away, and the dragon shot up the side of the ridge, higher and higher into the moonlit sky. We were going so fast that I could feel the pressure on my face and shoulders as I looked up at the spray of high and bright stars spread out above us, still visible in the graying light.

But I wasn't afraid, I realized. Maybe I was simply too stunned to be afraid. But all I could think was how beautiful the sky looked.

The black dragon appeared to reach the zenith of his power as the cold finally *did* start to bite, and with a rattling noise in his chest he snapped out his great wings and held them steady. My stomach lurched and fell as we hovered for a prolonged, delicious moment.

The black dragon wheeled in the skies, and I had the chance to look down to see the world from his perspective. What they called the World's Edge mountains lay spread out below us like a wide river of gray and white stone. It stretched as far to the south and to the north as I could see. To the west, the true Three Kingdoms of the Midmost Lands, all I could see was darkness, broken by the occasional rise of high foothills or peaks, catching the graying dawn.

But to the east?

I looked out to see the endless acres of the Plains. What the Middle Kingdomers called the 'Empty Plains' although I knew that they were anything but. They had shaken off the gray, eerie light of pre-dawn, and now I could see the first blushes of purple and ochre and even dim green in gigantic swathes; it looked like the washes of some titanic artist, using his dyes to paint the land.

The air was clearer up here, and in that moment I saw the small specks of things rising over the plains. The flocks of early morning Hooping Birds and Red Geese! I had forgotten what they had looked like.

But the pull of the earth was unstoppable, as my stomach lurched again and the dragon tipped himself forward in just a miniscule degree.

We slid down the thin and cold airs of the heights, gaining speed and momentum with every second. The great black dragon had no need to beat his wings at all, just hold them steady as the mountains started to rise up towards us again. I could hear the rippling of the dragon's wings. I couldn't believe that they were strong enough for such enormous pressures – just days after he had been so weak and ill!

"Skreeyargh!" The dragon roared, his excitement and savage joy in every note, and before I knew it, I was whooping too.

"Souda," the dragon said.

Said. Like, I could hear the words, but at the same time I could hear the chirruping whistle from the dragon above me. Somehow, that whistle was the same as the word in my mind, and I knew in that moment that, yes, Tamin had been right; the dragon *had* been talking to me.

"You – you can talk," I gasped. I instantly felt stupid. Tamin had told me that dragons could talk. And of course, a being as ancient and as powerful as a dragon could talk. It felt as natural a thing to me as a horse could gallop.

"Child of the Western Wind," the dragon said, and this time I focused more on hearing the words as they arrived in my head, not any other sound from my ears.

I could *feel* the dragon, I realized. I could feel it when he spoke. His words came with a sensation of soot and the smell of sweet frankincense. And beyond that, I could sense a greater, burning shape like a bonfire. That *was* the black dragon, I thought in awe. That heat, that feeling of strength and solidity and... *possibility* was the dragon itself, on the edge of my imagination.

"You. Me. Children of the winds," I heard the black dragon say, and in that moment all of my memories of the Soussa flooded through me. How it could scour and be fierce, or how it could keen high above the plains. How it brought with it the faraway sounds and smells of the Plains – and how it was always, forever uplifting to me. Possibility. Freedom.

"You feel it too," I said, smiling as tears welled in my eyes.

"Yes," I heard, but in my mind, I felt *of course, certainly, what else could I feel?* This dragon tongue was like a human, but it was also like the other animals of the Plains, I realized. When a deer raises its ears in alarm and sniffs in the direction of the hunter, it is not only saying *what is that?* to itself, but it was also saying *human!* – and, *watch out!* – to the rest of its herd. It was only we humans who had to split all of our feelings into smaller and smaller words – the other creatures of this world could contain so much more, in such tiny gestures.

"Deer?" The voice of the dragon arrived in my head, bringing with it a flick of ash and heat. I could feel the dragon's humor plainly. His claws tightened against my chest just a fraction, as if to show what incredible power he had.

"I wasn't saying you were like a deer," I said hurriedly, as there was a coughing, raucous noise above me. The dragon was laughing!

"Fish!" We were now swooping through the mountains, with peaks rising on either side of us and still the black hadn't had to beat his wings once. He simply raised one or flicked the edges of another this way and that, catching the drafts of air that swept up and down the different peaks and avenues.

And there below us was the long lake, looking black and deep in the shadow of the Masaka. The dragon swooped lower, and lower still.

He's showing off! I realized with a laugh as the rocks were barely two meters below us as we screamed towards the surface of the water.

Only for the dragon to turn both wings at the last moment, slowing us down and keeping us above the water as he kicked out his back legs. There was a roaring sound as two plumes of water exploded from his outstretched claws on either side of us – and then he was beating his wings, rising in slow, awkward stages, with fat and silver lake fish skewered on the ends of each of his rear claws.

"How did you heal so quickly!?" I asked as we began a much slower, steadier flight back to the ledge and his cave, with the sun breaking over the ridge of the Masaka.

"*Dragons heal,*" his thoughts came to me in a disjointed fashion, but I got the sense that there was far more behind them than just the words. I sensed *strength. Fire. Sun.*

As we crested the ridge in the first glares of the sun, I could feel his mood abruptly change however. A shiver ran through his entire body, and I felt the sick nausea in my stomach that I had felt before. I realized that we could see the work camp clearly now, and Inyene's keep on the outermost arm of the mountain. It was an ugly place to the eye and the heart, and I knew that the dragon felt the same way too.

"*Bones,*" the dragon said, and this time the heat of his words was pressed right up against my mind, burning hot and angry. I couldn't see them, but I knew that the dragon's eyes would be flushed a crimson red. "*Bones and blood and scales.*"

I didn't follow what he meant, but I could feel his anger directed to the three dark, motionless shapes that sat next to each other on the terrace beside the smelting sheds. Each one towered over the rough stone buildings, looking down into the main yard as if ready to pounce.

It was the metal dragons. I could see no light, heat, or feel any spark of life from them – but they were wrong in every way all the same. *And there were now three of them,* I realized. Inyene must be working around the clock to churn them out.

She must have been planning this all along. All of our finger-breaking effort must have been working towards this goal. Years of mining iron and copper ore for the skeleton frames. And finally, the strange Earth lights as well. We'd had years of collecting dragon scales to rivet to their sides. Just how many wagons and carts and tons had we slaves produced over our time?

And how many dragons could that make? I thought in horror.

"Skrargh!" The black dragon let out an accusing burst of flame and wheeled sharply, angling us towards his ledge and his cave, both of which were now sunlit. Tamin had finally awoken from his deep sleep and was waving both arms at us. I wondered what he must have thought when he saw us, with his goddaughter being clutched to the belly of a fully grown bull dragon like another catch.

But the black dragon was nothing if not delicate as he beat his wings, hovering for a moment over the ledge to release me into the outstretched arms of Tamin.

"Oof!" I tumbled, and Tamin caught me, holding me tighter than the dragon had! With a small flick of his wings and a swish of his long barbed tail, the dragon hopped lightly onto the ledge, pausing only to flick the fish from his feet, and leaning down to crunch his way through more than half of them.

"Nari! Are you okay? You're not hurt?" Tamin was patting my shoulders and back, but I brushed him off urgently.

"I'm fine, Uncle, really." I was more worried about the black dragon, as I could feel his disgust radiating from him in waves. He hadn't felt this angry even when Fankin had hit him!

"Dragon, thank you for the flight." I said awkwardly, moving towards him.

But the black swished his tail against the wall of the mountain in annoyance. He didn't hiss at me, and I knew that his anger wasn't meant for me, but I realized that he, too, must have a temper. Just like me.

"Ymmen," I heard his voice say clearly in my head. *It was his name,* I thought. *Dragons have names!*

But as I stood in wonder, abruptly all that dragon-sense of heat and fragrance and warmth was gone from me, as he withdrew into his own reptilian mind. It felt like missing a step in the mines – that sudden lurch and anxious fear before you jolted as your foot hit solid ground again. I was left feeling smaller somehow, without the dragon beside my thoughts.

"Ymmen!" I said, not wanting our contact to be lost so quickly, but the black dragon ignored me as he stalked back down into his cave, not stopping until he had reached the very back. He was still *very* angry at what he had seen. Which I understood, as those metal things were wearing the scales of skins of his kind. Perhaps dragons that he knew. Scales I had surely collected.

"It was the first time he saw them," I said, misery on my face as I looked up at the worried frown of Tamin. "The mechanical dragons." My god-uncle nodded slowly, looking at the ground for a long pause, and then back up at me.

"The dragon gave you his name," he stated. It wasn't a question; it was a statement of fact. "For all the nightmares that we are living through – you should remember that. I don't think such a thing has happened anywhere in the Midmost Lands for years."

"Yes, Uncle," I nodded, although I still felt awful – both for the slaves out there on the other side of the mountain as well as Ymmen right here inside of it. *What must it be like to know that people are treating your kind as nothing more than cattle?* I thought.

Pretty much the same as if they were treating you as slaves, I thought heavily. Even though the bright sun was rising now, and dawn had done its work, it was hard to feel the thrill of that flight. Everything had been marred by Inyene.

"Nari," Tamin was prompting me, and I looked up to see him regarding not me, but the dawn sky. "Indulge an old man for a moment. Let me tell you the tiny bit of dragon lore that I know."

"Please do," I said. Anything to take my mind off the terrible feelings of betrayal and disgust that were emanating from the dark recesses of the cave.

Was Ymmen feeling angry because I had spoken his name? I thought suddenly.

"Not you. The abominations." Ymmen's fiery words blossomed in my mind, and with it came the knowledge that he meant the mechanical dragons. He was disgusted that they even existed. That his kin had been used in such a way.

"The Histories of Torvald cited that a dragon's name remains hidden to humans, given to it by its Brood-Mother and for it alone. Should the dragon choose to share it with a human, it is invariably because that dragon has chosen that human to be its bonded partner," Tamin said.

"Bonded partner?" I asked. "Like the Lady Artifex and Maliax?"

Tamin nodded. "Precisely. But names are like gifts. The importance is in the giving of them. Once given, the dragons' names are recorded and can be used by others – but the first human to hear it is always the one that the dragon chose to share not just its friendship with – but its soul." The older man was speaking softly, reverentially.

Bonded with a dragon. I couldn't believe it. In truth, I didn't understand it. Tamin must have seen my confusion plainly, however, as he continued:

"With a bond, all of those things that I mentioned before – the joining of minds, the strange powers – they all become possible," he started to say.

"How?" I asked quickly, my thoughts quickly overtaking my mouth, "if I can learn how to do these things – break mountains, whatever else you said – then I could defeat Inyene! I could free the Daza!" *Is that what Lady Artifex could do?* I thought in wonder. Suddenly, a door of possibility had opened in my heart. We finally had a way out of this nightmare!

"Nari, Nari," Tamin's voice was calming – the same infuriating tone that I remembered him using when I had been a child and throwing a tantrum. Could he not see how important this was? "Dragon Lore is a strange branch of knowledge. Only the scholars at the Dragon Academy of Torvald might know the answers to your questions. And to ask them, you would first need to ask permission from the King of the Torvald and the Middle Kingdom itself!" He made it sound impossible.

"The gifts that bonding with a dragon brings can be unpredictable. They do not bring the same for every person. One of the earliest tales tells how a dragon could give its very life force to its bonded partner – making them stronger, quicker – even bringing them back from the brink of death itself!" Tamin said in awe. "There is a tale of the Dragon Riders Rigar and Veen, who lived far, far longer than their natural span of years. And then there was the Lady Saffron, once a queen of Torvald itself, who could wrest rocks from the ground with just her mind." Tamin looked helplessly at me.

"There is so much that is myth, that it is hard to know what actually happened and what didn't – but we do know that there were once schools of Witches and Monks and Wizards who would spend years learning the ways of their dragons, and honing their craft."His gaze turned back to the northeastern horizon, where Inyene's camp stood. "I fear that we do not have the time to learn these secrets, and neither can we really know what gifts you might get from your bond with the noble Ymmen."

I was adamant not to give up on my dreams of saving my people personally, just like the Lady Artifex on Maliax would have. "But still, Uncle – even if we were just using the dragon's strength and skill and his fire – that might be enough!"

"Would it?" Tamin looked doubtful.

I gritted my teeth in frustration. I knew what Tamin was doing. He was trying to be practical. He was trying to think things through in the careful, orderly manner that had made him such a good senior clerk for Torvald.

But I was certain that the time for orderly action was gone. I had an idea. "At least this then," I proposed. "If Ymmen agrees, then I will ask him to fly me to spy on Inyene's keep. There is one person there who knows Inyene and her plans and the workings of the metal dragons better than any other," I said.

Tamin's eyes widened. He knew just whom I was speaking of. "Lord Abioye," he said.

"Inyene's brother." I nodded. *He* would be the one to know how to stop the metal dragons. And I was sure that if it came to it, he would see the sense in answering my questions now. Especially if I was riding atop a fire-breathing bull dragon.

CHAPTER 13
POISON BERRY

It was clear that my bond had changed everything now. It was as if, as soon as I had a name to call what was happening to me, everything accelerated. During the rest of that day following my flight, it was hard to keep my thoughts focused on the small jobs of our hasty encampment.

Looking now at our smokery, our small collection of branch-woven or branch-sharpened tools – they looked futile. Silly, even, compared to the magnitude of the task ahead: sneaking into the keep. We had settled into spending most of the day in the cave, lest any of the mine scouts venture this far up the Masaka and discover us. During my time to sleep I dreamed constantly of flying, of soaring high over sunlit lands and low over fields and seas – even though I had never even seen the ocean before.

And I dreamed of the metal dragons. Or rather, I had nightmares about them. I would be flying or floating towards them in that way of fever dreams, and suddenly their eyes would blare with blue Earth Light, and they would raise their metal faces to look at me.

But in my dreams, now that I saw them, they weren't just dead and lifeless machines. Now, they had some ghastly semblance of life. Their borrowed scales made them look like a half-dead creature, still grotesquely clinging on to existence.

I woke up with a start, knowing that I could no longer wait. "I have to do this tonight," I said as I approached Tamin, who was once again tending the smokery and his newly caught fish that evening. The sky was turning a deep orange-red, and it made me think of the color of the fireball that the metal dragon had breathed.

Tamin looked up at me in alarm but nodded. He knew the stakes as well as I. It wasn't just that every day that we spent up here was a day that our friends and families were down there in the mines. Perhaps they were dying. Perhaps they were being beaten.

It was that every day, Inyene was working to add more metal dragons to her horde, I thought dismally. *Forcing my people to be complicit in the creation of the monsters that would bring about their own demise.* How long before there were too many – if there weren't already?

"We," Tamin said, standing up straightaway. "*We* have to do this."

I shook my head immediately. For some reason, my heart knew that Ymmen would not take Tamin. It wasn't that the two disliked each other, but Ymmen had chosen me, and had given *me* his name. I was the one that the black dragon – still only a scant few days from being seriously ill – had trusted.

"It has to be me, Uncle. You know this," I said, and Tamin hung his head.

The only thing left to do was convince the dragon of my plan.

"Skree-ip?" I heard a chirrup behind me, to see that Ymmen had silently followed me out of the cave. His eyes were gold, shot through with the reflected red of the sunset. I felt as though I didn't even have to tell him what I had been planning, but I did anyway. "Ymmen, noble dragon," I said, bowing my head in the most reverential way that I had seen my mother greet the Imanus from other tribes.

"I want to try and stop… *that* from happening over there." I pointed in the direction of the work camp, and Ymmen hissed in agreement.

"I know someone, a human, who might have the answers." I thought of Abioye's strange confession in the Western Tunnel, that he hoped 'we can all be free' – did he mean free from his sister? It was a tiny hope, but right now we needed all of the hope that we could get.

"He might know how to put an end to those *things,*" I felt my top lip curl in disgust as I thought about Inyene's dragons, just as Ymmen's top lip did the same. The feeling of indignation was burning between us, a shared fire that we warmed our rage upon.

"And my family, my friends, my people – they are being held prisoner by the one to blame for those creations. They are not free. They cannot feel the high or low winds on their faces, as we can," I said gravely, not knowing how to address a dragon really.

Ymmen, in response, cocked his head to look at me, and blinked slowly. *"Bones. Blood and Scales."* The outraged thought hit me again, and the burning hatred I felt in the dragon's heart was enough to make me gasp. He stood up slowly, walking daintily around us to stand expectantly on the edge of the ledge.

"He agrees," I said quickly to Tamin. "I will be back as soon as I can. And I will be as careful as I can," I promised, forestalling his inevitable advice.

"Be your mother's daughter," Tamin said gravely – which was the highest praise as well as the most serious task that anyone could ask of me.

"I'll try." I nodded, turning to reach up to the dragon's front leg, intending to climb it and find any space I could hunker down on Ymmen's back.

But the black dragon had other ideas of how I would be traveling, apparently. With a rush of air, he unfurled his wings with a thunderous snap! The blast pushed me back several paces, and I saw, above me, that he had flung from his wings the greenish 'scale' of the healing poultice that I had made, and in its place was a white lightning branch of healed skin. It was incredible how quickly it had worked, and I thought again of what Ymmen had told me of his gifts before: *Fire. Strength. Sun.*

With another beat of his reformed wings he had hopped several meters into the air, and once again I felt that thump as his claws clamped over me and pulled me up into the skies. I heard a sharp intake of breath from Tamin below, but by the time that I managed to look down he was now just a doll figure, small on the ledge below and raising one fist above his head.

Without pausing, the dragon dipped his wings and we swooped down into the gorge at the foot of the cliff below us, and Ymmen once again snapped his wings where the gorge widened out, and we were in the air, higher than before.

For a moment I was lost in the exhilaration of flight, feeling the crisp mountain air on my face as we wheeled and turned. Ymmen was turning away from the northeast and the workcamp, and instead taking me southwest, around the back of the Masaka where the light was still strong.

"We have to be quiet!" I gasped, my throat burning with the cold of the air. "Quiet and unseen." I thought about hunting on the Plains, creeping through the tall grasses and pausing every now and again as our hunting parties fanned out.

"Ha!" Ymmen's voice of fire surged into my mind with an accompanying snort of fire above me. "I know how to hunt, child," he said – but I could sense no disdain from him, just amusement. In that moment, through our bond, I got a sense of just how old Ymmen had to be. It made me imagine a measure of how it might go between us – with him being the more willful, even than I?

We'll see about that! I thought. I was still the woman who had, after all, shouted at him the first time we had met.

"Strong. That is why." The dragon's disjointed thoughts, along with his mirth, flowed through my mind like hot steam. He was saying that was why he bonded with me? Or that was why he hadn't eaten me?

"Both," he answered, as he took me on the long, circuitous route around the far side of the Masaka to eventually turn into a place where the Masaka ended and the next mountain – Old Giant – began. I had never been this far north before, and I saw that there was a pass

where the two mountains held themselves apart from other as if snubbing their rocky fellows.

And in the far bottom of that pass, was a thin ribbon of a road.

Where does it lead? I thought excitedly. I realized then, with some chagrin, just how close I had come to it on my previous escape attempts. Another day of traveling on foot, two or three of hiding perhaps, and I would have reached it!

"Smelly people. Cities. Tasty cows," Ymmen informed me, as a whole new revelation opened itself to my mind. Ymmen could read my thoughts!

"Thoughts?" The dragon sounded confused as he flicked his wings to bring us up the near edge of the Masaka, where there were many broken ledges and outcrops of rock. He alighted on one of these outcrops carefully and released me gently to scramble to the stone below. The sun had fallen at our backs in the West, but it was still warm. "Speak. Sing. Smell. Hear. See." He dragon-explained to me – or tried to, but I couldn't grasp what he was saying. It seemed that he didn't have a word for thoughts, and the closest he could come was to name all the other senses and abilities he had.

"No! Speak. Sing!" Ymmen repeated in my mind more forcefully as he appeared to be waiting for something.

"You want me to sing to you?" I said, confused.

"Skrargh!" He gave another snort of flame and his large tail slapped against the rocks behind us. "Thoughts," he repeated slowly, and I could feel his great impatience at how slow I was apparently being. "Songs."

Thoughts are like songs? I thought. And then, in a flash I got it. The other creatures of the Plains had many senses that we humans did not. The buffalos would start lowing before the rains came. A dog or a wolf could smell game many, many leagues away. Surely, dragons must have senses that were far removed from our own! Maybe whatever happened inside their minds to them *were* songs, just as the wolves could smell prey on the wind.

"Not all songs. Just." Ymmen struggled to put the words into my head. "Narissea."

It was the first time he said my name, and when I looked up, he was regarding me with his golden eyes. He might think me slow, but I could feel no contempt from him. I opened my mouth to say thank you, although I wasn't sure what for – but Ymmen was already raising his snout with a flick. *Just like a boy who doesn't want to seem weak,* I thought, and earned another slap of a tail against the rocks behind me.

"Now. Hunting," Ymmen said in my mind, and I turned my head to see what it was that the black dragon had been waiting for. The sun was well past fallen in the west, which meant that night was on its way in the east, aided by the tall and cold shadows of the World's Edge Mountains, too. I couldn't see the work camp from where we were perched, but I could imagine that it would be dark save for the circle of torch lights around the palisade walls.

"The sky is clouding," I said and nodded. *Good.* The sickle moon was thin anyway, and the clouds were obscuring both it and the stars. Less light to reveal our movements. "We hunt," I agreed, reaching up my arms as Ymmen's gigantic claws once again wrapped themselves around me, and we took off.

We swooped through the night, as silent as a whisper. From this height Inyene's workcamp where I had spent almost a quarter of my life looked so... *futile.* The four great wooden sheds where they housed us were small boxes, and the other assembled buildings – everything from the guard towers to the stone factory sheds – looked shabby and ill-made.

But my superior viewpoint revealed an ugly reality: I could see the open-topped rectangle of another great shed going up. They could fit almost a hundred Daza in just one, I knew. And then there was the constant smoke from the smelting shed. From up here in the clean mountain air, I could smell clearly how greasy and poisonous they were. Totally unlike dragon fire, I now knew – which to me smelled clean and purifying.

"Ssss…" Ymmen announced his concern, although he didn't need to. Another two dragons had been added to Inyene's three, in just the short time that we had been away. I growled in sympathy with the dragon.

"Abioye," I tried to concentrate on our task at hand. He had to be down there somewhere – but where? I had a hunch that he would either be at the sheds or at his sister's keep, and my gaze lifted to regard the place that had stood sentinel over my incarceration.

Inyene's keep sat on the last saddle of rock before the Masaka foothill eased into the dark-lit plains beyond. It didn't look as though it had ever been anything other than a martial place, and I struggled to imagine it as somewhere nice, and not just a blot on the landscape.

Her keep was built of old stone, vast gray blocks at its base that were almost as large as some of the sheds, growing smaller as the walls climbed. The walls weren't terribly high, only about four or five stories I guessed. But they were wide and thick, and joined onto a taller inner keep built of the same gray granite. From this height, I could see that there was a wide walkway on the inner side of the wall, just under the battlements, and that constant fires burned in metal dishes around its circumference.

The entire keep looked to be hunched and snarling, and the only part of it that was in any way graceful (although I hesitated to even use that word) was a singular tower that sat on one side of the Keep. I could not know of course, but I rather thought that it had been from here that I had felt Inyene's wave of power.

Maybe... The tangle of rage in my chest forced me to consider the possibility: *Maybe we could.* I thought of what I wanted to do. Kill Inyene. Make her pay for all the suffering that she had caused to me, my family, and friends – to everyone. But it was an ugly, nasty thought and it felt sour in my mind. Ymmen sensed my fury and was already turning his slow, soundless flight towards the keep.

But there was no light in any of its windows. The tower looked empty, and the only movement came from the small ant-like figures of the guards as they moved around the battlements.

Pheet! The thin sound of a whistle rose over the workcamp, and I watched a batch of slaves making their way out of the mines, feet dragging and heads bowed.

I wondered whether Oleer was a part of their number.

"They've increased the guards," I whispered, seeing how the thirty or forty strong work team of slaves were flanked by Inyene's mine guards. Maybe half to the number of slaves, I guessed, but they would all be armed just the same.

I shook my head. We could not attack the keep, however much I wanted to. "Their numbers are too strong," I whispered, knowing that Ymmen would hear me. "And a lot of the slaves would be injured before we could free them." I sighed. A lot of people would die.

So instead, I would have to concentrate on finding Abioye. He would know what Inyene's weaknesses were. And he would know how to stop these metal monsters. And I was banking on that one hope – that he had wanted to be free.

I realized I was putting a lot of faith in just a few half-heard words.

"Poison Berry," Ymmen said cryptically in my mind, and I had absolutely no idea what he was referring to. For a moment, I thought that he was referring to the smoke from the smelting shed, or perhaps some way to get at Inyene.

But then, in my mind, there was suddenly the smell of… *wine?* I had only tasted wine a few times, but the Daza people had their own berry-presses and vats. And the Traders who came through the Plains in their caravans always had barrels and barrels of it.

"You think we should get the guards drunk?" I said as we wheeled high over the keep. I had to admit – it was a great idea. But where was I going to find enough wine to intoxicate quite a few hundred guardsmen and women?

"No. Poison Berry – look." Ymmen dipped his wing low so that he

made a sharp turn, and then I saw that there was someone staggering along one of the terraces, illuminated by one of the wall's bonfires, lurching across the ramp that led up to the smelting shed, and moving past it, towards one of the metal dragons.

From his fine cloak, the flash of his fine linen shirt, and his hair – I knew that it was Abioye.

And he appeared drunk.

"That's him!" I said. But we'd have to land right in the middle of the main yard if we wanted to have even a chance of getting near him. *And that wasn't going to happen,* I thought. Not with a crowd of Daza slaves surrounded by thuggish guards nearby.

We lifted up from our flight, watching as Abioye lurched to the first metal dragon and appeared to be fiddling at its stomach for several long, fraught moments.

There was a sudden burst of steam from the thing's mouth, which turned into tendrils of rising black smoke. Abioye climbed up the creature's leg as its face smoked, and then promptly slid back down. It looked painful.

Apparently the young man who had offered me a chance to fold his laundry for a living was undeterred however, as he clambered slowly back up again to perch in a pre-made groove just behind the thing's shoulders.

"What under the stars does he think that he's doing?" I asked, before Abioye leaned forward as if he were hugging the brutish machine, and suddenly the eerie, unsettling blue Earth Light flooded from the creature's eyes.

"Ssss!" Ymmen flapped his wings in alarm, taking us higher as the wave of discomforting nausea swept over us.

Abioye was fiddling with something at his belt – it appeared to be hooks or straps or something, as the metal dragon raised its head straight up, and looked up.

If it was any normal, living and breathing creature it would have seen us, but if it did then it made no sign or sound of recognition. A shiver ran through the dragon above me, too, but the metal thing below us did nothing, at first. Abioye was still fidgeting on the creature's back, but suddenly the beast moved forward, taking a strange step with its forelegs, and then another as it raised its hind legs and unfurled its creepy bat-like wings.

"He's going to fly it," I breathed, and without even having to suggest anything the black dragon was carrying us aloft, higher and further so that we were just a dark shadow in the night. But we could still see the blue radiance of the metal dragon below. It was beating its wings in an almost lifelike way, before it jumped into the air – and with hisses of foul steam and the clatter and grind of metal gears – it flew.

Ymmen changed course. We were going to follow it, and him.

The metal dragon was easy to follow. It made a terrible whirring sound as whatever strange engines and wheels inside of it churned. From its snout it emitted trailing plumes of heavy black ghastly smelling smoke, that Ymmen was more than careful to stay above.

How could Abioye ever think that thing was anything like a dragon?

I thought in appalled shock. I remembered how the young man had looked at the Lady Artifex's journal, and how his long finger had caressed the fine drawings within. I had thought he had a love for dragons. A hiss of disdain came from Ymmen above me.

"Poison Berry," he repeated, and I realized then that it was his *name* for Abioye. I would have laughed, were it not for the horror of what we were hunting.

But still – I couldn't reconcile these two different parts of the man that I had met. For just the briefest of moments, he had seemed as if he might have understood. He had been the one to tell me the truth of Dagan Mar and our imprisonment there, after all. Not that he had done anything about it! I thought, just as quickly. Abioye's 'answer' to the fact that Dagan Mar would rather see us all dead than free was to simply offer me a position changing his bed sheets. He was either a fool or arrogant, or both.

We had flown well past Inyene's keep and the east-west path that led through the Masaka, and now I saw Abioye's real destination. There was a singular spire that rose from the craggy foothills of the mountains, tall and without any surrounding buildings. Ymmen gave a wide circle as we watched the metal dragon alight, and for Abioye to fall off its back with a grunt of pain.

"Magic," Ymmen said to me, and I knew that he wasn't *just* talking about the metal dragon below us. He seemed to be talking about the entire tower. Or something within it.

Abioye had stumbled his way to a trapdoor, pulling the handle and shouting, "Montfre!" before he climbed down. There were narrow windows in the body of the tower, and as we circled, I saw a light kindle first in one of them, and then another.

But the windows only start halfway up, I saw. And then I realized that, as we circled, I couldn't see any doors at the base of the tower at all. How did whoever was inside leave? Or get food?

From the air, of course. There was a bundle of ropes and bags beside where the metal dragon sat, and I figured that must be some sort of pulley system to deliver supplies. Ymmen was wary of approaching closer, but the metal dragon once again appeared to have fallen dormant. Wisps of smoke still rose from its mouth, but its eyes were dark, and there was no movement from its body.

"I think it's safe," I said – although I wasn't sure 'safe' was the right word for it. At my encouragement, Ymmen dropped closer until he had landed on the edge of the tower top itself, his rear claws clutching the crenellated edges delicately as he set me down. He extended his nose to sniff at the scales of the stilled metal beast beside him before curling his lips and hissing at it, and pulling back.

"You smelled magic from in there," I whispered to the black dragon. "And those things are powered by magic. There must be some kind of connection." I crept to the still-open trapdoor to see a circle of winding stone steps descending into the tower. Muffled voices came somewhere far below. I wished that I had any kind of weapon at all with me, and cursed One-Eye for taking the Lady Artifex's dagger. But without even a rock to my name, all I had were my fists and my luck.

Come on, Nari, you can do this, I told myself, and crept downwards.

CHAPTER 14
ARGUMENTS

"Well, at least it's not that horrible Northern wine that you drink!" a man's voice grumbled below me.

I had crept down several flights of the stone stairs, passing wooden doors at every landing. This place smelled odd, a touch of wet, damp stone but also the passing scents of stranger smokes and fumes. A little like the smelting works, I thought, although one room I passed reminded me of the herbarium in which my mother spent a lot of her time, constantly storing, crushing, or drying some wild Plains flower or another.

The stairs were lit by the flickering radiance of a fire just around the corner from me, its pop and crackle mingling with the creaks and shifting noises of furniture, and hiding the sound of my approach – at least I hoped.

"It's Torvald brandy. The very finest, my friend." I recognized

Abioye's voice, although it sounded different from how he had spoken inside the mines. It was thick and a little slurred from his excesses, and lighter and a little more carefree than it had been before. It was almost fascinating to hear how he acted in a place where he clearly felt more natural.

Almost fascinating, because at every turn I remembered that all of these same comforts – from fires to horrible northern wines or Torvald brandies – were not afforded to slaves at all.

"Finest," the unknown man's voice coughed bitterly. He didn't sound very old at all. The second man – *Montfre?* – sounded as young if not younger than Abioye did.

"Hey, what's this?" I heard Abioye say, and there was a shuffle of things knocking each other, and then a loud smash of glass on hard floors.

"*Gah!* What are you doing! That was my very last batch of magewort tincture!" the younger Montfre shouted, and I heard the sudden sound of things being rearranged and moved.

"Oh, sorry," Abioye said. "What's magewort anyway? Does it taste good?" Some more lurching steps.

"Just, please – sit down over there, Abioye!" this Montfre said in frustration as the sounds of the younger man cleaning up continued. There was a heavy thump as I assumed that Abioye had fallen more than sat.

"Shouldn't that be *Lord* Abioye?" he said in a high-minded way.

A moment's pause, and then Montfre's voice returned, lower and sullen. "Of course. I forgot for a moment who it was I was speaking to. I thought it was my friend."

"Montfre!" Abioye burst out, "I was joking. Forgive me. It's the wine. Of course you're my friend – how long have we known each other now, ten years?" Strangely enough, I heard real alarm and sympathy in Abioye's voice at that moment. As if he really *wanted* this Montfre to be his friend and couldn't understand why he wasn't.

I knew the answer however in the next moment, as there was a heavy rattle of chains.

"Six years in these, Abioye," Montfre said heavily, and I heard him glug and swallow.

"I... I know." Abioye was quieter. "How many times do I have to say that I am sorry? I had no idea that Inyene was going to throw you in chains! I really didn't." The air was tense, and I could tell that there was a story here between these two. I wondered if it was something that I could use against Inyene, so I moved a couple of stairs closer, towards the edge of the door.

"And you did try to blow up her laboratory," Abioye reflected, and I once again despaired at his drunken, quicksilver moods.

"It was *my* laboratory!" Montfre said with real passion, taking another glug from, presumably, the Torvald brandy. "I had put four years of work into that place, and your sister used me!"

I waited to see how Abioye would react, curious as to whether he would defend his sister.

"I know." He sounded crestfallen. "Everything that she's managed to build comes from your work. If only she'd never seen those little toy dragons you made." Abioye sounded regretful.

"I know. I wish that I'd never made the damnable things." Montfre took another glug, sounding just as depressed as Abioye did now. "You know, the madness of it all is that I had made those toys to bring joy to the world. I thought there were children in Torvald who would be delighted to be able to play with a dragon – albeit just a tiny one."

"I know," Abioye agreed. "But Inyene was always like that. She has always been years ahead of everybody."

"Uh-huh," Montfre agreed. "She saw how they could be scaled up." He was silent for a moment and then shook his head. "And to think – I thought she believed in me, in my vision. She made me feel important. If I had known at the start what she was trying to do, then I would never have shown her about the Earth lights or made her that scepter – I thought she just wanted to play with the toys."

"I was really hoping we wouldn't find enough, or that the Earth lights wouldn't work to control something so big," Abioye said. "But… did you see how I got here?"

Earth lights? A scepter? My ears pricked up. So that was how Inyene was doing it. That was why her metal dragons' eyes glowed an Earth Light blue.

That was the key, I thought. *If I can get a hold of that scepter…*

"Huh!" Abioye agreed lustily as there was a sound of a hand slapping wood. It seemed as though complaining about his sister was one of his favorite past-times. "You should try being in my shoes! At least you get the freedom here to do your own thing, kind of. To have some peace. She treats me like a slave. I have to fetch and do this or do that for her all the time." Abioye was warming to his subject.

Spoiled Poison Berry. I scowled.

"But it's gotten worse still, my friend. She's talking about building more mechanical dragons. Many more. Enough to," Abioye's voice faltered and lowered a little, as if even he were scared of what he might say. But he did in the end, anyway. "Enough to attack the citadel. Torvald."

"*What?*" Montfre said. "Is this because of that thing she has about being related to the high queen?"

"Yeah, precisely," Abioye agreed. "The old High Queen Delia. The first High Queen of the Three Kingdoms. The one to tame the dragons. All of that epic Torvald stuff." Abioye sounded frustrated. "She tried to show me some new family charts she's unearthed that prove we're Delia's last living relatives, but to be honest it was too complicated for me to follow." Another pause. "But anyway. That's what she's talking about now. She wants to raise a flight of your mechanical dragons that are strong enough to be able to take back the Three Kingdoms for her, so *she* can be the new High Queen!"

"*Pfagh!*" Montfre snorted in disgust, which was good because it covered the sound of my own gasp.

But though I was shocked and it was horrible to hear all these crazed plans of my oppressor – there was a certain sort of satisfaction in finally knowing *why* she had treated my people the way she had.

She was insane, that's why. She wanted to rule the Three Kingdoms, and to do that had used some weird ancient lawyer trick to turn my people into slaves, so that she could build her monstrous armies.

"But I just don't get it," Abioye whined. "We could lead perfectly happy lives without that, you know? Inyene's worked hard; I've worked hard—" *I doubt that.* I clamped a hand over my mouth to stop myself from sniggering, "—you've worked hard all these years. We could live comfortable lives now. We managed to get on the Middle Kingdom's Noble's List, for goodness sake!" Abioye ended in a petulant plea. "I don't want any part of what she's doing now!"

My suspicions were true! I could have stamped the floor in celebration but refrained for obvious reasons. Abioye *was* cowed by his sister, but if he detested what she's doing – I bit my lip – *then he might help us.*

But, despite my glee at the thought, it was still pleasing to hear that Montfre had just as much time for Abioye's childishness as I did.

"By. The. Stars, Abioye!" Montfre shouted at him. "Inyene is *your* sister! Why do you come over here, where your sister has me locked up in a tower"—another rattle of the chains to prove his point— "and complain to me? You think that you're as much a prisoner as the rest of us – but look at you, with your fine clothes and going off to the city to get drunk every night! If you're a prisoner of anything at all, then it's only your own cowardice!" Montfre said.

I think I like this guy, I thought.

"Please, if you thought me a friend at all then you'd stop coming around here, and pretending that I understand your pain"—Montfre went on—"because I really don't! Come back when you've set yourself free!" There was a smash as the now drunken Montfre must have thrown his bottle of Torvald brandy at something.

"*Urk!* Okay, I'm going! I'm sorry!" Abioye's chair slid and Abioye jumped to his feet. *He was going to come this way,* I realized as my heart jumped into my throat, and, without thinking, I turned and ran back up the stairs.

CHAPTER 15
THE MAGE MONTFRE

"It's the scepter!" I gasped eagerly to Ymmen as soon as he lifted me up in his arms. Abioye was still climbing the stairs of the tower below us, too drunk to either be hasty or notice that I had been there.

"Scepter?" Ymmen echoed in my mind, and I could sense his confusion. He allowed himself to glide down the edge of the foothills as we heard the sputter and cough of engines from behind us. Ymmen didn't betray our position with the snapping beat of his wings, and instead moved further away, as silent as a ghost.

Not that Abioye was in his right mind to notice, I thought disdainfully. Poison Berry indeed. As we wheeled lower and lower to the ground, I watched as Abioye finally got the mechanical dragon to work and felt that ripple of unease as its blue eyes shone out into the night once more. It leaped from the tower and, rather ungainly, started to clack and growl its way back towards the keep, as Ymmen skimmed the surface of the lower lands.

My heart was still thumping in my chest with everything that I had heard, and the excitement of everything that had occurred. I now knew a way to stop the mechanical dragons! I knew a way to stop Inyene's crazed plans.

But what of my people? I thought as Ymmen stretched out his rear hind legs to catch the ground at a run, slowing as earth and rocks sprayed around his claws to slowly hunker down once more. He put me down without looking, as his snout was still concentrating on the distant mechanical dragon, winging its way into the dark. I could sense his impatience at the edge of my mind like the coals of a fire sending up sparks and tongues of flame.

"I know," I said wearily. "But we can stop them now," I assured him. "Maybe without the dragons, the mine guards would take one look at you and run off, abandoning the mines," I thought out loud, hopefully. It was the best plan that I had yet.

"Bad magic." Ymmen sniffed at the air and snorted flame. *"Never good."*

The black dragon sounded as though he was speaking from experience, and I would have asked him what he meant – had the weight of the situation not been heavy on my mind. "It *is* bad magic," I said out loud. "But that young man in there knows how it works. Maybe he could tell us how to undo it."

And besides which, I cast a more critical eye up at the tower, if he had a part in bringing it into the world, then he sounded as though he would be happy to help remove it from the world, too!

"Can you take me back?" I asked Ymmen seriously, nodding back up at the tower top. I was aware that I had already asked him to do many things tonight – and even though he wanted to help destroy the mechanical dragons and the 'bad magic' – I knew that, though I had curbed his temper this night, I did not know how long the Bull dragon would be able to keep his temper in check.

"As long as you." He surprised me as he turned his head to look at me. His eyes were shot through with red, but I could sense that it wasn't me that he was angry with. There was a fierce sort of humor to his voice in my head and I was starting to get used to a mirth rooted in claws and teeth.

"Deal," I said, and found that I was grinning back at him.

"Then after: fish." Ymmen huffed his sooty breath at me, a small admonition and reminder of just who and what he was.

"I promise," I said, and held up my arms as Ymmen clutched me to him and jumped into the air, silent and graceful.

The tower top was less imposing without the mechanical dragon sitting sentinel atop it, but no less eerie. Ymmen rested lightly on the battlements as before and allowed me to clamber down, while he sniffed at the air and the stones around him. I hurried to raise the trapdoor to find that there was still light coming from below, as well as a high-pitched, tinkling sound of chimes.

Is that… music? I thought. It was unlike the pipes and strings of the Plains, but it had a certain repetitive, melodic quality like a bird. I did not feel threatened however, as I crept back down the stairs.

Montfre was still in the room where he had his 'audience' with Abioye, and it was from here that the light and the sound was coming from. I reached the landing and sighed deeply to prepare myself.

"I can hear you, you know!" the imprisoned man on the other side said loudly, and there was a sudden crash as an empty glass beaker flew through the open archway and smashed on the opposite wall. "I told you not to bother me again, Abioye!" the man inside shouted.

"Uh – I'm not Abioye," I said gingerly as I stepped out from around the archway and into the light.

I knew that the person speaking to Abioye would be young from his voice, but I was shocked by the sight of the actual person that I saw standing there. Montfre had white-silver hair that hung loose to his shoulders and clear gray eyes, as well as pale skin. He was young – only a few years older than Oleer and just a few years younger than Abioye himself. He was also tall, with a strong build that would have earned him a place on the first hunting parties of the Souda – were it not for the obvious toll imprisonment had taken.

He had sunken eyes and the harrowed, slightly shocked look that I knew only too well. I had seen that same look on the faces of every other Daza that I had ever come across in the camps. After the first year your face sets into a permanent serious expression. I wondered if I still looked like that after my taste of freedom.

He had the pale skin of one confined indoors, and the stooped shoulders of one who had spent a long time only moving through small spaces.

And of course, he had a heavy pair of manacles attached to his feet. The very same sort of ankle chains that Dagan had forced on me, more than once. I knew just how heavy they were, and just how they stopped you from ever stretching your legs fully. I wondered how he had managed to wear them for six years without being completely crippled, but he didn't even seem to notice them as he shuffled across the room towards me.

"I'm Montfre," he said, extending a pale, long-fingered hand. It reminded me of Abioye's fine hands, apart from the fact that Montfre's fingertips were callused and scarred, presumably from his work; which was all around him.

This appeared to be some kind of workroom, but its furnishings weren't anything like the long wooden benches where my mother had worked with her herbs and incenses. Instead, all three walls of the narrow tower room had long tables abutting them, each of which held wooden trays upon which sat grouped different types of substances. The longest table held different trays of bronze parts – some of which were large cog wheels, and others were so small as to just cover the pad of a finger. Next came thin rods or slivers of metal, each in exactly the same size and color.

Everything was ordered to exact detail – which was something that I did not expect from an Imanu, and I had figured that a 'mage' would be similar – but clearly not.

The next table had trays with more organic components – heaps of powders of different colors, along with trays of different colored and shaped minerals. One heap was clearly the russet-red of iron, and next to it the bright greens and the orange yellows that would eventually turn into copper, and eventually; bronze. Next to these sat trays of glass beakers – all grouped according to exact size and shape.

And then came the last table, which sat next to the large, padded leather armchair where Montfre must usually sit. It mostly held papers and books, but in its center was also a strange device: a small wooden box with its lid open to reveal a delicate wire frame, upon which hung singular crystal beads, interspersed with entire hollow 'rings' of glass. The entire contraption was revolving, with different parts moving at different speeds, and as the glass rings slid against each other or the crystal beads hit each other, it created that ethereal, twittering chimes of music like birdsong.

"Ah, you like it?" Montfre saw me looking, and I realized I had been staring at the device and hadn't even introduced myself. Before I could say anything more, he was rushing to pick it up and present it to me with a big smile on his face.

"It's a Crystal Euphonia. Entirely mechanical. No magic used whatsoever." He sounded proud of it, and a second later I understood why. "I designed it," he added, before his face fell "a long time ago."

I didn't want to hurt his feelings. It really was a beautiful thing, but I did have to wonder: why make a thing that sounded almost like birds when he could have just gone to listen to the birds?

Apart from the fact, obviously, that there were no birds in a box, I looked around his room. One thin window, in which there was a singular candle burning.

"Do you want to see more?" Montfre appeared giddy, excited like a child of ten on his name-day. "My collection room is the next floor up. If you like this, you should see!" he said, beckoning me already to the door.

Before he suddenly paused and shook himself a little straighter, as if he had realized something. "Only Abioye comes to see me. Or Inyene." He turned around slowly, and this time his gray eyes seemed hard and bright, as if with an inner light. "Which one sent you?"

"Neither," I said quickly. This young man had clearly been addled by his years in confinement, as I had seen many others become. But that didn't mean that he wasn't sane, or a nice person. Just that he wasn't used to this strange new change in his routine. "My name is Narissea, of the Daza Souda," I said formally.

"The Daza…" Montfre's anger subsided, to be replaced by apparent interest. "The people of the Empty Plains. Tribal groups, some twenty or more distinct tribes, spread across over at least thirty documented villages, covering a vast land." He spoke like he was repeating words that had been told to him.

And why does everyone keep on insisting that the Plains are Empty! I bit my tongue. Westerners!

"That's right," I nodded, although he was wrong. There were at least thirty different tribes that I knew the names of, and I'd heard tell that there were more the further out you went... But at least he didn't regard us all the same, I considered.

"Does that mean that you…" Montfre flickered a look to the window. "Are you one of the Lady Inyene's slaves?" A new concern crept over his features. "How did you get in here?"

It was my turn to impress him, as I said, "Come with me, and I'll show you."

"It's a dragon," Montfre said, in almost exactly the same tone that Tamin had used when he had first met Ymmen.

We stood on the circular top of the tower with the cloudy skies above us, and the light from the candle Montfre had insisted on bringing up with him shone over Ymmen's scales, making them shine in the darkness. I studied the young man's face as he looked at the black dragon, who had turned his head to regard the small person quizzically as he was studied in turn. Ymmen's pupils had turned to slits of black instead of their rounded ovals, which I knew meant Ymmen hadn't decided yet whether he liked Montfre or not.

"He's... he's... *magnificent!"* Montfre said in a rush, and I felt a surge of warmth through my mind.

"Not all *Bad Magic,"* Ymmen said in my mind, as his pupils became a little rounder.

"I mean, look at his wings!" Montfre burst out, which were folded now tight against Ymmen's back, but we could clearly see how long his pinion-bones were, at least. "His wingspan must be... twenty meters? Thirty? How much uplift can he get from that!?"

It was like the mage was speaking a different language from the one I knew. I had heard Tamin talk like this, when he had come back to our village to talk of *clauses*, and *propositions,* and *precedents* – and I had no idea just what either had meant, but I thought Montfre at least was trying to explain how awed he was.

"My wings are big, little mage!" Ymmen said, twittering through an almost closed maw as he lifted his shoulders and slowly unfurled his wings over us. I could clearly see the paler lightning-bolt where his

tear had healed, and his wings stretched far over the entire stretch of the tower top.

"I underestimated you," Montfre said, nodding his head gravely. "My name is Montfre Veer, of the citadel and kingdom of Torvald, and I am honored to meet you." He bowed deeply.

I was struck by just how different – and immediate – that Montfre's respect had been. Maybe it was that he was a mage, but it seemed that he was following a custom that I did not know. A ritual giving of names?

"He is of the people of the sacred mountain." Ymmen struggled with the words. *"Many years with dragon kind."*

Oh, I thought, and felt a pang of jealousy that Montfre had grown up learning how to be a better dragon friend than I was!

"Bah!" Ymmen snorted flame and fire into my mind, a laugh that threw aside my concerns. *"Heart-friends don't bow… but it is nice,"* he opened his maw to loll his tongue out at me, as if he were laughing, but he still seemed pleased with the reaction he had inspired in Montfre.

"Narissea," Montfre turned to me. "I take it that you are bonded? That hasn't happened in a generation!"

"So my uncle says," I agreed, although it seemed to me as natural a thing as breathing. "I'm sure if more people made the effort to talk to dragons, then they'd see that dragons aren't—"

There was a snarl from above us as Ymmen let out a small puff of smoke and flame at what he knew I was about to say.

"Dragons *are* incredible," I settled for, and felt Ymmen's acceptance of my words in my mind.

Beside me however, Montfre appeared agitated, but in an excitable way. "I'm afraid I have to correct you, Narissea. The problem isn't that there aren't people willing to become friends with dragons – in the citadel of Torvald at least – but that there are fewer dragons now than there ever were. It is a mystery." He looked up at Ymmen expectantly. Ymmen who merely blinked slowly. I got the sense that, whatever he knew about why the dragons were disappearing from the world, he was not going to share it with us just yet.

"Anyway." Montfre coughed. "This is a great cause of celebration! We must get you to the Dragon Academy at once!" His face fell. "Somehow," he added uncertainly, looking over his shoulder, back towards the south where Inyene's keep and the work camp would be. And his own mechanical dragons.

"I don't care about academies and schools and courts," I said. To me, they all seemed to belong to the same world that Tamin had run off to, and that Inyene had come from. Laws that weren't really true but were just tricks. *Debts,* I thought with derision.

"I need to free my people," I said, and I knew that Montfre understood my need from the light in his eyes and the chains around his feet.

"Then you must understand who it is you are up against." Montfre spoke seriously, and up there under the dark sky, he began his dark tale.

CHAPTER 16
A DARK TALE

"I first met Inyene and Abioye when I was twelve years old." Montfre's voice was hushed. He sat on the side of the battlements of his tower, the candle at his feet casting a circle of light that was flickering and hesitant.

"Or rather, I should say that Inyene met me. I don't think Inyene stumbles into anything. Not since she was a child, anyway." His eyes went far away, as if looking through a window to some old and forgotten room. He shook himself and changed tack. "The Veers aren't a poor family. We were one of the Named Nobles at some distant point in Torvald's history – but that was many, many hundreds of years ago."

"My parents were Valuers. They worked at Main Gate in the Merchant Houses," he said. All of these names and jobs were completely foreign to me. "We were comfortable I guess, a small townhouse on Beris Lane. But my mother got ill early in life. A coughing pleurisy of the chest, and my father had to borrow more and more money to make ends meet. We were fast becoming poor by the time Inyene sought me out."

"I went to school like any other Torvald child, but in my tenth year they realized I had a gift for... *devices.*" He said the word with a certain amount of pride. "I was sent to the Artificers for extra training, and it was *there* that they realized I had some magical aptitude."

The young man with the silver hair smiled at the memory. He had been proud of that, I saw. "And so, I was inducted into the Dragon Academy—"

No wonder he wanted me to go there as well, I thought a little irritably. It sounded like the place that made him feel the happiest.

"—but it couldn't last for long, with my mother's ill health. Although training at the Academy is free, paid for by the King in the promise of future service to the crown – I couldn't leave my parents like that. They were struggling already, and they needed an income that I could provide with my skills," he said, his face falling. "And so, I took to making toys and oddments like the Crystal Euphonia you heard downstairs. A whole range of them. I borrowed materials and workshop space at the Guild of Artificers, and I sold my creations at Central Market, paying back the Artificers and my father's debts. It was hard, very hard work – but I think I was good at it."

"Undoubtably," I murmured. Although I could not understand these strange devices that the young man took such pride in, it was clear, just from what I had seen, that he had skill. And it moved me that he had put his family first, above all other concerns. I hoped that I was honorable enough to do the same when it came to it.

"And it was at the market that Inyene sought me out. I had

constructed a range of mechanical toy dragons, each one no larger than a house cat," he said. "They could walk and pounce and glide, and I was working on one that would be able to beat its wings." Montfre creased his brow. "But the problem was always trying to make them come back, of course. I hadn't discovered the secret of the Earth lights back then."

What secret? I wondered. That was what I needed to know if I was to defeat Inyene's dragons.

For a moment the worry captured me that Montfre might even try to stop me from destroying the metal monsters. But the young man looked so sad-eyed, and so wounded by his past.

Still, I had best bite my tongue and listen. At least at first, I decided, until I knew for sure that I could trust him.

"Inyene was taller, older, beautiful, wealthy. I learned later she had been married to a wealthy young lordling, who allowed her access to the minor circles, balls, and dances of the Torvald lesser Named Families, and when he died, she had his wealth and small house – and his contacts – to use however she wanted. And what she wanted, I thought, was my creations. She showered me with compliments – she seemed amazed at what I had achieved and bought every one of my mechanical dragons. She said that if I had any more marvels to bring them to the market the next day, where she would be sure to buy them, too!" Montfre looked up, a sad look on his face. "Can you imagine what that felt like to a twelve-year-old boy?" He shook his head before he continued.

"The very next day she returned as she had promised, but this time with a retinue of men around her – Dagan Mar was one of them, her right-hand man, her thug and strongman, even then, though I did not realize it – and she did not buy my Euphonias and Light Refractors. She instead presented me with a contract."

Laws. Debts. "She's doing the same to my people, too." I couldn't keep the contempt from my voice. But this could be my chance to win the mage over to my side – our stories weren't *so* different, were they?

I cleared my throat and thought about what Uncle had told me. "Inyene came into the villages, promising everything – but it was all a trick so that she could send in her guards to clear the Plains and bring people here." I nodded down to his set of manacles. "I know how uncomfortable those things can be – I can't imagine having to wear them for years."

Montfre gave me a piercing look with his unsettlingly light eyes before nodding. "Not so different, perhaps. I imagine that Inyene uses the same term for your people that she did for me! It was an indenture – that means that if I signed, I would agree to work for her and her alone, and she would pay me and provide me with food and lodging. On top of that, she was offering a small fortune – well, a fortune to me at the time – that would go to my parents." Montfre scowled. "I should have realized then that Inyene already knew fully well who I was and what my problems were! But I was young. I finally had a chance to save my parents from the mess they had fallen into. So, of course I signed the form, and within a day I was riding out of the citadel forever as one of Inyene's retinue."

It sounded ghastly to me, although I could understand why the younger Montfre had made the choice.

"For the next four years, I worked hard for my personal queen. We were a small band back then, traveling all over the Three Kingdoms as Inyene sought the information and people she needed to make her dreams come true."

"To be the next high queen." I repeated what I had overheard, and Montfre nodded.

"Yes. She has some fool idea that she is a descendant of High Queen Delia, just because her family name is D'Lia. Inyene's mother always thought that meant Delia, as in *the* High Queen Delia – the very first!" Montfre shook his head as if it was a truly outrageous notion. When he saw my look of incomprehension, he must have realized that we Daza did not have the same histories that Torvald did.

"She was the mother of three princes, each one ruling either the northern, middle, or southern kingdom," Montfre explained. "She was the ruler of the Midmost Lands entire. And it was *she* who made a deal with the Great Dragon King Zaxx, which allowed the Dragon Riders of Torvald to be born."

"Zaxx the Gold," Ymmen said suddenly, his head turning to hover over us. His eyes were shot through with a crimson red.

"What's wrong?" Montfre asked, his face blanching paler (if such a thing was possible).

"I don't know." I looked up at Ymmen in confusion.

"The Gold was a bad dragon. Cruel," Ymmen stated, before he swiveled his head back and ruffled his wings indignantly.

"He doesn't like that dragon you mentioned," I explained, wondering what had caused such a severe hatred in Ymmen at just a name.

Montfre coughed and resumed his tale. "Anyway, the point was that none of us could see – even back then – how zealous and twisted-up Inyene was inside, and just how this one idea of her fictitious birthright totally ruled her. Or what she was really prepared to do, until it was too late."

"What was that – make her metal dragons?" I asked.

Montfre nodded. "We traveled everywhere, with Inyene adding tough, strong, and capable people to her entourage. She even married, once, which I later found out was a second time – to a wealthy merchant of the Southern Kingdom, who died not long after their wedding night..." Montfre raised his eyebrows. I understood what he was trying to say.

"First, she was searching for ancient scrolls, anything to do with the first days of the Torvald Kingdom, and the Dragon Monks – a type of mage, like myself, but the very first type. And it was in those scrolls she found talk of something called the Dragon Stones... a type of Earth Light, I think. So, then she searched for alchemists, and finally she searched for mines. I didn't know it at the time – but this was all a part of her plan to eventually build her own army of dragons. In those four years she kept filling me with confidence in my abilities, encouraging me to study more of the magical scrolls that she had amassed, and directing me to study the power of Earth lights."

I nodded that I knew what they were. I had mined them, after all.

"The Earth lights capture light – we all know that. But ancient scrolls talked of how they could capture other things, too. Thoughts. Emotions. The alchemists were trying all sorts of doggerels of incantations and old rituals – but nothing seemed to work." Montfre's face filled with a deep crimson blush as his voice faltered. "It was *my* idea to try and use the new techniques that I had learned as an engineer. The science of refraction and concentration, prismatics and so on that we started to be able to harness the power of the rocks, and to me it was a matter of scientific exploration."

Oh, Montfre, I thought, feeling at the same time both sympathy and horror. Imagine knowing that you were complicit – in some way responsible – for the evil that Inyene has brought into the world?

But apparently, it even got worse.

"The alchemists disappeared overnight," Montfre said. "We were in an old abandoned Estate on the edge of the Middle Kingdom at the time, and Inyene kept everyone in their own halls. One for the guards, one for the alchemists, one for the servants and so on."

Just like she keeps the Daza in their warehouses now? I grimaced. She thought about people like they were sacks of grain. Keep them here, bring them out when you need to use them, put the leftovers back again.

"I had been sent into the hills with a couple of Inyene's guards to harvest supplies for my work, it was an overnight mission, but when I got back the next morning the alchemists' hall was empty. But not of their equipment," Montfre said ghoulishly. "Only their clothes, their most personal belongings, the alchemists themselves had vanished! I should have seen it at the time for what it was: No alchemist will *ever* leave their refractors and magnifiers and mortars and half a hundred other tools behind!"

I shuddered at the mystery of what must have happened to them as

Montfre continued. "She started to trial my prototypes on newer, dog-sized mechanical dragons that she had me create for her. I had found a way to use the Earth lights to harness the residual etheric vibrations of matter," he said, his voice speeding up a little.

"The what?" I said, before a feeling of fire raged through me, like an inferno. It was Ymmen of course.

"The Songs," the black dragon hissed, and his tail lashed against the tower roof – causing several of the opposite battlement stones to crack and chip.

"I didn't know it would be so awful!" Montfre cried out at the black dragon's apparent outrage. "Truly, I didn't. I had discovered that all matter – all earth, rocks, stones, trees, scales – it had a sort of energy. And the Earth lights naturally concentrated it. Once I knew that, it was a simple thing to tune those Earth lights to only capture the energy of the dragon scales that Inyene had been collecting."

Montfre's voice broke as he sobbed, and I saw just how upset he really was. "Inyene needed a way to control the toys, she said. So, I made her the scepter, which allowed her to animate all of the mechanical creations, so long as they had Earth lights and dragon scales on them."

The young man looked at me with haunted eyes. "Believe me, I would do anything to undo what I did."

He would? Now was my chance. "Help me," I said, "Help my people escape." Montfre looked at me seriously, and we held each other's gaze for a long moment – but then he nodded.

"Can it be undone?" I asked immediately.

Montfre wiped a hand over his face. "I've thought about it often, but I've never found the perfect equation. The problem is, that without my staff..." He sounded lost.

"Why do you need a staff? Is it because of the chains?" I asked, though he looked perfectly capable of walking to me.

"Mages need a focus for their power. In ancient times, a mage was often one who was bonded with a dragon, but I have never bonded, and so my magic is erratic and unpredictable. Inyene broke my last staff so that I couldn't destroy her work. As soon as I realized – almost six years ago – that she was building an army of monsters, I tried to burn my research and destroy my workshop. She stopped me with the power of the scepter that *I* had made for her. She broke my staff and imprisoned me here."

He's a mage. And all he needs is a staff! My mind was a whirr of possibilities. "Look, Montfre – I will get you that staff! Look at Ymmen; look at how powerful he is!" I was saying excitedly. "Between us, with your power and this dragon – if we could even get Abioye to let us into the keep then we could steal the scepter!"

Montfre seemed to take interest for a moment, but then his eyes dropped as he sighed deeply.

"You see, I want to, but... you have no idea just how..." the mage searched for the right word, "*cold* Inyene is," he settled for.

She doesn't know how fierce I can be! My thoughts crackled, but Montfre was like a hurt animal. He was cautious. Wary. He needed to lose his pain and fear of Inyene before he would fully commit.

"It came from her childhood, I think," Montfre mused. "Both she and Abioye did not grow up as rich or as powerful as they are now. They were orphaned when Inyene was just thirteen, and Abioye was only a toddler. That's why he's so loyal to her – she's the only mother he's ever had."

"Inyene was forced to take her young brother and herself into an alms house," Montfre said.

"An alms house?" I asked. I'd never heard of such a thing.

Montfre looked surprised at this, but he explained. "Well, alms houses were meant to be places of charity, to help those in need be useful and get back on their feet, but really, they had become debtors' prisons. Anyone who was unlucky enough to end up there became the slaves of any merchant or workshop owner or lord who wanted to hire them."

"So that's where she got the idea for her mines," I said, mostly to myself, and if Montfre noticed, I couldn't tell.

"Abioye says that he doesn't remember his childhood, and I often wonder if that is the truth or a lie that he has told himself," Montfre said, his voice low. "They stayed there for only four years, until Inyene took her then seven-year-old brother and fled. They traveled to Torvald, living on the streets, amongst thieves and pickpockets until Inyene found a way to claw herself and Abioye out of their tragedy."

I was rapt at the story, although it gave me the chills to think of it. I had come to regard the cities of the west with suspicion a long time before this – but I had never thought that they could be this cruel. Such things did not generally happen on Daza land. I did not think of my people as being cruel – or perhaps we were only cruel when we absolutely had to be. If a Souda stole, they were given a chance to make amends. If they did it again, they were driven from tribal lands. If a Souda had nothing – if by some calamity or ill health they could no longer hunt or weave or plant – then we would look after them. There were always many ways to be a part of the village, after all, and we were stronger together. The idea of casting people away because of bits of paper seemed strange and ugly to my heart. But I had not grown up as Inyene and Abioye had, being used and seeing others as tools to profit by.

She uses all of the people around her just like she uses the Daza, I thought. Something made me wonder at that. At just what could make a person so twisted that they couldn't see just how similar they were.

Montfre was from an unlucky family like she had been, I listed. *The Daza are being forced into this 'debt', which Inyene knew from a personal experience.* It was madness. Sheer madness!

"Pain can be anger," Ymmen spoke into my mind, and it chimed almost exactly with a saying that my mother had often used.

"Hurt animals growl," I repeated, earning a strange look from Montfre, that made me go on. "Inyene D'Lia has been so twisted by her experiences that now she's like a crazed lone wolf."

Montfre nodded. "Yes, I suppose she is," he said. "It's enough to almost make me feel sorry for her. Almost."

"Apart from the fact she should know better!" I said. "After having gone through the same pain that she is now inflicting on others!" My own four years of torment, and seeing my friends have their health ruined, lose fingers and toes and break bones, would never let me forgive Inyene.

To my surprise, it was Montfre who shared my savage judgment. "That is what I have been trying to tell you, Narissea of the Souda. You already know that Inyene is cruel, and that she doesn't care for anything but her goal of becoming High Queen – but now you know just how ruthless she also is. And clever," Montfre said with wide eyes. "She managed to get from nothing and nowhere to be a noble-woman with riches and wealth, a private following of hundreds of mercenaries, as well as four or five hundred slaves."

"As well as five mechanical dragons," I added. Montfre was right. If she had managed to amass all of that – seemingly by the strength of her wits alone, then I was certain that it wouldn't take her long to build her army of mechanical dragons.

"But now that you are here," Montfre said, his voice dry from all the talking, "we have some hope," he croaked, looking up at Ymmen sitting beside us.

The black dragon was looking resplendent, with the sun glinting across his snout and side. Just looking at him brought me hope, and I'm glad that Montfre shared my feelings.

The sun! I gasped, suddenly realizing how late – or early – it was. We had spent so long talking that the sun was already rising over the eastern plains, turning the sky a dim, suffused pink. "I have to get back!" I leaped up to my feet. *Tamin.* I had left him all night at the cave – he had food and water, but he would be beside himself with worry!

"Montfre – I thank you for everything that you have shared with me;

I promise that I will return," I said, already reaching my hands up to the sky as Ymmen stood up, stretching out his legs and wings.

"With a staff!" Montfre called out to me. "Just bring me a straight and strong staff. Rowan, oak, or ash if you can find it!"

I nodded, told him that of course I would, as Ymmen's claws closed around me and I felt that familiar rush of being plucked into the air.

CHAPTER 17
FATES, STORIES, AND STAFFS

"——And then he said that he needed a staff, otherwise he wouldn't be able to perform any of his magic!" I said, somewhat breathlessly, to Tamin.

We sat just on the inside of Ymmen's cave, with the light of the morning strong across the mountainside beyond. Tamin had already damped down the smokery, and it was still early enough that I knew none of the work shifts would be making their way up the mountain yet. *In fact, no work shifts had come up the mountain since we had escaped,* I realized, pausing my story of last night.

Ymmen had retired to the dark recesses of the cave, grumbling that he was tired. The more time that I spent with him, the more I came to think of him as an older dragon.

Not old! There was a distant tail thump from behind us, making me smile.

"What was that?" Tamin asked, looking warily between me and the shadows of the cave. He still had trouble getting used to my bond, I saw. The thought made me pause for a moment. Why wasn't *I* just as surprised by this new ability to hear the dragon's thoughts? To have the dragon hear mine – much better, I had to say.

Strange, but my bond with the black dragon felt *almost* natural. Almost, because it was still difficult to understand precisely what he was trying to say in my mind. But that was the limits of the awkwardness. Like getting to know a new horse – you might not understand each other perfectly, but there was an easiness to the relationship that was often lacking with people.

Honest, I thought. No bits of paper. No laws. In response, I felt a rising glow of warmth spread through me, and I knew it was Ymmen's approval.

"So." Tamin coughed. "That's your plan, is it? To steal this scepter that this mage Montfre made, and do what with it?"

My mind went blank for a moment, confused at why he would even ask. "Destroy it, of course. That way, Inyene won't be able to animate her mechanical dragons."

"Hm." Tamin nodded, clearly approving of my answer. "But, presumably this scepter will be well-guarded? Inyene is building an army. She will not leave her most precious item lying around, will she?"

"We have Montfre. We have Ymmen," I pointed out. A mage and a mighty dragon. *Why was Tamin being so difficult?*

"Ah, my fierce Nari," Tamin said softly. "I tried to explain to you before, when we first came here." He meant the cave. He meant bonding with the dragon. "You cannot see it, but what you are doing here sounds more like the old legends of Torvald and the Middle Kingdom. It sounds like you have come to the attention of *fate*," he said mysteriously.

Was that a bad thing? I wondered. Maybe my god-Uncle was just having cold-feet, I thought. I patted him on the shoulder.

There was a sharp and high-pitched *pheeet* that echoed over the Masaka, instantly cutting through our conversation. From its long, drawn-out wail I knew it to be the sound of either the morning work shifts beginning or the night shift ending. It made me anxious for every minute that I had to spend up here, hiding away.

"The thing with fate is," Tamin said in a quieter voice, "and what many people do not understand, is that it is about *stories.*"

"Songs," I heard Ymmen suggest, and the dragon-word in my mind was hazy with lizard-sleep.

"Most people's stories are *not* straightforward – but they are understandable. They begin with their parents, they tell themselves through the course of their life, and they are passed on after they have left this world," Tamin said.

I had never been very good at philosophy, but I listened all the same.

"But some stories are much deeper, and much older. They are told through generations, centuries, entire ages," Tamin said.

So? I thought.

"You said that Inyene believes herself a descendant of Queen Delia?" Tamin asked, and I nodded. "Then let me tell you a little of the story that is associated with her." My god-uncle scowled to the northeast, where Inyene's camp was.

"Even though the high queen is taught as the mother of the Midmost Lands, there are still far too many *stories* associated with her that are not so wholesome. Stories of the compact she made with the dragons of the sacred mountain and how it might not have been so good-hearted as people believe." Tamin's voice was serious. "Magic, the very stuff that Montfre and Inyene are using, is rumored to come from that time. And there are clear accounts from people who called themselves the Western Witches that the High Queen Delia did something terrible in order to yoke the dragons to her will and release their magic. Something unspeakable."

There was a slow, reptilian hiss from behind us in the cave. Even though I trusted Ymmen implicitly, I still did not think it wise to poke any more at this subject.

"Uncle," I said. "We Daza have our own stories, do we not? We may never have ridden dragons – but we do now. We will write our *own* stories! Maybe *fate* had better prepare for *us!*"

"*Foulness!*" I awoke to a sudden storm of fire in my mind with a gasp. It was Ymmen's thought, of course – and it took me a moment to center myself and work out what had enraged him so much.

But then I heard it – the clattering, whirring sound of one of the mechanical dragons, far above. I had slept through the day and it was sunset, the entrance of our den was filled with a blood-red light as the clacking, grinding, whirring sound only grew closer.

"Hgh? What is it?" Tamin woke up – an irritated Bull dragon was a hard thing to sleep through, even for Uncle.

"Ymmen, calm, please." I reached out to my friend with both my hands and my heart. Even though it was gloomy here in the cave, there was still enough light to make out the wall of shining scales, rising and falling as he huffed his disgust towards the entrance.

His scales were warm to the touch – almost hot, and the instant that I touched them his outrage only swept through me all the stronger. *Please, calm!* I tried to counsel him. *We can't let them know that we're here!* I was sure that Ymmen, with all his terrifying strength and ferocity, would be able to beat one of those clacking, rickety dragons – but now was not the time. Bringing down one might mean bringing four more upon our heads.

Not that we had much choice, apparently – as I heard the unmistakable sound of a guard whistle, and it sounded nearby.

"What! They can't have discovered us, could they?" I tensed, as behind me Tamin was already getting up.

Pheet! Pheeet! The whistles were getting closer. I froze. I didn't know what to do – we couldn't stay in here – but if we fought I wasn't sure that we could win.

"I can beat anything!" Ymmen hissed. Suddenly, in my mind, I received a picture of what the black dragon sensed. No – a picture is the wrong word for it. It was a collection of senses – images, smells and memories and sounds all rolled into one – and even though I had never thought in this way before, somehow this collage made sense.

I am seeing with Ymmen's senses, I thought in wonder. This was a totally new experience for me.

The clearest experience came together in Ymmen's and my mind as: *The cruel human,* and at the same time the memory of a metal bar coming down on scale. Fankin!

And then another collection of scents and sounds of distant voices.

'Are you sure you came this way?' The words were heard by Ymmen's sensitive ears, and *I* could hear them too. And recognize them. Overseer Maribet One-Eye.

With them, the dragon relayed, were a handful of others – all with the heavy tread, leathers, and whistles of the mine guards. They appeared to be searching the mountainside for us.

"I will burn them all!" Ymmen started to quiver in rage.

"Is there another way out of this cave?" I asked quickly.

"Why? We can fight!" Ymmen responded in my mind. Our connection was growing stronger – I didn't know if it was Ymmen's anger which made his thoughts so clear, or whether it was the fact that I had my hands touching his scales, but the thoughts flowed between us seamlessly.

And I knew that there *was* another route through the caves. I could sense it clearly in Ymmen's mind, as I was doing to him what he could do to me – picking the thoughts and memories from them! The cave wound to a larger hollow of smoothed rock that Ymmen had made his home, but a tunnel led up and out, narrow at first so that Ymmen didn't like squeezing through it, but it emerged on the western side of the slopes.

My way is better, I spoke into his rage, showing him in my mind my plan: Escape. Steal the scepter. Stop the mechanical dragons. And after that – scare the mine guards away and free my people. I threw that thought at him of swooping down, scattering the panicked guards left and right with his mighty wing beats.

"If we attacked now, then the mine guards will only compare you to the mechanical dragons," I said, as sternly as I was able. "Don't you want to be the only dragon in the sky? The largest, fiercest dragon that ever was?"

That seemed to mollify him a little, as the thought of even sharing the winds of the world with such awful creations was an insult to him.

"Everyone will see how fierce you are, the guards will run away in terror, and we will free my people," I concluded.

"Everything is meant to be free," Ymmen growled, but strangely it didn't sound like an agreement. It sounded like he was trying to make a point. "Humans. The wind. The rocks. Songs. Dragons."

But that was already what I was trying to do, wasn't it? *What do you mean?* I thought at him – only to be met by scaly silence. I might have averted disaster, but I knew that time was running out. Ymmen might not hold his anger in check for long, and Inyene's army of dragons would surely only increase. I let Ymmen lead the way as he turned with a sighing, rattling hiss of scales in the tunnel, his body rippling and flowing as it moved through the dark.

"Uncle, quickly!" I said, reaching out to grab his hand as we crept after Ymmen into the dark.

"Here." Ymmen shared with me the scent of fresher air and the last warmth of the rocks that edged the exit to the tunnel. The sun had set, but it was still only a purpling dusk on the western side of the Masaka. But on the eastern side, under the shadow of the mountain, it would already be full night.

Ahead of us were dark shapes of the rest of the mountains, spearing into the gloaming sky, and the thin silver of the lake far below. I could still hear the whirring clatter of Inyene's dragon, but it was distant and far, having moved southward through the mountains. I couldn't hear the whistles of the mine guards at all.

"The staff!" I thought suddenly. There were more of those healing trees down by the lake that I had used to fix Ymmen's wing. They had grown straight and tall, and for some reason it felt *right* to make the mage's staff out of a tree that had brought life – to combat the scepter that brought death.

"Stand," Ymmen said in my mind, and I knew that he was including both of us as I directed Tamin to stand at my side, arms up in case he didn't want to get them clamped to his torso and unable to move. Ymmen ducked and, with each claw folding itself around us, held us to his chest as he jumped into the night airs.

"Oh!" Tamin made an astonished gasp as we swooped low over the hillside towards the lake. I looked over to my god-uncle to see that, although his eyes were wide with the shock of the experience, he was also grinning broadly and open-mouthed.

"It's... amazing!" he shouted in awe.

"Now you understand!!" I called back as Ymmen alighted by turning his wings and pulling his back feet forward to grasp the rocks below him, right in front of a stand of the trees.

As soon as Ymmen had set us down, I was already racing to one of the smaller ones, setting a hand on its silvery-white bark for a moment before pulling my flint blade from my wrap of a belt. It was tough work, but Uncle and I chopped away at the trunk, before pruning the staff of its smaller branches. To finish, I left a disjointed Y-shape near the top. It was taller than I was, and although I had no idea how a mage went about using a staff, I wanted it to at least be a serviceable walking stick if nothing else!

"Good." Tamin tested the staff first, leaning against it and pulling on it to feel its flexible strength. Thus pleased, he handed it back and I slid the staff through the wrap of cloth and old rope serving as my belt, and we held up our arms to return to the skies.

"Now, we get this to Montfre and stop Inyene's madness!" I said.

CHAPTER 18
THE WINDOW

Montfre's tower was burning with light when we approached it on the wings of night. But the place did not appear homey at all, mainly due to the mechanical dragon that sat stilled on its roof.

"*Hsssss!*" Ymmen let out a strangled hiss of rage at the merest sight. But its eyes were dark and there was no smoke rising from its maw at all. It was dormant – but what did it mean? *Had Inyene set a dragon to guard Montfre? Had she already uncovered us?*

No, I considered as we circled high above the tower. "The dragon is useless unless it's been lit, or brought to life," I pointed out. The only benefit of it being here was as a carriage to carry someone.

Abioye, I thought with a grimace.

"Nari?" Tamin called towards me from where he was clamped to the dragon's chest as well. I could sense his alarm in his words, as I shook my head.

"We go ahead with the plan." I was adamant. Now we had the chance to free Montfre *and* capture Abioye. Maybe by the time morning's light broke over the Plains this would all be over and my people would be free!

And besides, I considered. We couldn't afford to go back and hide in the cave now, could we? Fankin had been working with the mine guards, probably leading them straight back to the cave. *He must have been recaptured,* I thought, *either that or handed himself in to Dagan Mar with the promise of revealing us!*

Whatever. What's done was done, and there was no sense bemoaning a bad apple, I thought. You just had to throw it away and get on with it.

"Take us down," I said, and I could feel Ymmen echoing my fierce attitude with one of his own. He approved.

The only weapons I had were my ridiculous flint blade and the staff, but Tamin was behind me as well. Even though Abioye was larger than me, and probably had a fine blade – I was sure that I would be able to outfight him if it came to it. *Poison Berry.* I remembered Ymmen's name for him and sniggered. *He was probably going to be drunk, anyway.*

"Down here." I lifted the trapdoor and, taking a breath, unslung the staff and started to creep down the stairs. Once again, there was a radiance coming up from below, and, just as before, there were muttered voices that became clearer the closer we tread.

"We have to act now!" I heard. It was Abioye's voice – not slurred like last time, but tight and high with anxiety.

"Wait. Calm yourself, *Lord* Abioye," I heard Montfre's voice returning. He still sounded annoyed with Inyene's brother. *As well he might!* I thought of the chains that the young mage wore. It was a burden that I knew only too well.

"No, you don't understand – the window is closing – even as we speak!" I heard Abioye say, and we were so close now that I could hear him shuffling nervously from foot to foot. The lantern light of Montfre's room illuminated the arched door and the corridor outside of it, and I could see a shadow cut across the wall.

"Just wait. There is someone you have to meet – an ally," Montfre said.

"An ally? How on earth have you managed to find an ally in here!" Abioye burst out.

I held the staff low in front of me and stepped out into the doorway. "Some people are more resourceful than you can imagine, *Lord* Abioye," I said grimly, mimicking Montfre's condescending tone.

"You!" The young man whirled, his scarlet cape flaring about his broad shoulders as he did so, and his tousled hair quivering. His eyes were large and wide as they looked at me, and his face flushed a crimson.

"Seeing a ghost, *my lord?*" I said, unable to keep the grin from my face. "Don't move," I said, jabbing the staff forward a little. I didn't hate him, I realized in that moment. What I had overheard between

Abioye and Montfre, and what the mage had told me just last night, made me pity him if anything.

But he could be so much more than he is. The frustrated thought flashed across my mind. Maybe it was my Daza childhood – it wasn't that we Plains people were 'tough' – what a ridiculous claim! – it was that we had to get things done if we wanted to live the life of the Plains. There was no time for bemoaning our misfortune, especially if it was perfectly in our power to change it!

"Narissea – wait!" Montfre was shuffling forward however, holding his hands out between both me and Abioye (not that Abioye had made any attempt to guard himself or threaten me, I noticed). "Abioye has come to help us," he said to me earnestly.

He has? I frowned.

"I have?" Abioye echoed, looking from me to Montfre uncertainly.

"The window," Montfre said out loud, while gently tapping the edge of the staff I held to bring it down. "You said that there was an opportunity to defeat your sister."

"Oh, right." Abioye blinked, shaking his head as I saw him cast another glance at me as if he still couldn't believe that I stood there at all, and then look up as Tamin stepped from around the doorway too. "Dear stars – has there been a breakout?" he murmured.

"And why would that worry you, Lord Abioye?" my uncle said sternly to the finely

dressed noble, with all of the authority of an older man scolding a younger.

"Oh, no – I mean good, if there was," Abioye prevaricated quickly. "But a breakout would mean that it might already be too late."

"Montfre," I handed the staff to him, the strange young man's face lighting up. "No, there's been no breakout, but yes, my uncle and I have been surviving in the wilderness, and please-please could someone explain to me what this plan is you're talking about!"

Abioye swallowed nervously, nodding. "My sister has been beside herself since one of the criminals came back. He *walked* back to the mines; would you believe it! Pounded on the outer palisade gates and demanded to be taken to Dagan Mar, shouting that he knew where a large black dragon was hid!"

Fankin, I thought. It had to be, didn't it? "The plan, Abioye," I said. I really didn't want to hear anything about that creep Fankin again, but Abioye was insistent.

"This returnee said that the dragon was not far from the Masaka camp, and that it had eaten you two!" Abioye looked at us in astonishment. "He promised to lead the way to its lair, in exchange for a post as one of Inyene's guards."

"He probably realized that he wouldn't survive a night out in the mountains on his own," Tamin muttered under his breath.

"My sister sees it as an opportunity. Track down the living black dragon, use her mechanical dragons to kill it, and then harvest its scales, even though she has enough now for twenty or more of her own."

"Skrearch!" There was a distant sound of a roar, muffled and far

above us, but it was still clear just how furious Ymmen was at the thought.

"Oh, dear stars," Abioye breathed. "It's here!"

"*He's* my friend," I growled, with a touch of the soot and fire of the dragon anger in my own voice.

"He's..." I could see the lordling struggle to grasp the concept. "Does that mean that you two...?" Abioye's cheeks flushed pink once again. *Was he jealous?* I thought wryly.

"Narissea is bonded, if that is what you mean," Tamin said sternly, stepping forward at my side. When he next spoke, his voice sounded strong and clear – and proud. "Narissea of the Souda is the first of our people that I have ever heard tell of to become a true dragon friend."

"Oh," Abioye said.

Whatever. I wondered whether Abioye was stumped by the fact that *he* was no longer the one who could 'save the day'. But I still wanted to hear his plan, however. *Maybe we'll even let him help us out,* I thought charitably.

"Inyene's not in her throne room." Abioye cut to the chase. "She's with Dagan Mar, preparing the capture of the black dragon...I mean – they *can't,* because he's here, right – but anyway," Abioye said quickly. "She's left the scepter unguarded, and she's raised the other mechanical dragons, and they are scouring the Masaka's southern slopes for the dragon. There might never be another chance like this again!"

I held Abioye's gaze for a moment, making sure that I could see the truth in what he said. He appeared too high with emotion in order to be lying, so I nodded. "Then we have to go, *now.*" I turned to Montfre. "The staff – will it work?"

The young mage was busy doing things to the staff, running his hands up and down before stopping at various places as if on a whim, making small notches or markings with a blade, and then beginning again. As I watched, his eyes took on a strange intensity, and I could almost see them giving off a certain brightness – although I couldn't be sure in this lantern light.

"Aldarn wood? Oh yes, yes indeed," Montfre muttered, shutting his eyes and raising the stick, point-wise, upwards in front of himself.

I felt something in my stomach, a jittering sort of feeling. But it wasn't the cold, uncomfortable dis-ease that the mechanical dragons inspired. It was similar, but not the same.

"Strength of wood, whose roots burrow deep into the earth," Montfre muttered, raising the staff still higher. "Whose limbs withstand the strongest storms, whose might can split mountains!"

Crack! There was a resounding snap of thunder and a flash of light as the mage brought the staff straight down against the manacles between his feet. When the flash receded from my eyes, I saw that the iron manacles had split apart, and that the rounded end of the staff was now scorched and blackened.

"I think she will do very nicely," Montfre said, testing the newfound reach with his legs.

"It must be powerful enough to destroy the scepter!" I marveled, but Montfre had different ideas.

"Oh no. I'm afraid we won't be able to destroy the scepter so easily!" he said, appalled.

What? My heart clutched. That was the whole point, wasn't it?

"It took me three moons to create it, and twice as long in preparatory rituals," Montfre said. "Although it won't take nearly so long to unmake the sorceries binding it together – it will still be no easy feat!"

I opened and closed my mouth for a second as I tried to rethink. *Nothing changes,* I thought. "We steal the scepter. Inyene won't be able to use her mechanical dragons against us, and then we send Ymmen in." I grinned.

"Ymmen? Is that your—?" Abioye said lightly.

"My friend, yes, it is. Come on… you'll get the chance to meet him!" I said with a victorious smile and turned to lead our small party up the stairs, and towards freedom.

"Poison Berry!" Ymmen greeted Abioye as soon as he got to the top of Montfre's tower.

"He's… *big,"* Abioye murmured, almost making me laugh out loud. *Why are people always so surprised when they see him?* I rolled my eyes.

Ymmen enjoyed the attention though, filling his chest and rising up on his haunches so that he was even larger. Abioye gulped and sank to one knee. "Sir dragon, I am Abioye D'Lia," I heard him say in a tremulous voice. "And I fear that my family has done you a disservice."

"They have." I heard Ymmen's words clearly in my mind as he lowered his head towards Abioye very, very slowly. The meaning was clear – Ymmen did not forgive him *yet.* For his part, I saw Abioye nod seriously that he had understood, and back away, and for Ymmen to relax his posture once again. Strangely, I felt approval from the part of my mind that was Ymmen. The older dragon seemed to value honesty very highly indeed.

But there was no time left to lose, I knew. Who knew when Inyene and her guards would be heading back to her throne room – if they weren't there already? The only problem left, was…

"How many people can you carry, Ymmen?" I looked skeptically at his claws, and then at the four of us.

"No – we can't use the mighty dragon," Montfre cut in, with a gracious nod to Ymmen. "Although I cannot wait for the opportunity, sir dragon," he added. "But as soon as the guards see this magnificent beast approach the keep, I am sure that every alarm will go off in an instant. We will need to gain access to the throne room without raising alarm." The mage's eyes turned to regard the dormant mechanical dragon on the other side of the tower top instead.

No! I thought immediately. The very thought of sitting atop that beast was insulting.

"Nari," Tamin said, and although he looked as disgusted as I did, his voice was somber as he said, "It's the only way if we want to have a chance at freeing out people."

I growled in frustration, and it was echoed by Ymmen above. But even in my anger I could see the sense of his words. "Okay."

"If Ymmen will take me, I will stay with him," Tamin said, looking abashed for a second. "My fighting days are long over anyway... and this way you will have an extra pair of hands on the outside."

Once again, I had to agree. I wasn't eager to throw my god-uncle into the middle of a fight against Inyene's guards if it came to it. But...

"I don't have any weapons aside from a sharpened bit of stone," I said, and Montfre suddenly exclaimed, "Aha! Perhaps I can now help with that!" He turned and, with his recently freed legs, ran down into the recesses of the tower, only to return a little while later carrying a bundle of cloth – and in it was the knife with the curved blade-point, engraved with stylized dragons.

The Lady Artifex's dagger. I recognized the weapon in surprise. It was the same one that had been in the shrine-chest Tamin and I had uncovered. But I had been certain that Maribet One-Eye had stolen it for herself, just like she had pilfered the Earth lights in the shrine. But I remembered how nervy my old overseer had looked when Abioye had started talking about 'those who steal mine artefacts'. *She must have returned it to the box when no one was looking.*

My mouth went dry when I looked up to see that Montfre was presenting the dagger to me. I knew that Montfre trusted me, of course, but to be given the weapon that the dragon-lady who had seemed so strong and independent herself had wielded. I felt humbled.

"It was once carried by a dragon friend, so I see no better reason for it not to be given to another!" he beamed. "Inyene brought it to me to investigate a few days ago." He scowled a little. "She knew that, even if I had a weapon, she still had me under lock and key anyway and could easily overpower me with her guards."

"Well, not after tonight, my friend," I said, as Abioye vaulted onto the back of the mechanical dragon, waiting for Montfre and I to follow suit.

No, not after tonight, I promised myself. *Tonight is when everything is going to change.*

CHAPTER 19
THE KEEP

Riding on the back of the mechanical dragon with Abioye in front of me and Montfre behind me was unlike anything that I had ever experienced.

It was awful.

It was uncomfortable. It was smelly. The heavy, bitter tars of lamp oil mixed with something fetid and putrescent. The small straddle 'seat' that was installed between the girders of its back ridges kept on jumping and twisting up and down, and I was forced to throw my arms about Abioye's waist (*of all people!*) for fear of flying off! By the time Inyene's keep rose into view, with the lights of its burning wall lanterns making it look like a vast crown in the night, my thighs and hips felt battered and bruised with the constant knocks of the wood and metal supports that the outer plates of scales were riveted atop.

But pain, at least, was something I had long ago learned to bear. I gripped Abioye's waist tightly (*surprising how slim it was,* I thought, having imagined he would be pudgier under the soft linens that he wore) as I peered around his shoulder.

"How are you flying this thing!?" I shouted, and Abioye leant to one side to show me where there appeared to be, at the front of his seat, a series of handles that he could either pull or push to direct the thing's flight.

"A lot of it is instinctual!" Abioye called.

It has no instincts! I hissed but held my tongue. Anything I could learn about these monstrosities surely would help defeat them.

"The Earth Light energy, or whatever it is, seems to make it respond a lot like a living creature, anticipating my actions and movements. It'll keep beating its wings without me, for example – *Look!"* He suddenly let go of all of the different levers, and I let out a small yelp of fear as the entire dragon fell downwards by a couple of meters.

But the gears and levers carried on jerking, twisting, and swaying all on their own nonetheless, as the mechanical beast did indeed, continue to beat its wings.

"Ha!" Abioye said, and I realized that he had been showing off.

If you want to impress me, I thought, *maybe NOT using the reanimated bits of a dead dragon is the way to go.* Before I could point out this bit of wisdom to him however, the walls of Inyene's keep were already rising ahead of us.

"Narissea," Abioye suddenly hissed to me as we rose in a swoop that would take us over the outer wall. "You'll have to pretend to be a servant, I – I'm sorry," he said.

"Just what you wanted," I mumbled and felt him cringe under my hands.

"And what about me?" Montfre however, clearly not so eager to relinquish his first taste of freedom in more than a decade, ever since he had first started working for Inyene. "Do I have to be your servant too?"

"Well…" Abioye didn't sound sure. "If anyone asks…"

The walls of the keep swept below us, along with large bronze lanterns blazing on their metal tripod legs, surrounded by groups of Inyene's guards holding their crossbows slung over their shoulders underneath them. Surely the guards should have been looking out over the mine or the mountains – but most of them were more concerned about being warm. I wondered if that also meant that they weren't a hundred percent loyal to Inyene and would rather run than try to stop a black dragon.

Ymmen? I thought, knowing that he would be able to hear me.

"Of course, I can hear you. Ymmen and Nari are—" He said a dragon-word, which I didn't understand. But it came with the feeling of wholeness, like the way that the Plains are whole with all of their different animals and habitats and weathers, all being a part of the same thing. That was us, me and the dragon – different, yet a part of something greater than either of us.

The thought gave me courage and joy that I would be able to do this.

"I am close," Ymmen's thoughts in my mind reassured me. He was faster than the mechanical dragons, and so long as we could get back to the battlements or a rooftop I trusted Ymmen to be able to get us

out. Through our bond, I could feel the dragon raise himself up and start to sweep higher and higher far above us, with Tamin in his claws. I hoped that Tamin was still enjoying it!

On the other side of the outer walls were three wide halls that connected the defenses to the central keep itself. Each of them had long flat walkway-roofs, and it was one of these that Abioye used as his landing spot. The wings of the mechanical dragon clattered and whirred in fury, and once again the entire construction started to shake and judder as we were lowered to the roof before finally coming to a halt. Abioye released the handles and, as soon as he had slid down from the thing's back, the blue Earth light started to fade from the creature's eyes, leaving just the black smoke rising from its maw.

"Narissea." I was surprised when Abioye had turned to raise his gloved hand up at me. For a moment I looked at it, wondering what on earth he meant, before I realized that he was offering to help me dismount. I accepted his hand, feeling the steady grip he had on my forearm as I slid from the saddle and down the dragon, his touch lingering even after I'd caught my balance.

"Oh no, don't mind me," Montfre grumbled beside us as he wobbled and half tumbled to the stones beside us.

Even though I had spent almost four years seeing Inyene's keep, I was still unprepared to see it this close-up. There were distant towers and ruins here and there across the Plains, but now that I was right next to its huge stones I could only marvel at all the time that must have gone into fitting them together. I marveled at the effort – and also the stupidity.

Why would a people be so scared as to need such high walls? I thought. But even I had to admit that there had to be a fair bit of skill involved too. Abioye was already marching towards the archway into the large round keep itself, the entryway decorated with stylized dragons, one on each side forming the outer pillars, and leaning over to capture the keystone in the center, which looked like a crown.

"Ah, this was an old Torvald outpost." Abioye saw me looking. "I think it's why Inyene chose it," he said distractedly as we swept into a wide hallway, lit with lanterns. The floor was a checkerboard mosaic of black and white tiles. "My sister had some crazy notion that High Queen Delia had this place built, so, naturally that is why we ended up here," he said as we walked.

On either side of us were more archways, and when I looked into them, they appeared to lead into large and airy rooms, some with banqueting tables and others just with tables piled high with guards' shields and suits of armor. The keep looked deserted and under-used for such a large space.

To be honest, the inside of the keep was a bit of a letdown. I was expecting lines of thuggish guards in every room, brandishing clubs and swords and crossbows. I wasn't expecting it to look so... *haphazard.*

"Down there." Abioye pointed to where the hallway ended in another door, but also with a grand set of stairs leading to the left. He took us down them and I saw that they were curving around a large interior room. There were more lanterns on the stairwell, and I started seeing drapes as well – all of a deep red velvet. The stairs and walls looked swept and gleaming clean. We turned the corner once again.

And there I saw her... Inyene the Queen, standing there in all her power.

But it was only a statue, standing to one side of a set of iron-bound double doors. I shuddered at how lifelike the stone was. Its edges were crisp or smooth, with no signs of weathering – clearly a newly carved installation. It showed a righteous Inyene standing proudly with her chin up and with long hair flowing around her shoulders. Crouching at her side was a perfectly carved dragon. On her brow was a crown, and in one hand she held a scepter – clearly a replica of the one that Montfre had made as he gasped in outrage when he saw it.

"Hail my sister the queen," Abioye said skeptically, throwing us a dark glance as he pushed open the heavy door.

To reveal the *real* Queen Inyene, sitting at her throne and surrounded by guards.

"Ah, brother dear, do come join us!" Her voice pierced my heart like ice.

She's not meant to be here! I froze behind Abioye, with the glare of a hundred crystal lanterns in my eyes. Was this a trap? Had Abioye deceived us? For a moment I cast a look to Montfre, who was looking just as appalled as me, but then Inyene was speaking again.

"Come in! Don't dawdle by the door, letting the draft in – guards! Get that door closed!" Her voice was like cut glass, hard and sharp, with each syllable and consonant hard-edged and exact.

Suddenly there were guards moving across a wide, oval-shaped room towards us. These looked to be larger, better equipped versions of the mine guards outside, I saw. They were all men and women in their third or fourth decade, I thought – and had the grim, expressionless faces of those who knew their jobs well. I took in the better quality of studded leather, a bit of ring mail, and the fat leather belts that bristled with both small and larger weapons.

Should I try to kill her now? My hand was already moving to Lady Artifex's dagger under the flap of my tunic, but suddenly Abioye's hand was on my shoulder, pulling me forward beside him. His grip was like iron.

"So many guards just for a door, sister!" he said breezily.

"Do you not think that ones such as we need our protection?" his sister countered, and I could hear that when she said 'we' she meant 'I'.

Abioye walked us across the middle of the throne room, once again paved in the checkerboard mosaic, to where there was a long line of what looked like purple cushions on the floor. *Huh?* I thought in confusion, before Abioye pushed me down beside him as he kneeled on the cushions, with Montfre doing the same on the other side.

In front of us were a set of black and white marble steps, leading up to the higher end of the room where Inyene's throne sat. I found myself staring up at her in amazement.

I've never seen her before, I realized. It was strange to finally come face-to-face with her.

She was thin, but square-jawed like her brother. Too thin, was my next thought. The sort of thin that I had once seen in the faces of the Mitika tribe of the Plains. They lived much farther to the south than us, and once, when I had been young, my mother had insisted I travel with her on a rescue party, delivering water because their more arid region hadn't had rain for almost an entire summer. I remember being shocked by their sunken eyes and the way that I could clearly see the veins on their temples and around their hands – and it was the same sort of emaciation that I saw here in Inyene.

But she could obviously afford any food or water she might want, I saw from her rich white robes, embroidered in stunning gold and lapis blue – as well as the throne itself that she sat upon, golden and encrusted with fat rubies.

It was also apparent that her physical stature made her no less imposing. If anything, it only added to her intensity as she leaned forward, her eyes bright and sparkling as they focused on Abioye.

"You didn't come to our hunt, my brother. Why is that?" she said in her exact, clipped tones. "Luckily, I had my man here to help me." She inclined her head just a fraction, and there, limping in from the shadows of the alcove where Inyene's throne sat, came none other than Dagan Mar.

Dagan, his small frame appearing even more twisted with hate than usual, blinked when he recognized me. I gritted my teeth, my hand twitching towards the dagger hilt hidden under my folded arms.

But Dagan didn't say anything. I saw his mouth pursed tighter, but he remained silent as he stood next to the Throne, glaring down at me, Abioye, and Montfre.

And he's inches away from the scepter too, I thought in frustration, which lay across Inyene's lap. It was a horrible, black-iron thing with different sized humps and rings and ended in the largest floret of Earth Light crystal that I had ever seen in my life. It glowed eerily against Inyene's too-white hands, making her look more like an apparition out of some ghastly fairytale.

There was no way that I could wrest it from Inyene without Dagan Mar being able to stab me in the back, as well as two or three dozen of her guards jumping on me. I scowled.

"I could not assist you in the search, my sister... because I—" Abioye faltered at my side and swallowed nervously. His voice rose a notch. "I believe I have found the Stone Crown!"

The what? I thought.

"The Stone Crown," Inyene said very slowly, drawing out every syllable like they were ripe fruit and she wanted to extract every goodness from them before she spat them out. "Her Majesty, the High Queen Delia's Stone Crown," she said, and her hands on the scepter gave a small shake of excitement.

"Yes, my sister! Yes – and these two have the clues to where it is hidden!" Abioye said in a rush.

I beg your pardon? All breath left my body as Inyene's eyes swept over me, and it was like the rolling thunderhead of a storm.

"This *slave?*" Inyene frowned at me as I looked, aghast and quite probably stupefied, back at her. Why would Abioye lie like that? I inwardly screamed. How could he be so stupid? *This is insane! I*

don't know anything about any Stone Crown! My temper flared in my chest. *But of course, he's a spoiled, selfish lordling. One who would do anything to save himself, wouldn't he!* I felt betrayed.

"And I see that you have also released Montfre." Inyene's gaze swept away from me, discarding me as easily as if I were a beetle crushed upon her shoe. I blushed at the shame I felt, and my jaw clenched tighter.

"*And* you have given him a staff." Inyene sounded less than pleased.

"My sister – I did," Abioye once again lied, ending in his anxious high note. "I knew that Montfre would be able to help. And Narissea, the Daza girl—"

I growled to myself. I didn't want my name thrown to the oppressor of my people so easily. I wanted her to learn my name and know what it *felt* to be me.

"Her people have legends about where the High Queen Delia hid the Stone Crown, out in the Plains. Between them, the girl and the mage, we will be able to decipher the map that I brought to you!"

Lady Artifex's map? I concluded, as my shame and anger only deepened. When I saw Dagan Mar's victorious little smirk behind Inyene, I had to lower my head and hide my face in my hair, staring daggers at the stupid purple cushion on the floor.

"The map you suggested that I send to the King of Torvald?" Inyene said sternly. "I seem to remember, brother dear, that you were suggesting that I would need to curry favor with the monarch of the Dragon Riders, and that it was imperative that I send it to him as quickly as possible?"

Abioye stammered beside me, but with no intelligible words appearing out of the jumble of sounds.

"Luckily for both of us, I have no desire to parlay with that fool of a boy," Inyene said with obvious scorn. "*He* is the one who should be trying to entreat with me!"

"So, uh – you still have the map?" Abioye swallowed.

"Of course, I still have the map!" she snapped. She snapped her fingers and sent one of the guards off to retrieve it. "Now tell me about the Stone Crown."

"Well, it was the High Queen Delia's—" Abioye said.

"Not you!" Inyene hissed at him, and I was surprised at the anger in her voice. Apart from the obvious physical similarity, they didn't sound like they were siblings at all. I was thinking this thought when I heard what she had to say next, and my blood ran cold.

"It's not *you* that I want to tell me about the Stone Crown. *I* was the one who first told *you* about it, in case you had forgotten, brother mine – I want *her* to tell me about it!" she spat.

And I realized that the Lady Inyene, oppressor of my people and decimator of my village, was talking about me.

CHAPTER 20
THE STONE CROWN

All eyes inside the throne room turned to me as I continued to stare down at the purple cushion. I was painfully aware of the dagger handle that was poking into the bottom of my ribs, hidden by my folded arms.

Could I pull it out? Run up the steps and plunge it into her black heart?

In the back of my mind I heard a hiss of flame as somewhere, far, far above, Ymmen voiced his own opinion. *"Attack! Kill!"*

But I had never killed anyone before. Not any *person.* All of my long nights and days and seasons and years of anger froze in me, like the winter frost that stilled the grasses of the Plains. Now that I was sitting here, with the dagger at my side and my target just a few meters above me.

I balked.

I'd like to think it wasn't fear that stayed my hand – although in truth, my heart was hammering like a galloping jackrabbit. But it was the crisis of the moment. The decision. Was I the sort of person to attack a woman sitting down, even a woman as evil as Inyene was? To attack her without giving her any warning?

It's not that she gave the Daza any warning, an angry, almost dragon-like part of me thought. But no. If I was to defeat her, I wanted her to see what it was she had done. To understand *why* I had done it. I raised my head to look up at her.

Her bright green eyes regarded me quizzically. There wasn't even any malice in them as she looked at me. Just a sort of detached interest.

"The Stone Crown?" I heard myself say in a small voice. I even wondered what it was that I was going to say. Should I lie to her? Or should I tell the truth?

Which would expose Abioye's lies, and probably have him punished and Montfre killed. My confusion started to clear as I realized that I couldn't give into the anger now. People would die. I would abandon the Daza, and Tamin, and Ymmen.

"No!" Ymmen's voice blew like a strong gale through my mind. Even though I could feel the dragon's thirst for justice, he also had no desire to see me killed by Inyene's guards. I could sense Ymmen's feeling of frustrated impotence at being so far away, and also, strangely, a deep fear.

"You cannot die. I will not feel my bond partner die!" Ymmen was adamant, and I realized then that our bond meant that he would feel everything. It made me feel ashamed. *Who was I to throw my life away so recklessly, and hurt Ymmen in the process?*

"She clearly has no idea what you are talking about, brother," Inyene's eyes flickered from me in an instant. "Take her back to the mines, someone…" she started to say.

I can't let that happen! I thought in horror. *Dagan had said if I was caught escaping again I would be branded – and it would be my last chance.* And now, as I saw Dagan Mar puff his chest out and limp down the first step, I knew that the chief overseer would not hesitate to kill me as soon as I was out of sight. "I'll gladly see to it, my lady —" the chief overseer began.

"Although we have no legends of any Stone Crown, Your Highness", I burst out quickly, "there are ancient Torvald ruins all across the Plains. I grew up seeing them in the distance.".

"Wait." Inyene held out one long, emaciated finger, and Dagan Mar stopped, as obedient as a dog. Her bright, unnerving eyes held me in their icy clutch once more. "Go on."

I swallowed nervously. I was speaking the truth – or I had started off by speaking the truth, anyway – but the scant fragments of folk lore and history that I was ransacking my mind for felt to me like lies. "There used to be dragons that flew across the Plains regularly," I said out loud, remembering what the Elders and even my mother said.

"And I was told that Torvald had towers and way stations out here, but which are now broken open and overgrown," I continued. "We Daza people have always avoided them in the past, because we thought they were haunted." That bit I made up. "And so, we have to know where they are, in order to steer our cattle and herds away from them."

I paused, to see that Inyene was still regarding me intently, judging every word.

"We Daza people travel far and wide across the Plains; it is our nature to follow the herds, and for those of an age to spend a season out on the trail," I said, trying to impress on her that our tribal knowledge was deep.

"And there are places where great battles were once fought," I said – although this was the flimsiest piece of rumor. It was true that in some areas of the Plains the plants grow rambling and wild, and the ground was unusually churned up. Once, I had heard my mother suggest that is because that was the site of a great battle or a slaughter. I didn't know which facts would be of interest to Inyene so I blurted them out.

"We Daza have our own names for the places of the Plains," I continued. "There are the Bone Canyons, the Lakes of the Sun, the Darkening Caves…"

"The Darkening?" I heard Montfre say, but it wasn't in awe – it was in a sort of aghast horror. "That was one of the very early enemies of the kingdom of Torvald – a magical storm that could suck the life from your very bones!"

"Enough." Inyene silenced him. "I am satisfied that there might be *some* use to this theory." She cleared her throat as she beckoned Abioye closer. I watched out of the corner of my eye as he stood up, with his head still bowed, and ascended the first few steps to once again kneel down, right at the foot of his sister's throne.

"Ah, my dear, sweet, innocent Abioye," I heard his sister say in a lower voice – but there was nothing soft about that tone. If anything, it sounded like a threat. "When you first came in here, talking like a crazed child, I was certain that you had been a coward or worse – a liar to me," she scolded him, reaching down with one almost skeletal-pale hand. She lightly grasped his chin between thumb and forefinger, pushing his head back so that he couldn't avoid staring back at her.

"I thought that you had refused my call because you feared the combat with the dragon, or that you doubted me." It was a question, and I could hear that it was a loaded one.

"No, not at all, sister!" Abioye said, his voice slightly garbled from Inyene's grasp.

"No," Inyene agreed, giving his chin a little disapproving shake. It was a cruel gesture, and I could see the relationship that they must have had even when they had been young. "Have I not always looked after you, Abioye? Even when everyone around us has betrayed me?" she asked.

"You have, sister." Abioye swallowed nervously.

"Have I not shown you that we D'lias must be strong? Strong in mind and spirit. Stronger than anyone else if we want the world to listen to us?" she asked.

"You have," Abioye mumbled.

"You are my beloved younger brother, Abioye, and I would never change that. But sometimes, even I wonder if you will ever be able to accept my birthright," she said, and I saw

Inyene's brow crease in confusion as she wrestled with the question.

She's frog-hopping mad, I realized. She was so convinced of her own importance – and the *right* to be important – that even she didn't see how mad she was.

"I understand, my sister – my queen," Abioye mumbled, and Inyene beamed at him, letting him go.

"Then let us find the Stone Crown and finally take back Torvald!" She raised her hand, gesturing to where the doors at the back of the room had opened, and I turned to see two guards carrying the large metal box that my uncle and I had found.

"Hmph." Inyene's eyes narrowed as Montfre and Abioye carefully unpacked the contents of the box before her, first unrolling the large painted image of the Lady Artifex and her dragon Maliax. It was strange to see the image again, and I was struck by how similar (red hair, green eyes, pale skin) and yet how completely different the Lady Artifex and the 'Lady' Inyene were. The Lady Artifex looked hopeful, where Inyene scowled. Artifex had been painted healthy and strong, whereas Inyene appeared desiccated by her passions.

Like they were two versions of the same person, one good, and one—

"Just the map," Inyene said, her casual disregard for the image of the woman insulting. I wondered if this image of a stronger, healthier version of herself was what upset her so much.

"If I may, sister," Abioye said nervously. "The journal and the map have to be understood together." He put both of his hands together into one clasping motion. He picked up the leather-bound book as Montfre unfolded the old vellum map on the marble floor.

It was larger than I remembered it, and I found myself starting to lean closer automatically. Down one side were the sharp, stylized triangles of mountains – with several of them displayed prominently, or with broken gaps between them.

The largest, middle space however was mostly empty, save for waving lines back and forth, leading to other, smaller pictures. I saw 'X's and other, rounded curls with arrow heads on the end.

"This is the keep, where we are…" Montfre announced as he pointed a finger over the edge of the mountains. There was a small picture of a tower, and a tiny asterisk. Suddenly, the entire image came into focus for me, a little like when Ymmen had shared his senses with me and they had seemed chaotic at first, until they had finally all come together to make sense.

If that's the keep, then that is the pass that I flew over with Ymmen, to the north of us. Spreading my eyes outwards over what had to be the Plains, it was looking down at them from a great height, able to see all of them at the same time! I saw the Southern Plains, where the warmth grew oppressive and the summers arid – and they were marked differently from the Middle Plains, where I came from. Here, the map was dotted with more waving lines and more tufts of what looked like stands of grass.

And that meant that up there had to be the Northern Plains. I saw more hills and trees and small circles – and I knew from experience that the Northern Plains were certainly a hillier and forested, colder land with many lakes.

"Do you recognize anything here?" Inyene asked me pointedly. I had to nod.

"Yes, Your Highness." I said, pointing to one of the places where the small, curving arrow was situated. "That's one of the old ruins of a tower," I said matter-of-factly, and scanned for the next one. *Yes, it seemed to fit.* I tapped the vellum just over the next curling arrow.

"I've seen something like that before…at the Academy." Montfre was frowning, tapping his chin. "That arrow – it's something to do with the Dragon Riders, or what was *before* the Dragon Riders perhaps… The Dragon Monks."

Ha! I suddenly saw the small image for what it had to be. The curling, forked tail of a dragon.

"And so – everywhere that we see that image we can also presume that is where the very first Dragon Monks made an outpost." Inyene was smiling, congratulating herself. "Abioye? You may study the map and the journal. Learn *everything* you can from it – I must know what Her Majesty, the Empress Delia, did with our Stone Crown, and where she hid it!"

Inyene crowed in delight as she sat back in her throne, but all I could see was a woman on the very edge of all reason.

"We will start the preparations for our expedition immediately," Inyene announced.

Expedition?

"Sister – we don't even know where the Stone Crown is hidden," Abioye said from his place beside me, sweating. *Was he saying all of this stuff just to buy us some time?* I wondered.

Inyene had stood up, and looked down at her brother, kneeling on the floor between Montfre and me – the slaves. "Brother," she said coldly, exactingly. "I am certain that with your intelligence, and with those fine tutors I brought for you, that you will be able to decipher the map and the journal's secrets. Either tonight or on the way," she said with a small smile. "You *are* up to the task, aren't you?"

Abioye blanched, but nodded. The implication in Inyene's words didn't have to be said aloud – she would find someone else to do his tasks if he could not. And then what use would her brother be to her?

"Good. Then, as a reward you will lead my expedition to recover the Stone Crown, and you will leave as soon as we have amassed the supplies!" She raised the scepter in her hands and brought it down on the metal arm of the chair to the sound of a dull clang, just like I had seen Tamin do sometimes when he had deliberated on village disputes.

"I will need to take these two!" Abioye said quickly. "The Daza girl will act as a guide, and Montfre – well, you know the marvelous skills that Montfre has," Abioye said, as Inyene was already turning to go.

"Fine." Inyene waved her hand. "Take who you need. But my guards – and dragons – will go with you." She said with finality, before turning to stalk out of the throne room. I saw Dagan Mar throw me a sharp, poisonous look before he, too, followed her.

What have you done? I thought as I looked to Abioye. I didn't know

how to feel about this. I would be farther away from the scepter –
unless Inyene was going to come with us? I would be farther away
from my fellow trapped people here.

But I might also be able to send word to the rest of the Daza on the
Plains, I thought.

CHAPTER 21
SOME STUPID RELIC

"An expedition! To find some stupid relic!!" I hissed as I followed Abioye through the Keep. I was holding one of the heavy rings of the metal box while Montfre was holding the other – as Abioye had announced that we would start our research right away.

"My apartments are up here." Abioye nodded to a set of winding stairs, flanked by two heavyset guards. I kept my eyes lowered and my head down as they respectfully touched their fingers to their foreheads as Abioye passed. As soon as we had rounded a few turns of the stairs however, I could clearly hear the guards snigger behind us.

Whatever position and prestige Abioye has, it completely relies on being the brother of Inyene, I realized. The guards here didn't respect him at all.

The stairs went up a few more turns before opening out into a wide hallway, one side illuminated by the silvery-gray moonlight of the large arched windows, while the other held wooden doors. Both Montfre and I had slowed our steps, and I had a chance to look out of the windows to see that we were quite high up now – the black mountain side swept down across our vision, and there – in the distance, I could see the telltale lights and bonfire of the mines of Masaka.

I dropped the box with a heavy clang.

"Ach!" Montfre continued walking a step, to an awful scraping noise.

"Narissea?" Abioye turned and looked at me, still wearing the worry on his face that I had seen in the throne room.

"You sleep up here," I said. It wasn't a question; it was a statement.

"Yes," Abioye said, at first in confusion before he followed my gaze out of the windows to the clear view of the mines below. I knew that Abioye wasn't an *evil* man. Not in the same way that his sister was so twisted up that there was barely any bit of soul left inside of her anymore. But the fact that for the last however many years, he was still able to walk out of his 'apartments' every morning, set my teeth on edge. He had seen us slaves down there, toiling and working hard and getting picked on and beaten by his sister's guards, and he had done nothing to stop it. It awoke all my old feelings of rage once again.

"Ah." Abioye clearly saw what was on my mind. "Please, not here," he said, gesturing to the largest set of double doors, and looking back down the corridor to the stairwell. "We can't talk out here – Inyene has her servants and spies everywhere."

I didn't budge. "When," I said, remembering the words that I had overheard Montfre say to him just a few nights ago. "When are you going to step out of your sister's shadow, Abioye?"

The young man cast a look once again back to the stairwell, and then to me – and finally to Montfre, who appeared stony-faced.

"Now," he hissed desperately. "Tonight. I have a plan." If I hadn't just seen how he was with his sister, and if he had said these exact same words back at Montfre's tower when I had cornered him, I might not have believed him. But I could see in his eyes all the shame, all the guilt and the embarrassment his sister had made him feel. He appeared desperate – angry. "This cannot go on. *I* cannot let her go on doing this!" he hissed.

Good, I thought. Anger wasn't for everyone, and neither was it a particularly useful tool – but sometimes it was necessary. If you are cornered by a Plains lion, it doesn't matter how peaceful you want to be. Sometimes you need to be able to spit and snarl and to fight.

But my long years of incarceration had taught me that there were limitations to that need to strike back.

Like Rebec, I thought. She had always been angry, just as I had for the entire first year. Constantly furious. Constantly glaring at the overseers – and with good reason, too! But anger had a way of eating you up just as much as it empowered you. It was the memories of my people, and of the wind on my cheeks, that had kept me going. Kept me alive.

But for some – I nodded to myself as I looked at Abioye – some people needed a touch more fire in their belly, and it looked as though Abioye had just discovered his. The young lordling had already hurried to the larger set of double doors, using a key from his belt to unlock it, before turning around to look at us.

He still didn't offer to carry the bleeding box, though, I thought a little wryly as I grabbed one end and Montfre picked up the other, and we went inside.

My feelings of resentment didn't exactly subside as I saw the sheer opulence that Abioye lived in. Even though he had called this place his 'apartments' – for some reason I had expected it to be 'rooms.'

It wasn't. I had walked into what can only be described as a large reception hall, with high-backed, gold-inlaid chairs around low stained-wood tables, and with further large, leather-backed seats comfortable and large enough to sleep on. The room was deep enough to extend to the far side of the keep walls, where three bay windows stood, currently half-shuttered with wooden frames. There were huge earthenware pots filled with tall, large-leafed plants the like of which that I had never seen before.

And the wonders still did not stop there. On one side table (with the most ridiculously thin, curving legs that I had ever seen in my life – how was that any use as a worktable!?) sat a diorama made out of painted clay – a double-mountain with one side totally dominated by cream-white walls of a citadel.

"Torvald," Montfre said with a trace of awe to his voice, as we set the box down in the center of the room and moved across to it.

"Seems like a silly place to live," I muttered, even though my heart quickened a little at the sight of it. I knew that I was being a little childish – finally seeing the place that had always been talked about and mentioned through my life made me feel awkward. Out of place.

But there was something to it, I had to admit secretly as I examined the sculpture. One of the mountains wasn't really a mountain at all – but was instead a vast crater, and inside it I could see terraces of carefully sculpted rocks – and even dried grasses and sprigs of bushes that had been carefully pruned to look like trees!

There was a ridgeway that connected the crater to its sister mountain, and, nestled just under the peak of painted purples and browns, there was another grand old building. A little like this keep in fact, but much wider.

"What are these?" I pointed at the strange half-moon shapes in the walls. They dotted this top keep as well as the rows of terraced walls of the citadel itself.

"Dragon platforms," Montfre said, his eyes shining at first, before he blinked and looked sad. "My mentors and masters at the Academy said that each platform would be filled with dragons, all through the sunny days when they stood guard over the city."

"Guard over the mountain!" I heard Ymmen breath into my mind. *"Dragon mountain,"* he breathed – but my mind translated it as *sacred* mountain.

"Dragons and mountain are one. *Were* one," he said mysteriously in my mind.

"Then why aren't they there now?" I said, part in question to Ymmen, but it was Montfre who answered me, thinking that I was talking to him.

"The dragon numbers started declining a generation ago, I think," Montfre said, looking sadly at the diorama. "There are still dragons and Dragon Riders, but only a fraction of what there used to be. No one knows for sure why they went – or where to." Montfre sounded wistful, and I could only agree. I got a sudden appreciation of the model in front of me as only half of what it could be. The citadel itself with its curving streets and high walls, weirs and guard towers and small plazas, looked very fine indeed, but the *other* half of the model looked empty and barren – the crater and the mountain tops.

"It's meant to have dragons," I breathed, and felt Ymmen's assent. Once again, I sent the question up to him that I had asked before: *Why did the dragons leave?? Where did they go?* But once again I was met with only a scaly silence in my mind. It was either something that Ymmen wouldn't – or couldn't – talk about. Maybe he didn't even know, I considered. It was a hard thing to imagine a creature that powerful and that large experiencing any type of pain, but I dreaded to think of the scale of the trauma that he and his dragon kind must have gone through, secretly, if they had abandoned such a sacred place.

There were still more rooms to discover in these apartments I saw, as Abioye opened one of the three doors in the main reception room to reveal another room, this time lined with books. "Come, it's a bit more… secluded in here," he said, casting a wary eye at the main doors. "I have my chambers there, and a small servant chamber besides"—he indicated to the other two doors behind us—"which either of you are welcome to use."

"Uh, I don't think so," I said under my breath. The very word 'servant' irked me far more than 'slave' did. They both meant the same thing in Inyene's household, right? At least 'slave' was the more honest.

"But there's two more rooms beside mine," Abioye said quickly at my distaste. "I think this whole wing must have once been for courtiers or royal relatives, once. Inyene has pretty much given this floor to me alone, saying that we needed to keep an air of dignity about us D'Lias." He shook his head, moving into the study room.

Once again, I shifted the heavy metal box with Montfre and shared a slightly comical look with the young mage. Abioye doubtless still had a lot to learn about how to make friends.

But whatever. There would be enough time to tell him that he shouldn't treat other people like glorified manservants if he wanted to have any sort of friendship with them.

But Abioye was at least trying, that I could see, as he had pulled out three chairs around another one of those ridiculously small tables and set down a carafe of pale pink wine and three long-stemmed glasses.

"Please, sit," he said encouragingly, pouring me some of the wine, and then Montfre, before going back and topping up his own glass so that it almost brimmed.

"My plan." He cleared his throat, taking out the map and setting it on the table, folded. "As soon as I saw this map, and started to read the Lady Artifex's journal and saw what it meant, and how important it was going to be to Inyene."

And just what is this master plan of yours? I thought.

"This journal is written in Old Torvish, and luckily, as my sister was adamant that we were the rightful heirs of the Three Kingdoms, she had me learn it. It appears to be an account of a lengthy expedition by the Lady Artifex." Abioye reached to draw out the journal next, carefully flipping through the pages. "I believe that the Lady and her dragon were actually on a very different sort of mission," he said.

Abioye flipped open the map, to point towards the various small dragon-tail insignia, as he outlined his argument.

"One: The First Realm of Torvald, under High Queen Delia, had already mapped out quite a large part of this area, as it seems that as soon as the high queen found the power of dragons, then she sent them off to explore and expand her empire."

"So why send out another expedition at all?" Montfre said pointedly.

"Precisely." Abioye nodded. "And two: The Lady Artifex doesn't seem to follow any sort of pattern in her journeys. She's not following a river to its source, or skirting a line of mountains to their end, or heading in one straight direction as far as she can go." His finger dotted here and there around the Empty Plains. "Which is what I would expect to see of an exploration mission. No, instead, it is almost like the Lady Artifex was just taking what currents interested her." Once again, his finger moved back and forth.

"Although I am probably wrong on the details of her journey," he admitted. "There are many places and details in the journal that I couldn't find on the map at all."

I thought about that erratic sort of journey, and it made me think of the only two explanations for why a Daza would perform strange here-and-there travels.

"If it was the Souda doing that," I said. "We would either be visiting people and places that we already knew and had a reason to go to," I said, "Or…"

I looked up at each of the young men beside me in turn. "Or we would be attempting to throw off a predator from our trail."

"Then why make a map at all?" Abioye frowned, looking at the parchment. "If the Lady Artifex was trying to conceal her movements."

"Well." Montfre cleared his throat. "There's nothing here that suggests a straight-line destination. Maybe the Lady Artifex was clever enough to know that this information shouldn't be lost forever, and that there might come a day when, in the right hands – the Stone Crown could be useful."

"Hsss…" I felt a hiss of annoyance from Ymmen in my mind, but before I could reach out to him Abioye had continued talking.

"When Queen Delia died, she left the midmost lands in turmoil – three lands given to each of her three sons, and then devolving into the Land of the Three Kingdoms, as it was for almost a thousand years," Abioye said seriously. "But she *did* leave behind the Dragon Monastery."

"There's something I don't understand, however," Montfre piped up. "It is well-known that during Queen Delia's time, they *used* dragons, but no one *rode* them. It was only when the first king of the Middle Kingdom learned to ride one that the Dragon Monastery turned into the Dragon Academy." He pursed his lips. "But you say that this Lady Artifex was a Dragon Rider under Queen Delia?"

Abioye nodded, moving to the front of the journal and opening it once again, to clear his throat and read out the dedication just as I had heard Tamin doing.

"This being the journal of Lady Artifex, detailing my attempts to chart and plot the confines of the World, under the rule of High Queen Delia the First, with my faithful companion Maliax," he read.

"Impossible." Montfre shook his head. "I was *at* the Dragon Academy remember – admittedly, only for a couple of years, but they made a *BIG* deal of history up there. It was the first king of the Middle Kingdom that rode dragons. No one before him."

I squinted at the map, with all of its intricate glyphs and squiggles. "And these places are Dragon Rider outposts," I said. "So… either the map is much newer, or the journal is, or—"

"Or someone is lying." Abioye frowned at the title page of the journal before a slow smile spread across his face. "Of course. This whole box is a puzzle, don't you see? Lady Artifex, if she rode a dragon, *had* to have been alive fifty years or more *after* the High Queen Delia's death. Which would make perfect sense if she had been sent to the ends of the world to *get rid of the Stone Crown!"*

"Why would that make any sense?" I asked out loud, totally confused by the looks of victory between Abioye and Montfre. "Didn't this new Torvald King want it? What was wrong with it – too ugly?"

Or too many bad memories? I wondered, remembering what Tamin had told me – that there were some very bad rumors attached to the first ruler of the Midmost Lands.

"It's why my sister is so fascinated by the Stone Crown," Abioye said quickly, as Montfre nodded. "The old legends go, that although it was the High Queen Delia's sheer strength of character that made the dragons respect her – she made for herself a magical crown that would forever call the dragons to her aid when she needed them."

Well, that certainly sounded like something that Inyene would want, I thought. She had imprisoned entire villages in order to create her own army of mechanical dragons – why not go for the one object that would mean she could summon the rest, as well?

I growled in annoyance. "I don't know why your sister doesn't just try to get to know a dragon," I muttered under my breath. Maybe that was what she had always needed – to be able to share her heart and have her mind *seen* by another being as close as a dragon bond.

But then again, I knew only too well what would happen if Inyene had ever plucked up the courage to actually try and talk to a real dragon. Somewhere in the back of my mind, I felt the white-hot embers of Ymmen's anger. *They would have seen straight into her black soul and swatted her like a fly!*

"But the Lady Artifex took this Stone Crown far away, and attempted to hide it?" I concluded. Both Abioye and Montfre nodded. *And something must have chased her along the way, as well,* I thought, poring over her zigzagging, backtracking and forward movements.

There was only one question left really. "Why didn't this new king of Torvald keep the Stone Crown?"

Had the Lady Artifex stolen it, I wondered.

"Those are questions which we may sadly never find the answer to," Montfre said sagely. "All we know is that it vanished from the history books – and what Abioye has deciphered here is probably the best explanation that any have had as to where it might have gone." The mage nodded calmly before looking up to the young lordling. "Your plan, Abioye?"

Ah yes, I thought. *The plan.*

"I realized that the map might lead to the Stone Crown," Abioye said to us in a quieter voice, "but I couldn't let my sister have it. That was why I was trying to convince Inyene to send the map to the King of Torvald. If Inyene has the power to summon real, living dragons…" Abioye shook his head.

I suddenly realized the game that Abioye had been playing. Even though he had been unwilling to directly oppose his sister before – he had been attempting to sabotage her plans this whole time!

But now, his sister would be too dangerous to sabotage, I saw. *Even Abioye, her brother, could see that.* He needed to stay close now, in order to get his hands on the map. And the Crown, I now realized as he continued to explain;

"We go on the expedition. Inyene says that she wants me to lead it – that will give us the perfect excuse to get to the Stone Crown before she can, and then send it to Torvald!" He appeared pleased, before looking at me. "You could even ask your dragon to take it to them! He'll be able to fly faster than any of Inyene's mechanical dragons!"

I nodded that all of the above was true. But there was still something that he was forgetting.

"My people. The Daza slaves out there," I said sternly. "How long will it take to find this Stone Crown, and to send it to Torvald, and for Torvald to do—" *To do what with it?* I thought. Did Abioye expect the Middle Kingdom to come to his aid, when they had so far apparently ignored Inyene and him completely?

"I know," Abioye said quickly, "but Torvald has Dragon Riders, and soldiers and armies…" Clearly, he was trying to placate me – but it had completely the opposite effect.

"No, Abioye, *you don't know!*" I pointed out, thinking of his plush rooms all around him. "You don't know that every hour, or every day, there are innocent people down there suffering. Some are losing fingers, toes, going blind, breaking limbs," I said hotly. "You don't know what it is like out there on the Plains. There can be dust storms and thunder storms. Wild cats and tar pits and worse. Floods and heatwaves. Every day that we spend out there crossing the Plains is a day that can see one of my people – one of my *friends* die!" I thought of Oleer and the others. Even sour-minded Rebec.

"But…" Abioye shook his head. "What other option is there!? You can't suggest you attack Inyene with your black dragon – alone! She has fifteen mechanical dragons now, and the smelting works are running day and night!"

But I'd heard enough. I stood up, tired of talking. "Abioye, you have a good heart, I'll give you that," I said. *But not a strong heart,* I almost added. "And your plan is a good one, even – if we were willing to let more Daza die. And I am not." I turned to the door as both Montfre and Abioye jumped up, trying to stop me.

"Narissea!" Montfre called as I stormed into the main reception hall of Abioye's apartments. "You can't. Even with my staff and your dragon… *many* Daza could die!" he said.

That thought made me stumble, caught between one evil and another. "I can't just sit around and talk!" I spat. The fact that I wasn't doing enough to help my people was eating me up. I would sneak out of here and find Inyene, I thought. Just as Lady Artifex had taken a long and dangerous journey alone, then I would be as brave as well.

All of this Stone Crown business will take weeks, months even. I would find Inyene now and put my blade to her throat until she handed over the scepter. And *then* Ymmen could free the Daza first, before we went to find the Stone Crown.

My temper flared as I snatched one of Abioye's rich green cloaks from a stand beside his apartment door, throwing it on to hide the Lady Artifex's knife at my side as I turned, ignoring Montfre's and Abioye's aghast looks.

But just as my hand grasped the door handle, there was a sudden rapping from the other side, and a familiar voice called out. "Abioye – open up in the name of Queen Inyene!"

It was Dagan Mar.

CHAPTER 22
ANGER

*D*agan! I involuntarily took a step back from the door, my hand already on the blade handle.

"Open up, Abioye – don't make me get the guards to kick the thing down!" Dagan snarled through the door.

Had we been discovered? I turned to look at the others, both of whom appeared similarly appalled. But how could Dagan know what we had been talking about? I had no idea, but I prepared myself for the worst. It was surprisingly easy to do.

"Stand back," I heard an unexpected voice say. It was Abioye, as he strode up to stand in front of me, pausing briefly before he reached for the door. "These are my apartments, and I'm still Inyene's brother," he whispered to me. "I said that I was on your side Narissea, and now I guess I have to prove it."

He pulled the door open to reveal an irate Dagan glaring on the far side, and with two of the largest mine guards that I had ever seen at his side.

"What is the meaning of this!" Abioye bellowed, and for once his voice didn't raise in anxiety.

The cruel little man on the other side of the threshold blinked, as if confused at this newer Abioye who stood before him. But then a cruel smile of victory took over his face instead. It was one that I had seen him use before, gloating over any misfortune that he had managed to cause to those of us in the mines that he had taken a special dislike to – like me.

"The queen has decided that it is unsafe to have you left alone with these two," Dagan Mar said, flicking a glance to me and Montfre, but mostly to me. At the older man's nod, the two guards beside him marched into the room around Abioye. One for me, and one for Montfre.

I growled.

"This is ridiculous!" Abioye shouted as I looked up at the guard who was coming for me, and what he had in his hands. It was a pair of leg manacles. The guard's eyes were cold and uncompromising, and besides the short sword at his belt he also had a long metal rod – either of which I knew he wouldn't hesitate to use against me. *Well, he has another thing coming,* I thought, as my hand tightened on the knife.

"No! I forbid it!" Suddenly, Abioye was there, in front of me and between me and the guard. He was holding out a hand to stop the guard. The second one, who had already cornered Montfre by the model of Torvald paused as well at Abioye's sharp and commanding tone of voice.

"The queen's orders," Dagan crowed victoriously.

There was nothing Abioye could do, I thought. We had to go with my plan. We had to attack.

"No." But Abioye had already turned his back to me, defiantly facing both the guard and Dagan Mar.

"Are you disobeying the queen?" Dagan Mar was almost breathless with excitement. I could see in his eyes just how long he had been waiting for this moment.

"No, I do not think that it was *my sister's* orders to manacle my... aides," Abioye said. "My sister has never got herself involved in the *uglier* side of the family business. You know that only too well, don't you, Dagan?" Abioye said pointedly.

Inyene had been using Dagan for a long time. I remembered Montfre's story. Possibly even to help one or both of her unfortunate husbands become unfortunate.

"In fact, the queen would expect me as a D'Lia, to look after myself, to be strong!" Abioye spoke with passion. To me, it sounded filled with self-hatred – but that was only because I had heard the other, more vulnerable side of him as well.

Dagan licked his lips calculatingly. But he didn't deny anything that Abioye was saying, and now I saw how right Abioye had guessed. This petty act of making sure that Montfre and I would be put back in manacles and chains – that we were reminded of just how powerless we were – was all Dagan through and through. I doubted that Inyene had even thought once about me after I had left her sight.

"This came from *you,* Dagan," Abioye echoed my own thoughts perfectly. "And, from where I am standing, I am pretty sure that I heard *my sister* ask me to lead her expedition. Not even you, because you are nothing more than her manservant." Abioye spat the words at him, and it was like watching the chief overseer get slapped in the face. His lips pursed, his eyes squinted, and his cheeks blushed a deep purple.

"I do not need to remind you, Mar, of your place here. I am my sister's representative – not you! And if I say that my aides will remain un-manacled, then they shall. Are we clear?" Abioye's voice had taken on a deeper register as he demanded, and I realized that was what his 'real' voice sounded like – when he wasn't either too drunk or too nervous to think straight. Strangely, he also appeared taller somehow as he stood in front of me. Like maybe he *was* a lord after all.

"For now," Dagan Mar muttered in a tight voice, his eyes flaring at the younger man in front of him, and then alighting on me in a look that could have sparked fires.

I glared right back at him.

"You will be gone a long time, *Lord* Abioye," Dagan said in a murderous tone as he nodded for the guards to leave the room. "I can only pray that you have a safe journey," he said acidly. It was the kind of statement that would have kept me up at night.

Dagan and his guards left, and Abioye waited until he had closed and locked the door behind them until he let out a shaking sigh. All the color blanched from his face as his eyes widened. I had seen the youngest of hunters look like that after their first major kill.

"You did well. You were strong," I said immediately, moving to his side. It was important to hear these things at such times.

"Was I?" Abioye said, his voice returning to its lighter version. "What if I have only made everything worse? Dagan will be watching us now – I am sure of it."

Yes, he would, I realized. I wouldn't be able to creep through the keep tonight. I wouldn't be able to confront Inyene and seize the scepter. Which meant that there was only one plan of action – Abioye and Montfre's plan.

I can't, I thought immediately. If Dagan was going to be left behind with Inyene, then he was the sort of man who would only take out his frustrations against the slaves while we were gone. *Not that he would stop if Abioye stayed here,* I thought. But I would be leagues and leagues away – with no way of stopping him.

But then again – how could I stop Dagan if I remained here? I was caught in this trap of hot and bold feelings when Abioye touched me – just lightly – on the shoulder. "Nothing more tonight," he said in a low, earnest voice. I nodded. It would be foolish to try and do something now, to hunt on anger and impulse and not patience and determination.

"There are rooms next to mine. Go to them. Dagan wouldn't dare defy me again so soon," Abioye said.

"Wouldn't he?" I said, but it was a rhetorical question. He was right. It's better to hunt when your prey doesn't expect it.

I was surprised that Abioye didn't once again try to insist that we both stay here with him, as his servants or 'aides' – but also pleased that it seemed that Abioye was paying much closer attention to how he treated us. It had not escaped my notice that he had told Dagan we were his aides. He escorted us out of his rooms to the doors on either side of his, unlocking each one. "Only I have the keys," he said. "You will be safe." And then he paused and handed first me and then Montfre each the key to our own door. "Lock it after you," he said seriously.

It was a small, inconsequential thing. A normal thing – but I had never had my own key to the many rooms and warehouses that I had been in over the four years. That small act, almost more so than seeing Abioye stand up for me, made me realize how much he trusted us.

"Maybe you're not so bad after all, Abioye," I muttered, turning into the room before I could see Abioye's reaction. And before he could see how embarrassed I suddenly felt.

He was being nice to me. Why? I found my thoughts jumpy and bothersome as I looked around my rooms for the night. They were nowhere near as large as Abioye's next door, of course – but they were still several steps up from a blanket on the floor of a cramped warehouse.

I wasn't sure if it was better than the cave, however.

Abioye is being nice because he's feeling bad, of course. He must have finally seen just how evil slavery was. And just how complicit he had been. *Although it's not really all his fault as well, right?* It was his sister's. And he had been trying to undermine her this whole time by attempting to alert the King of Torvald to Inyene's plans. I argued with myself as I started to take off the green cloak, and then left it on, and then decided that yes, I would actually take it off.

"What's wrong with you?" I snapped at my own heightened nerves. It had to be the confrontation with Inyene and Dagan.

But it was strange having people be nice to me, I thought – before once again turning on myself like a cat after its own tail. *Isn't Tamin nice to you? Ymmen? Oleer? Montfre?*

"Okay, it's weird having my oppressor's brother be nice to me," I settled for. That felt more true. Maybe it was the years that I had spent seeing Inyene's keep in the distance and seeing it as the source of all of my woes. It was strange to find myself here, in this room, with other people who were trying to help me undo the damage that Inyene had caused, who had the power to be successful.

The room itself was longer than our hut had been back in the village. It was mostly a bedroom, but there was another small door that, when I opened revealed a marble washing room, with even a hand cistern and an old terracotta jug with some very dried out and dead flowers in it.

And in the corner, a standing mirror.

We Souda had mirrors of course – the small pocket ones that some of the village had traded for from the passing caravans. But mirrors weren't such an obsession for us as they seemed to be for the people of the Midmost Lands. If we wanted to look nice for a village festivity, then we would borrow those small hand mirrors or – much more likely, we would get ready in our little groups. The lakes would provide reflections, and our friends would help us braid and decorate our hair.

So, it was weird seeing myself in the mirror now – and seeing just how much I had changed.

I was taller, for a start. Taller than four years ago, anyway. And I looked, I had to confess, *shabby*. My mining slave uniform could barely be called clothes, my hair was tangled in knots and there was a layer of grime under my nails. I growled in frustration.

Mirrors only make you feel bad, I told myself, as I pulled some water and did my best to wash out some of the mine dust that still clung to me, despite the few days that I had spent away from it. When I was done, my feet returned unbidden to the mirror to look again, despite knowing that it was a bad idea.

I looked older; I guess that was the most startling change in me. It was strange to see a young woman looking back, and not the girl that I had been when I had been captured – just after my Testing. I congratulated myself on the athletic, lean and wiry strength that I had, but as I looked, I saw that there was something else that was new – a harder light in my eyes. Gone was the carefree expressions of my youth.

And of course, then there was my collection of brands, the four heavy brown marks that swept up one of my arms. Only room for one more– which would be my last, according to Dagan's self-made law.

"Never be ashamed of scars," Ymmen roared into my mind again, and for a moment I imagined seeing, in my mind's eye at least, a small spar of orange flame behind my own eyes. It was good to feel the dragon there, so close. In that unconscious sense that we had

together, I could feel that he wasn't flying anymore – that he had landed somewhere nearby on the dark slopes, and that Tamin was with him as they waited.

"Scars are battles you fought and survived. And surviving is winning," he said.

"You're getting wiser and wiser." I gave a wry smile at the mirror, and at the dragon within my mind. *And, it was getting easier to understand him,* I thought.

"Always like this. Friendship starts slow. Builds closer," Ymmen said, and my mind could translate that when he said 'friendship' he also meant 'bonds'.

"You know a lot about this bonding," I said as I turned back from the mirror with a sigh, to tie my hair back in a simple knot and return to the main room. I'd had enough of preening in a mirror, thank you very much!

And then Ymmen did a curious thing in my mind. A wave of the normal impressions of heat and winds and soot and Frankincense – and then it pulled back, before returning. Almost like a dragon version of a stutter.

"Ymmen?" I prodded him.

Ymmen's presence remained fluttering, before it returned to my mind in full force. "When are you leaving that evil place!" he demanded, and I could hear the growl in his voice.

I have been in here far longer than I intended, I agreed sadly. "I can't," I whisper-thought at him as I looked around my new rooms. There was a wide bed, more of those ridiculously low and flimsy tables, along with some more sturdy chests. On investigation, these were filled with blankets, and I took out the whole lot and threw them on the bed. It was going to be strange to be sleeping in comfort, as well!

But then I crossed to the singular window to open the shutters wide, revealing the glass archway behind. There was a pole sitting on the bottom sill with a strange brass-like hook attachment, and I realized that was for opening the top sections of these windows. I did so, letting the cool and fresh night breeze in immediately.

"Skreeeee!" I heard a high-pitched, thin whistling note of a sound from the dark, and knew it was Ymmen calling. I gave a long and high whistle back.

"You should return to the cave," I murmured aloud, knowing that the dragon would be able to hear my words in his thoughts as well as with his super-sensitive hearing. "No sense in you and Uncle freezing out there tonight." I thought about what Abioye said. It *was* too dangerous to continue with my plan now – but what about in the gloom of pre-dawn? Maybe I would try again, sneaking out to get the scepter?

"Not leaving," Ymmen said strongly – even defiantly. "You are in danger," he added with a mental hiss. Well, there was nothing new about that, I thought pragmatically. I tried to think of a way to convince him that everything was going to be quiet, at least until pre-morning.

"No. You *are* in danger. I can sense it," Ymmen said, and in my mind there flickered the dragon's sense-image of Dagan Mar, and it was knotted up with anger and outrage and pain. For a moment my mind stumbled – where was he getting this image from? Ymmen had never even met Dagan as far as I knew, had he?

"Dragons see the songs. We hear the songs," Ymmen said quixotically. I wondered then, if he had plucked those impressions of Dagan out of *my* mind? "I am always with you, Narissea. As you challenged the little limping man," the dragon explained. "Dragons know fire. We know anger. That human's anger is vile and will not stop."

I wondered then at the sharpness of a dragon's senses – that somehow Ymmen could see different sorts of anger and emotion – *and thoughts?* – as I might be able to read different tracks of the animals that I had learned how to hunt? But whatever – Ymmen was absolutely right that Dagan was still abroad, and would always be a danger.

"We are not leaving. Not while that human is close," Ymmen said, and the tone in his voice made me see that there really could be no arguing with him at all.

"Okay, wyrm," I said in a softer voice. I didn't know why I thought of that word, but it suddenly felt right – a fitting affectionate almost-insult.

"*Hsssss!*" He lashed his tail in my mind and withdrew, but I could feel that he wasn't really angry.

And as for myself – I crept onto the large bed, surrounded myself with blankets, and had to admit that it felt good to know that there was an adult Bull dragon out there in the night, and that he would be watching over me from far away.

CHAPTER 23
SACRIFICE

"*Awaken, Narissea, awaken!*" Ymmen's words tore through my panicked dreams, which had been full of tight, underground places and ice.

"What is it?" I gasped, my hand already finding the handle of the Lady Artifex's knife where I had kept it close under the blankets. I didn't need to ask as I heard a rattle at the door, and the handle starting to turn. But I had locked the door!

I gasped, rolling from the bed to land, barefoot, on the cold paving slabs below, facing the door. I was certain I had locked it – and the key was there on the low table by the side of the bed. For an instant my knife hand lowered – it had to be Abioye, didn't it? Something must have happened during the scant few hours that I had been asleep, and he had come to warn me.

"*No! Danger! Fight! Attack! Survive!*" Ymmen roared in my mind, so powerful that I staggered a little, putting one hand on the edge of the bed to steady myself. He was incensed, and his thoughts were full of fire and flame.

Whomever this was, it wasn't Abioye.

"What do you want?" I shouted, already snatching up the green cloak in one hand as the door opened.

It was, of course, Dagan Mar – and he held in his hand that hateful little hatchet that I had seen at his belt for four years.

"Oh, it's only me, Narissea," he hissed.

"Abioye! Montfre!" I shouted. I didn't think Dagan was coming to put a pair of manacles on me, and I was right.

There was a muffled thump and a gasp from outside in the hallway, and Dagan snickered as he raised his hatchet and stepped forward in a defensive crouch. "Oh, they're not going to save you, girl. They're occupied." He barged into the middle of the room and I jumped backwards onto the bed.

"It turns out that there are some guards who don't want to wander off into the sunset under that fool of a boy." Dagan lashed out with the hatchet, forcing me to jump backwards again, putting the bed between us.

"And no one trusted the mage-boy anyway." Dagan swayed from side to side as he edged around the bed towards me. At my back was nothing but the window – and then a few hundred feet drop.

Ymmen!? I thought, my eyes fixed on the glitter of cold malice in the man's eyes.

"I'm coming! I'll tear them limb from limb!" he roared in my mind.

"And Inyene won't miss you, you know. She won't even remember you after I tell her that you killed Abioye and we had to deal with you." He lunged at me suddenly in a fast snake-like snap. He was fast. Deceptively fast.

I yelped and bounded over to the other side of the bed again, as Dagan bolted after me.

Dagan's limp was clearly not as bad as he had pretended. He was going to reach me before I could ever have a chance to get to the corridor – *and then what!?* I threw myself backwards, kicking out at the low table as I did so, for it to scatter across the floor and into Dagan's legs.

"Grargh!" He gave a short snarl of frustration as he stumbled. There were now more thumps and shouts coming from outside in the corridor. Did that mean more guards?

"Slave!" Dagan roared, filling the word with every ounce of hatred that he had.

I had to kill him, I realized, with the knife in my hand. I couldn't run away.

"For my people." I ducked forward and lashed out with the Lady Artifex's dagger.

Clang! Somehow, Dagan had swung the hatchet up to bat the dagger away and then lunged forward, hooking the dulled edge of the hatchet over my wrist as he pushed my arm out – and then twisted.

What kind of move was that? "Agh!" My wrist bent back on itself and the pain was excruciating as I reflexively dropped the Lady Artifex's dagger. It was either that or have my wrist snapped, I thought.

I had never even seen someone use a weapon like that before, and panic rose in me as he forced me back towards the wall. Despite our relatively similar sizes, he was still the stronger of us two, and I was off-balance with my arm pushed back.

I had never been properly trained in weapons. Although the Daza *did* know how to fight – we'd had our wars and our raids as any other peoples did – all of the weapons that we Souda used were primarily hunting weapons. Spears, bows, javelins, or thrown bolas. We trained with them in order to bring down big game and scare off the Plains predators, and only rarely practiced fighting hand to hand against other armed warriors.

And I guessed my four years underground – with no combat practice whatsoever – showed as well, as he easily slammed my shoulder with his other hand, driving me against the stone wall.

"Narissea!" someone shouted. It sounded like Abioye, but it could have been in my mind, as my head bounced off the wall. For a moment, everything went black.

I leapt back into consciousness with the vision of Dagan pushing me by the shoulder against the wall, his hatchet raised back over his head in an overhead blow. Time itself had slowed down and every detail of the man about to kill me was in sharp relief. I could see his small eyes, sunken into his face but nevertheless still glittering sharply. As he roared I could see that he had two missing teeth in his jaw. I could even smell the tang of his horrid sweat as it came off of him.

"Fight! Attack!" Ymmen snarled in my mind, but I didn't have weapons with which to fight anymore.

"You have your claws!" he ordered me in a heartbeat, with all of the ferocity of a grown Bull dragon.

I did have my claws. I lashed out with my hand as if I were a wild cat, not caring as my cracked and dirty nails struck and dug into the side of his face.

"Gah! You little—!" Dagan shouted as he recoiled. But it wasn't enough. He was still in striking range, and I was still forced up against the wall. He still had his hatchet held high, and all of the muscles of his arms under his tunic bunched as he swung the nasty little weapon down.

"Yagh!" I did the only other thing I could do, throwing Abioye's green cloak at him, and managed to turn my wrist at the last moment, just like I was throwing a deer net. The cloak flapped and spun, wrapping itself over Dagan's face and arm as he gurgled.

I lashed out with my foot and felt an immediate thump of pain as I had used the edge of my bare foot against his shins, and realized that I should have stamped with my heel instead. But Dagan fell back, still entangled in Abioye's green cloak. Now was my chance!

I dove for the gap between us as Dagan tore at the cloak, ripping it from himself, his hatchet making a tearing noise as it cut through the heavy wool.

There was the Lady Artifex's knife, lying on the floor just a little way ahead of me. Dagan was right there behind – but having no weapon would be even worse for me, so I stooped to snatch up the blade.

Pheeet! Just as Dagan's hatchet whistled past my head.

I swore, pushing out with my feet to let my momentum carry me into a roll as Dagan hit the paving stones behind me. I was at the door-way, I could see the windows on the far side of the hallway, I was almost out.

"Come 'ere!" Dagan grabbed my hair that must have come loose and was billowing behind me. I screamed in agony as I was jerked back-ward – but, with a pain that was almost unbelievable, he tore a hank of hair straight from my head as I threw myself forward.

"NARISSEA!" Ymmen roared in my mind as I tried my best to scramble forward – aware of the pulse of something hot and wet at the side of my scalp.

"I got you now!" Dagan crowed as he lunged through the door.

Terror lent speed to my scrambling as I managed to half crawl, half run to the far side of the corridor, with Dagan slowing to a panting, loping stride behind me. *Where were Montfre and Abioye?* I wondered for a moment in panic.

Dagan was right behind me – but an Imanu's daughter wasn't going to be gutted on the floor like a boar! I turned over, holding the blade in both hands, my arms shaking with the energy of the fight. I could see the two other doors on this floor, Abioye's and Montfre's, were also open, and there were still the sounds of thumps and grunts from inside. From my low vantage point I could see a little way into

Abioye's reception room, and there were pieces of furniture and smashed terracotta vases all over the floor. For some reason, my eyes caught upon the upended and cracked model of Torvald and the sacred mountain of the dragons – and it was totally ruined.

I'm not dead yet, I realized, as I raised my head. My heart was pounding in my ears and now the side of my face was also wet with blood where Dagan had taken his gory trophy from me.

Ymmen? I thought, as my hands shook on the blade held before me.

"I'm coming, brave one!"

But Dagan was already towering over me, as it seemed that he had paused to take a breath. A wide smile lit his features and made them ghastly. "Here." He threw down the hank of hair he had torn from me to my feet. "I think this is yours? How fitting for one of your kind." He sneered, taking a deep breath as he casually tossed his hatchet from hand to hand. "Isn't this what you savages do out there in the Empty Deserts? Take trophies of your kills?"

No, it wasn't. If my fury had been stalled before by the pain, suddenly it evaporated in the incandescent, white-hot heat of a dragon friend. We Daza took horns, pelts and furs yes – and sometimes even talons or claws if we had to deal with a ferocious big cat or similar. But none of them – *ever* – was a 'trophy' in the way that I knew Dagan Mar meant.

They weren't 'prizes,' I thought as anger made my limbs shake and my teeth crunch together. Every piece of our kill that we kept was useful to us. If it was a prey animal then we ate it, or turned its marrow into tallow or boiled down its bones to put on the crops. If it was a predator animal that we had been forced to kill – always in self-defense – then sometimes we took a memento to serve as a part of the story of the animal and the fight. It was never for personal glory. It was to further the story of the tribe.

The Song. I realized in that moment what Ymmen must have been talking about, all along. Stories. It was all about stories. It was all about the generations that came before us, and all of those hundreds of thousands of tiny acts of bravery and compassion and honesty.

And my song was as a dragon friend to Ymmen the Great. The words enlivened me, as I heard myself start to growl up at the ridiculous little man. *And my song was as the daughter of the Imanu of the Souda.* I rose from my crouch, keeping my eyes straight on Dagan Mar as he, too, readied himself to pounce.

And my song was as the woman who got away from the mines of Masaka. And brought them to their end.

"It's not the Empty Deserts, you fool," I hissed at the man who had been my tormentor for four years. "It's called the Plains!" I swung for him.

Dagan grunted as he skipped back, before darting forward once more just as quickly, flicking his hatchet to swipe at me.

I growled, ducking under the blow. I wasn't little Nari anymore, the girl who had run across the Plains. And neither was I Narissea the slave girl either. I felt like I was a hunting wolf, or a falcon, or – a dragon!

"SKREAAYARGH!" Suddenly, all light from the distant camp and the stars behind us were blacked out in the same instant as there was a deafening roar – and the crash of glass. Instinctively I ducked as glass exploded outwards from all around me, and for the first time, Inyene finally had a real live dragon at her keep.

"Kill! Burn! Destroy!" Ymmen's roar of outrage surged through me, turning the insides of my mind into an inferno. And yet I wasn't afraid, and I wasn't thrown by his current of fury as I had been before. Now, it was as if his emotions perfectly matched mine, and we jelled.

We became one.

Ymmen's front claws clamped onto the stones of the broken windowsills, scratching their hard surface as he gripped onto the side of Inyene's keep. The gallery windows were just large enough to allow his head and neck to come through, just over my shoulder. The dragon's anger empowered me and protected me. It didn't feel like we were different creatures at all – but rather we were extensions of the same thing. Two parts of a greater, furious, fiery whole.

I raised myself up as the last of the glass and window fragments scattered ahead of me like a wave.

There was a look of pure terror on Dagan's face as he leapt backwards from the blast of the shattered window. Once again, everything appeared to fall into slow motion, and every detail was picked out exquisitely in that teetering moment. I saw Dagan's alarm turning into outrage, his body flexing as he moved, and the flickering flames of the wall torches as they guttered back into life. I could even see the sparkling glints of the torch light on the most miniscule fragments of glass at our feet – it was as if the dragon had overlaid his senses onto mine. Even the distant sounds of crashes and grunts from Abioye and Montfre's fighting appeared to have slowed.

And there was the gleam of bright light on the edge of the Lady Artifex's dagger in my hand as I moved forward.

With a sudden thudding of my heart, everything flew backwards into furious, fast-paced time. Dagan swung his arm holding the hatchet in an overhead throw and it spiraled through the air – not towards me, but straight at the dragon above me!

"No!" I ducked my head as the handle sailed past, inches from my bleeding temple. "Ymmen!" I shouted in alarm, to see the weapon hit his nose as he turned his head. There was a crunch as the hatchet was thrown with enough force to crack a scale.

Attack! Kill! I didn't know whether those feelings came from me or Ymmen, but they surged through my heart. *No one does that to my friend!* I threw myself forward, striking out with the dagger.

But Dagan was too quick; he was already dodging to one side, spinning on one foot (*where had that limp gone now?*) as he lashed out at me with his off hand.

It was a backhanded cuff around my head. The chief overseer was powerful enough and experienced enough that it made my head bounce backwards, but I was still on my feet as I swung for him again.

Dagan snarled as he grabbed my wrist in midair with one hand, while grabbing another handful of my hair with the other. He seemed too good at this brutal, nasty way of fighting.

Just as he was too strong for me! He was pushing my blade back down, using his wiry force to make the Lady Artifex's dagger point back towards my own chest!

"Narissea!" There was a roar and a heavy thump and a torturous screeching noise as Ymmen tried desperately to force more of his claw into the gallery, to scrabble and scratch at the man attacking his bond partner – me. But the space was tight, and I was in the way, and Dagan was already yanking on my hair.

I let my feet slide out from under me – partly because there was nowhere else to go, and partly to avoid Dagan pushing my own blade into my heart. At the same time, I reached to grab Dagan's tunic with my off hand, dragging him down with me.

We hit the floor together in a heavy tangle, and for a horrible, terrifying moment, all I could smell was Dagan's acrid sweat and see his pale and blotchy skin, sprouting uneven stubble. His body was bony and repulsive as I bucked, kicking out with my legs and pushing him *away, away, away!*

And then it happened. I caught a glimpse of my own hand around the Lady Artifex's dagger as if it belonged to someone else – as my wrist twisted and I sank the blade into his black heart.

Dagan made a strange little noise, as if he was surprised and confused, before falling backwards from me and hitting the floor, a wide circle of blood quickly pooling underneath him. The dagger was stuck in his chest as I saw that, horribly, he wasn't even dead yet. He gave me one last blink, and a sneer twisted the corner of his face, before his eyes finally closed.

No last words, I thought to myself. Not even at the very end – he had nothing to say to defend himself. Only hatred.

I had seen other people die before, of course. Death was not an unnatural thing after all – but back on the Plains it had been the deaths from accident or illness or of those much older, who had been surrounded by their loved ones and friends. I had also seen people die here in the mines. Horrible, terrible, tragic accidents that had crushed limbs and stolen breath.

But somehow, despite this life that I had lived – one where I had walked so close to death on a daily basis – I was still unprepared for this one.

"*He was your rival,*" I heard the dragon beside me whisper into my mind. And I knew that Ymmen was right. Dagan had dominated my life in a way that Inyene hadn't – she had been a distant shadow, a background menace always – but nothing more than that.

It was Dagan who had made my life hell. And now he was dead. I didn't quite know how I felt about that. In fact, I didn't actually feel any different about myself, or what I had to do – which in itself was strange.

But my dark thoughts were broken by the clamor of bells and the high-pitched *pheeet-pheeet* of the guard whistles. "We have to get out of here!" I whispered, as bonfires exploded into life beyond the dragon's shoulders on the opposite wall.

WHAM! There was a sudden explosion of sound from beside me as Montfre's door was blown open in a cloud of splinters, and the bodies of two guards literally flew through the air across the corridor to tumble against the floor, and for the young mage to follow it out, lurching, with the fresh-cut staff that I had found for him glowing an eerie blue at one end, and smoking.

"Montfre!" I gasped. The young mage's clothes were ripped and torn, and it looked as though he had one hell of a fight.

"We must leave, fierce one!" Ymmen was saying in my mind as he clutched onto the edge of the window.

Yes, I thought. We had to get everyone out – my heart thumped an instant later, *Abioye!* I spun around to his open reception room and ran forward.

The reception room was completely, entirely destroyed by the fight that must have raged in there. The ridiculous spindly-legged tables were all smashed and in splinters about the place, and even the wall hangings had been torn from the walls.

But my attention wasn't on the room – it was on the two mine guards who were lying dead on the floor – and on Abioye himself lying in the middle of them. In his hand was his fine, slim-bladed rapier, and it was drenched in blood.

"Abioye!" I said, running to him.

"Hgh... Nari?" he whispered as he opened his eyes. He had a graze down one side of his face, and when he tried to move he winced and hissed in pain, as I saw that there was a tear on his shirt, and the fine linen was dyed a deep red.

Thank god he's alive, I thought, and was surprised at the sudden strength of my emotion.

"Dear stars!" I gasped as I saw the size of the jagged wound on his chest. I didn't even give him a moment as I placed my hands above and below the cut and gently pushed at them. It was a nasty cut – but the blood wasn't flowing from it, I was grateful to see.

"Your ribs protected you," I whispered. I had seen similar grazing injuries when any of the tribe had lost a fight with one of the wild bull deer of the Plains. If the blade had been turned just a fraction in a different angle then it would have punctured straight into the young man's chest, and probably taken his life.

"Stand back," Montfre whispered urgently, as he lurched and stumbled in behind me. The clamor of the keep alarms were only getting louder, and I could feel Ymmen's agitation in my mind.

"Bolts! Fiends!" I heard him roar. The wall guards were firing on him – on *my* friend! But as I crouched here with Abioye, looking up at what Montfre was about to do, I heard a mighty, thunderous crack that I recognized as the wings of the mighty dragon snapping. I don't know if he was using them to blow the crossbow bolts out of the sky, or whether he was merely folding their thick, protective leather over his body.

"Uria-isia, las-vitae…" Montfre whispered above me, and then I felt as though all of the hairs on my neck stood up at once. I felt that strange breath of a wind that didn't move any hair on my head or the clothes on my body. The feeling of this mage's magic made my teeth grate in my jaw – but it wasn't the same, sickening nausea that I got from the magic of the mechanical dragons.

Montfre stepped lightly in at my side and lowered the end of his staff towards the groaning, wide-eyed form of Abioye.

"What are you doing?" I heard him whisper.

But Montfre's face was flushed, and his eyes were filled with a whitish radiance as he concentrated, and the very tip of the staff glowed a pale and hazy blue as he dropped it lightly onto Abioye's wound.

Abioye hissed and winced in pain before the blue radiance spread out across the cut, sealing it and leaving a wide, silvered scar. *Magic doesn't heal as well as a body can,* I saw. *But it works faster.*

"Up," Montfre said, and I could see just how clearly the effort that casting the magic had taken from him. He panted as he took his staff and slid it into the belt at his tunic, and even that effort appeared to cost him.

"Montfre?" I asked questioningly, as there came the clatter of running feet.

"No time! Hurry – I'll be fine!" the young mage snapped.

So, I hurried. I reached under Abioye's arms and pulled him unsteadily to his feet, allowing him to lean on me. Despite the fact that the young lordling was healed, I got the sense that it wasn't a *true* healing. Abioye was breathing shallowly as I almost had to drag him to the door.

Ahead of us, Montfre had seized up Abioye's sword and was hurrying in his loping, gasping weakness to Dagan's body. I saw the young mage wince, then pull the Lady Artifex's blade from the dead man's chest. He returned to slide the Lady Artifex's blade into Abioye's belt before standing back and raising the sword at us both – the sword wobbling slightly in the air as he did so – just as the first wave of guards appeared in the stairwell.

"Montfre!" I gasped. "No!" I could see precisely what he was intending to do. He was making it look as though *he* had been the one to attack Abioye and kill the guards. He had already killed two of them by blowing out his door with the staff – and it wouldn't be any great stretch to the imagination to assume that the dangerous young mage – who had already defied Inyene and destroyed her workshop before – would have acted again.

"It has to be this way," Montfre whispered as the guards surged into the hallway, raising their cruel black-handled crossbows to fire.

"Dear stars!" One of the guards fainted at the sight of Ymmen's giant head and coiled, hunched neck just inside the windows. The dragon had shielded us from the bolts of the wall guards and was doing his best to keep his head down *and* keep an eye on us at the same time. The other guards saw Ymmen and fell into a panicked commotion – as no one had clearly *ever* prepared for this.

"Not at Lord Abioye, you idiot!" one of the women of the guard – clearly some sort of captain – shouted from behind the terrified cross-bow-wielding guards.

Montfre barked a totally unimpressive and clearly fake victory laugh as he turned towards Ymmen.

Take him, I begged, but the ancient black dragon – who was far older and wiser than any of us in the room – had already understood Montfre's plan, already thought of what I had suggested. The dragon reached forward with a snap of his jaw, seizing the young mage by the back of the tunic, before throwing himself backwards from the wall.

It all happened in an instant, like watching a big cat on the Plains strike. And then there was another thunderous snap of his wings, and the dragon was gone – his dark shadow turning into a blur of claws and scales, with the dangling Montfre somewhere in its middle.

"My heart!" I threw the thought back at the disappearing dragon, knowing that he would be able to hear me.

"Mine," Ymmen said in my mind, and coming with it was a surging tide of savage affection, joy, victory – all mixed up with frustration at having to leave me behind.

"My lord!" The guard captain was hurrying towards us, her eyes flaring as soon as she saw me. "Unhand him! Get back, slave!"

"If I let go of him, he'll fall over," I said evenly. I was really far too exhausted and in too much pain to care anymore. And I had killed a man today, I thought, and my eyes inevitably found the stilled form of Dagan Mar on the floor, still with that cruel little sneer on his face.

I guess it's stuck there, now, I thought with a shiver of revulsion.

"It's okay, Captain Ennis," Abioye gasped beside me. "I'm fine – my... *aide* here was helping to defend me against Montfre." He struggled for words, and I wondered if that was due to his ordeal or having to denounce the only boy who had been his friend. "The mage went berserk," he said. "He was shouting something about Inyene, and the years that he had been mistreated, and how he was going to get the Stone Crown all for himself. He killed his own guards, and then when Dagan came to stop him..." Abioye shook his head sadly.

"Don't worry, my lord – we'll catch him. That one was always a monster!" Captain Ennis said with obvious distaste. But she shared a wide-eyed look with the other guards as they were all hanging around, looking faintly out of place as they surveyed the destruction.

It was the sort of look which said, 'I don't know how anyone is going to stop a dragon and a mage!'

Ha! I thought – moments before I had my answer to just exactly how a mage and dragon might be dispatched.

That feeling of cold-without-cold and nausea flooded over me like a wave again, just before I heard the deep whirring and clacking sounds of the mechanical dragons spring into the air from what must have been the keep's roof.

"Ymmen! They are following you!" I counted the sounds of metal thunder as each dragon soared after my bond partner. *Fifteen,* I told him. Anxiety clutched at my heart. Fifteen against one? Even if they were smaller and slower – each one presumably had that crescendo of fire that the very first one had.

"Have no fear, fierce Nari." Ymmen's voice in my mind sounded, if anything, enthused by the prospect – and not worried in the slightest. He sounded joyous as he hissed his soot-laden words into my heart, "Nothing under the stars can fly faster than a dragon."

Just be safe! I thought desperately, aware that the guard Captain Ennis was talking, but I was unable to concentrate on her. With any luck, she'd just assume that I was being a slave and not really care if I didn't talk.

"Safe! HA! Dragons are never safe in this world, little Nari," Ymmen said with a flick of thunder and flame in my mind and was gone.

"I'm telling you, I don't need a healer!" I blinked my eyes to refocus on what was going on around me. It appeared that Captain Ennis was trying to convince Abioye to be treated. *I can't leave Abioye alone with these people!* My heart thumped with panic. The thought of leaving Abioye's side, while there were clearly guards around here who wanted him dead, well, it wasn't going to happen. My hands clutched a little tighter at the young man.

"I can treat him," I found myself saying.

"You?" Captain Ennis was looking at me with a scowl of distrust, before offhandedly barking at the others, "Get these men moved! Clean this place up!" before turning back to regard me with some very high amounts of suspicion.

"We people of the Plains have many old and remarkable remedies that the people of the Midmost Lands do not." I put on a slightly thicker version of my accent just for the captain's approval. From each of my earlier dealings with the Midmost Land guards and over-seers, I'd learned they all seemed to have little disregard for the Daza – but I had also discovered that their complete lack of knowledge was accompanied by a sort of fear that we could do 'strange and unnatural' things.

"Oh." Captain Ennis looked at me warily a moment, and then at all the blood and mess that was around them. "Well, see to it, then!" she snapped, before turning to one of her men, "Astrid, find the Lord Abioye a room in the Western Halls. See to it that the Lady Inyene is informed of her brother's condition, and the"—I saw Captain Ennis look to the shattered windows from which Ymmen and Montfre had fled—"*situation* with the mage and the dragon," she ended a little uselessly.

"Yes, sir!" Astrid the guard nodded, flicked a desultory look at me, before nodding that we were to follow her.

As we marched away, my eyes found Dagan's body on the floor once again. No one had dared touch him. It was only then that I felt a weary sort of victory. He wasn't going to hurt anyone ever again.

CHAPTER 24
TO THE EAST

"**Y**mmen?" I whispered into the misty grays of the pre-dawn air.

I stood at the window of a new room, this time in another part of the keep called the Western Halls, and with Abioye's new suite of apartments next to my quarters just as before. This room seemed narrower and draftier than the other had been – not that I truly cared.

But what I *did* notice were the few small attempts that had been made to make this place a little more comfortable. There were fresh linens piled up – even vases of flowers. In just one day since the dreadful battle with Dagan Mar, the news that I, a lowly Daza girl, had saved the Lord Abioye's life had spread about the keep. I wondered if the small gestures of friendship that I received – as a woman carried yet another platter of food to my room and gave me a small smile – came from Inyene, or from the servants themselves.

This woman was like all of the keep servants, a Three Kingdom Westerner. Not the dark-haired Daza like myself. It felt wrong to be waited on by her, and I hurried to take the platter of food from her so she wouldn't think me lazy!

"Thank you," I murmured, catching the woman's eye. "I don't mean... I didn't ask..." I tried to express the depth of shame I felt by this.

"No, thank you." The woman had cherry-red hair, and although she had the same bags under her eyes and slightly harried look of all of those under Inyene's command her smile was genuine. "For saving Lord Abioye's life. He's the only one who tries to make our life bearable around here," she confided in me.

He does? I blinked. I had thought him a foppish fool before last night!

The servant must have seen my surprise because she nodded as she rearranged the linens a little. "He argues on our behalf with his sister – even for those working in the mines." A darker look passed over the woman's features. "Better food rations, more breaks, that kind of thing." She looked up at me, setting aside her harrowed look. "And he speaks to us. Like we're people."

"You are," I insisted, but my words had seemed to upset the servant woman, as she bobbed her head and hurried out of the room.

Dagan had been wrong about how Inyene's people feel about Abioye, I saw. Or, even if Dagan *had* managed to find some of the guards who would help him try to assassinate Abioye, then there appeared to be many others amongst the lower servant class who liked the lordling.

Because he's nothing like his sister, I thought. *Or Dagan.*

"I am here," the dragon breathed into my mind. He sounded sleepy, and his thoughts were fuzzy and warm. Around them, I could sense some kind of cozying dark, and – wind in the trees?

"Young Wood," Ymmen confirmed, saying it like it was a name, although I had never heard of the place. "It is north of you, in a valley untraveled by humans."

He had gotten away from the mechanical dragons. *"Of course!"* he whistled in his sleep, and my heart felt as though one more weight had left it at last. But there were still many more.

"Montfre? Tamin?" I asked. Tamin had been with Ymmen before Dagan's attack, and since I hadn't seen him at the window, I realized that Ymmen must have placed him down somewhere.

"I did. Can't fight holding an old human," Ymmen said with a flick of his tail.

Wyrm, I thought, with an edge of playful warning.

"They are with me, here. They agree this place is beautiful. You should let me bring you," Ymmen said in my mind. *"You can even bring the Poison Berry, if you like."*

It seemed Ymmen's distrust for Abioye had subsided an awful lot since they had their 'chat' on the roof of Montfre's tower, though I still sensed a vein of humor for the young man coming from Ymmen.

"I wish I could fly away," I sighed sadly. It was a nice thought, living free – out there in the forests and glades and mountains… and the skies.

"You are a child of the wind," Ymmen breathed his words into me –

and they came with all of the promise of the coming dawn, of the fresh chill of the rising breezes as they peeled off the mountain tops, to the higher and wider currents of the skies that brought with them the tangs of faraway places – touches of incense or woodsmoke, or green, living things.

You soothe me, dragon, I thought, as I allowed my eyes to close and my head to rest against the window for the briefest of moments. It had been like that out on the Plains. With the breeze in my hair, and the ability to read the scent of distant game as the breeze flurried and eddied. Only this dragon-sense was much, much stronger. For a second, I caught the wild possibilities that were out there, waiting for me in the future as I grew with Ymmen.

But the sound of the morning bells of Inyene's keep erupted, and they weren't the delicate sort of 'tinkling' that I would have expected from looking at the model of the Torvald citadel. Instead, they were the harsh clamors of guards beating rough-cast bells, awakening the slaves of the Masaka mines. *Well, those who weren't on the night shifts, anyway,* I thought.

"I can't fly away and leave them," I said, my heart clenching as I thought of Oleer (if he even still survived) and the others. "I have to see this to the end. I have to stop Inyene, somehow." Even despite Dagan's death – or perhaps especially because of it – I was even more aware now that the danger had not passed. Everything had changed and nothing had changed. The keep had spent the rest of the night in uproar, with guards running back and forth through the halls, checking windows and doors and lighting even more bonfires as Inyene had ordered every guard she had to the walls.

At least that meant there were fewer down with the slaves, I thought glumly. It was a very small sense of satisfaction.

But now, even despite their chief overseer dying, the morning bells were ringing once again, and the slaves of the Masaka were being dispatched down the mines. The terrible, torturous ordeal of my people had only continued.

And I should be down there with them. The angry thought flashed through my mind, hot and guilty. How dare I stand up here, surrounded by luxury and with plates of fresh and dried fruits brought up to me while my people – my friends – were down there in the dark. I thought once again of those ghost stories that we had used to scare each other with, of the Daza ghosts knocking on the stones and forever lost to the wind.

"We need to stop Inyene," Ymmen surprised me by agreeing. And not only agreeing, but by including himself in my quest.

Huh?

"Silly human. You? Me? We? There is only one thing. That is *Us,"* Ymmen said, and I got a sense that when he said 'us' he wasn't just talking about me and Ymmen, but by something much deeper, much more profound.

"Songs," I whispered.

"Songs. We are all a part of the same song. And Inyene threatens all," Ymmen said, and his mind grew brighter and hotter in mine as he turned his full attention to me. It was like I had been walking through a cold corridor, to suddenly open the door to find the heat of a blazing bonfire.

In those flames of his mind, there were flashes of images, snatches of words, feelings, and faces.

And almost all of them were dark and terrible.

I saw a great, boiling thunderhead laced with purple lightning rising over a rolling, green landscape, and it howled like the voices of a thousand lost souls.

I saw a great mass of people trudging and marching over muddied fields – but these people weren't moving like normal humans – they were *shambling,* and I realized that each and every one of them was one of the Dead.

"No!" I gasped at the horror, but the visions continued.

A woman sitting in an ancient cave, with hair that might have once been golden but had long since turned a platinum white, and as she cried and sobbed, between her hands grew a strange, twisted sort of vine with poisonous-looking purple thorns, thrashing and lashing out ahead of her.

And then I saw a singular white tower, standing high above the other walls and battlements of a vast castle – *no, a citadel,* I realized. It was Torvald, but Torvald unlike I had ever seen it before. The skies were black and boiling, and the walls of the citadel were topped with strange mechanical devices – great gears and wheels, and as I watched they moved, spewing out a torrent of lead shot – straight into an oncoming wave of dragons who were flying in formation across the sky, spiraling downwards.

"Torvald attacked dragons!?" I whispered in horror. This was against everything that I had ever been told.

"The Dark King once did, when he ruled there," Ymmen growled, and the visions shut off, leaving me gasping and sobbing. I wondered if he was showing me these things to try and put my troubles in perspective somehow. If that had been his motive, it hadn't worked – now the world of the Midmost Lands and the Three Kingdoms just looked like a litany of catastrophes and despots.

"Yes," Ymmen agreed, breathing fire behind his words. "That is one of the reasons why many of my kind have vowed to no longer have anything to do with the land of the humans," Ymmen explained. "We dragons can remember long, far longer than even *you* imagine, dragon friend," he said mysteriously. "And that means that we can see the melody and rhythm of the song long before any other creature."

"The same notes play out every time there are humans and dragons. Always there are the dragon friends, and there are always those others who steal our power." Ymmen said all of this, and I was amazed at how eloquent he was. Something had happened to the bond that we had between us; either I was learning to understand his thoughts better, or we were each growing closer, allowing more communication between us.

Because we were one thing, I remembered the dragon's philosophy.

"Inyene is as bad. Or will be," Ymmen said finally, and then there was a new image – of the fifteen circling the keep and the mines of Masaka, but from far up above – so high that I couldn't hear the racket that they made from my vantage point.

"They haven't stopped. Haven't slept. Haven't fed," Ymmen told me with great suspicion. "There is nothing that will tire them from their destruction."

And they had no fear. I nodded. And none of the natural instincts that any other animal had. If Inyene ordered them to attack the Plains – or even Torvald – then that is just what they would do – even once their wings had been ripped from their back or their sword-talons struck from their paws.

And she is only making more of them, every day, I thought in horror.

"Yes. We cannot let her get the Accursed Crown," Ymmen said, and I sensed that the dragons had an entirely different view of what the Stone Crown was, and what it represented. I nodded gravely. This was the only way to truly save my people.

I was about to ask Ymmen about the 'Accursed Crown' and what he knew of it (*why had I never thought to ask him that before?*) when there was a rapping on my chamber door. I jumped, whirling as the door was pushed open. For a moment my mind saw Dagan Mar standing there, miraculously alive and still intent on killing me – but it wasn't him, just another guard that looked a little like him. I hadn't been given the luxury of locking my door this time, I thought.

"C'mon, next door," the guard growled. He was one of the unfriendly ones, apparently, as he waited for me to grab my cloak and then halted me, patting me down for weapons. As I no longer had the Lady Artifex's knife, I had nothing. "Walk in three paces, bow, and kneel. And stay down!" The guard pushed me roughly on the shoulder the short trip past the complement of guards who lined the walls, and Abioye's open doorway.

The room was large and sumptuous, and it was gray with early morning light. Abioye himself lay on the wide bed, breathing shallowly but looking a lot better, propped up with pillows.

And there was Lady Inyene herself by her brother's bedside – sorry, *Queen* Inyene, I saw, as she had added an iron circlet to her brow. I froze briefly in the doorway as I saw her. She was dressed in many layers of gossamer white dresses, embroidered with the greatest skill in purples, reds, and gold. Over this was a long, floor length sort of coat, somehow in a silvery-white hue. When matched with her red hair and the drawn and pinched white skin of her face, her visage reminded me of the image of the Dead, marching ceaselessly, tirelessly. Inyene had something of that same relentless force of will about her.

But she was very much alive, her eyes gleaming with a hard intensity as she turned quickly to regard me like a falcon spying prey.

Three steps forward, bow and kneel, I remembered, doing everything the guard had said that I should. Inyene waited for me to perform the necessary honors that she demanded, a small, pleased sigh of air coming from her when my head lowered, and I knelt.

How insecure you must be, to constantly need everything around you telling you that you are strong! I thought with disgust.

"You are the slave Narissea, are you not?" Inyene said. I was about to look up and answer, but it seemed that the self-appointed queen did not even need any input from anyone else, as she continued. "My brother, the Lord Abioye, has told me of your bravery during the atrocious act of treachery by the mage Montfre," she said. It sounded like a speech, although she was only addressing me, the guard standing at my shoulder, and Abioye on the bed.

"A great ruler is also a beneficent ruler," she said, and it sounded like a familiar saying or a quote, though I had no idea from where that quote came. "And so, seeing that you are *so* smitten with your liege lord—" Inyene said with apparent hilarity. I blushed. It wasn't like that.

"—I will offer your village clemency for their crimes against the True Throne of the Three Kingdoms!" She ended on an apparent flourish.

The thrill I'd felt at the word 'clemency' died in an instant, giving way to fury. *What crimes! What is this 'True Throne' nonsense!?* I kept my eyes cast down, lest she see how outraged I was. This wasn't news that I could even *dare* to be happy with – nor could I dare to believe she would ever keep her word.

What about all the other Daza on the Plains? What about the Daza down there in the mines? I thought.

"Well, applaud, you imbeciles!" Inyene hissed when her dramatic statement was met by nothing but confused subservience from the guard and me.

I swallowed back a growl. If only I had the Lady Artifex's knife at my side about now. But though it pained me, I did clap, as did the guard at my shoulder, and even the guards who stood outside in the hall.

"My only condition for your village and you to be freed from their debts is that you return my brother, victorious, with the Stone Crown," Inyene said in a satisfied fashion.

Which was never going to happen, I knew as I kept my face lowered.

It wasn't just that I didn't know if we would ever be able to find her precious Accursed Crown. It was also the fact that the pride of my mother, and of a dragon, and of myself blossomed within me in that moment.

I will never trade the freedom of my people for your gain, I thought. The Daza – stars, all of the free peoples of the world – were worth far more than that. We were not pawns or bargaining chips. We were part of a larger song.

"And so, my dear brother"—the 'Queen' Inyene then turned her attention to Abioye, lying before her—"I graciously give you permission to leave. Immediately. At first light," she said with a beatific smile on her face.

"I... uh... now?" Abioye blinked in surprise from where he lay on his convalescence bed, with bandages wrapped around his head and wrist. It had barely been a day and a night since the fight.

"Yes, brother dear." Inyene's beaming smile faltered as a frown wrinkled across her forehead. "It has been made clear to me that there is now a pair of dangerous renegades on the loose about my lands. Montfre and the black dragon. We cannot allow them to halt our plans!" she said vindictively.

"And so, to that end, I am sending you and a full complement of guardsmen ahead, and I will also be rewarding you with a company of my finest dragons," she said.

Uck! I felt appalled.

"I will be sending more supplies and troops after you, but for now it is far more important that you get this done." Her eyes glinted cruelly as she regarded her brother. "Any brother of mine, one with the blood of the High Queen Delia herself coursing through his veins, will see this as an opportunity."

Abioye looked steadily at his sister and nodded that, yes, he understood – and when Inyene turned her back to the room to gaze out into the eastward dawn and continue her tirade against Montfre, the lord Abioye and I shared a look.

Yes. This was going to be our opportunity. Our determined eyes met. And we were going to use it to bring Inyene down.

END OF DRAGON CONNECTION
THE STONE CROWN SERIES BOOK ONE

Dragon Connection, 25th December 2019

Dragon Quest, 29th January 2020

Dragon Freedom, 26th February 2020

PS: Love dragon fantasy? Keep reading for exclusive extracts from **Dragon Quest** and **Dragon Called**.

INDEX

Daza: the name for all the peoples of all the tribes living in the "Empty Plains"; includes the Souda, Metchoda, Uoda, Jinda tribes.

Dragon Rider: graduate of the Torvald Training Academy; a human bonded with a Dragon.

Dragon Spine Mountains: the mountain range running north to south, running along the Middle Kingdom's western boundary.

Earth lights: crystal that glows green or blue when exposed to any kind of light and holds onto that radiance for long periods of time, used to power mechanical dragons.

Empty Plains: the Torvaldite (or "Middle Kingdomer") name for the Eastern Plains.

Imanu: the name for a Daza wise woman; a leader within the tribe.

Masaka Mountain: the location of the Masaka Mine complex; one of the mountains within the mountain range running north to south, dividing the Middle Kingdom from the Eastern Plains. The entire mountain range is referred to by the name Masaka Mountains by the Daza; see also World's Edge Mountains.

Metchoda: the name for one of the Daza tribes, meaning "People of the Open Places."

Middle Kingdomer: the Daza name for the fair-skinned people of Torvald; also Torvaldite.

Roskilde: an island nation, once considered enemies of Torvald.

Souda: the name for one of the Daza tribes, meaning "People of the Western Winds."

Soussa winds: the Daza term for a gentle wind upon the plains.

Stonedog: a creature of the World's Edge Mountains, a fierce predator the size of a small pony, with skin like plates of rock.

Torvald: capital city of the Middle Kingdom; also once the name of an Empire, ruled by an evil wizard-king, and consisting of the Three Kingdoms of the Midmost Lands (North, Middle, South).

Torvaldite: the name for the fair-skinned people of Torvald; also Middle Kingdomer.

Tozut: the Daza term for horse dung; an insult.

World's Edge Mountains: the Torvaldite and Red Hound name for the mountain range running north to south, dividing the Middle Kingdom from the Eastern Plains, last refuge of the wild dragons; see also Masaka Mountain.

THANK YOU!

I hope you enjoyed **Dragon Connection**. Please don't forget to leave a review.

Receive free books, exclusive excerpts and be kept up to date on all of my new releases, when you sign up to my mailing list at AvaRichardsonBooks.com/mailing-list

ABOUT AVA

Ava Richardson writes epic page-turning Young Adult Fantasy books with lovable characters and intricate worlds that are barely contained within your eReader.

Her current work is 'The Stone Crown Series.'

She grew up on a steady diet of fantasy and science fiction books handed down from her two big brothers – and despite being dog-eared and missing pages, she loved escaping into the magical worlds that authors created. Her favorites were the ones about dragons, where they'd swoop, dive and soar through the skies of these enchanted lands

Stay in touch! *You can contact Ava at:*

f facebook.com/AvaRichardsonBooks

BB bookbub.com/authors/ava-richardson

BLURB

She can save her people—or doom the world.

Narissea faces an impossible choice. Armed with a map discovered in the hidden shrine, she's forced to lead Inyene's heir through the wilds of the Plains to claim the ultimate prize. For only the wearer of the Stone Crown can command all dragons, and take the High Throne that rules over the three kingdoms.

To place the crown's power into Inyene's hands is unthinkable. Yet failure to obtain it means certain death.

But the small band is not alone. Vicious mercenaries seek the crown for their mysterious patron and attack Narissea's expedition when they least expect it. In the ensuing chaos, the map is torn in two, forcing Narissea to rely on her memories of landmarks and stories passed down by the village elders to make her way through the Plains and its treacherous Sea of Mists.

When Inyene suspects betrayal, she sends her mechanical dragons against the beleaguered band, and the sands erupt in an epic clash of forces. Narissea's desperate decisions threaten to alter destinies, but she'll do whatever it takes to save her people.

No matter the consequences.

Get your copy of **Dragon Quest**
Available January 29th 2020
AvaRichardsonBook.com

EXCERPT

Chapter One:

Nightmares in the Wind

Just as it always did in my dreams, dappled sunlight played over my face from the thin trees around me, and their branches sighed with the rising *Sousa* winds of the Plains.

Good, I thought. The sound of the breeze would hide my approach, and I took a careful step out from the straggly copse, towards where the tall grasses—like a blanket of gold and yellow—started.

My short bow was in my hands, and at my hip was my knife. I had everything I needed to complete the hunt…

There. A flicker of movement from the tall stalks. *It went against the flow of the Sousa,* I registered. My quarry was in there, trying to remain hidden. I crouched, trying to ease the excited hammer of my heart. My first solo hunt! If I could complete this—then everyone at the village could see that I was ready to start my responsibilities as the Imanu's daughter. My mother would start teaching me the more complicated stories of the Daza, the tales that only the wise women and elders called the Imanu would share with each other. I would learn the true names and proper-ties of the Twelve Sisters—plants and herbs whose use was restricted.

I would be trusted in village council meetings; my voice would be listened to, and they would ask me—Narissea of the tribe of Souda—how I would shape the future of our people.

I paused, nervousness playing through my body in flashes of heat or cold. I wondered if I was truly ready. Even after three days alone in the Plains, surviving just by my wits and what I had been taught—I still felt anxious.

But this was what I had been trained to do, wasn't it? I steeled myself as the winds plucked and picked at my dark hair like it was attempting to soothe my spirits. *'Step into your life, fierce little Nari...'* I remembered the parting words of my mother.

Yes. My future was waiting there for me, out in the Plains—and all I had to do was reach out and grab it—

Crunch. There was a sound from the grasses ahead, and I tensed—before remembering to unwind the knots in my shoulders and arms. You had to be calm to perform a successful kill. If I was going to take a life of the Plains, then I had to do it swiftly and as respectfully as possible. The animal that gave its life so that we might feast should suffer as little as possible.

A shadow appeared in the near grasses—dark, and taller than I was expecting.

I breathed in, pooling the breath in my chest as I raised the bow—

The creature stepped nearer, and the grasses wavered in front of its approach.

Calm, Nari, I told myself, before offering a heart's prayer that I would get this right—

"Slave!" A man burst from the grasses, his face twisted in a snarl of rage as he spat the word straight at me. He limped on a twisted leg, and his eyes were like small sparks of flint. And in his hand was the small leather-tailed whip that he had beaten me with many, many times.

It was Dagan Mar, the Chief Overseer of the Mines of Masaka.

And there on the left-hand side of his chest, jutting out horribly and spreading a sheen of red down his tunic was the handle of the knife I had used to kill him.

"Slave scum!" Dagan roared. Not even being killed could quench his anger as he lurched towards me—

"Argh!" I screamed, kicking at the coarse and heavy blanket that had been given me for a bed. I was not out on the Plains. I was not performing my three-day Testing.

And the undead shade of Dagan Mar had not returned to take his revenge on me.

"Dear Stars…" I breathed as I gasped and struggled to a crouch. Around me was the canvas tent, half-filled with boxes and barrels and sacks of our provisions of our expedition.

Well, Inyene's expedition, I corrected myself as I reached for the skin of water I had left by the side of my makeshift bed. Unlike the other Daza slaves who had been ordered along on this crazy mission, I was allowed to sleep in the store tent, on my own. To be honest, I would have preferred spending the night with the others—even if that did mean having my feet manacled together with everyone else's. As absurd as it was to admit—the gentle murmurings of quiet talk or soft snores reminded me of the Tribal Hall of the Souda where there were always people day and night—either working or sleeping. Many times, I had fallen asleep before one of the fires, competing for space with our hunting dogs as the voice of the Elders told one of the old tales.

And now, of course, I thought, *most of my people apart from the ones here were all back at Inyene's Mines.* Who knows how many of the faces that I knew so well were still alive? *And I was the Imanu's daughter.* If it was anyone's task to keep them safe right now—it had to be mine.

I sighed. Sometimes I didn't feel like I had done a particularly good job of that.

A foot stamped outside—it had to be my guard. Even though I had garnered enough trust for saving Lord Abioye D'Lia's life—the younger brother of the self-styled 'Queen' Inyene—to avoid being manacled, that 'trust' didn't go so far as not being kept under watch, as the canvas door flap was pushed aside and the gruff voice of one of Inyene's guards called in. "Hoi, what's going on in there!"

Ugh. I ignored him as I stood up and stretched, irritably grabbing my few possessions. The scowling guard at the tent flap didn't really care if I was having nightmares or not—just that I wasn't attempting to run away, or eating all of the provisions or something. I picked up my cloak and my belt pouches containing the few belongings I was allowed—a flint, some twine and hook for a fishing line, and a few of the dried and gathered herbs that I had managed to harvest so far—as the guard grunted again and stepped away, seemingly satisfied that I was just crazy—but not disobeying Inyene's rules.

Inyene's rules and her damned Laws! I kicked one of the sacks of grain, before wishing that I had at least thought to put on my sandals before I had done that. "Ow!" A sack of packed grain seeds was surprisingly solid.

That 'lady' of the Middle Kingdom had terrorized the Daza people of the Plains (*what the Western Three Kingdomers called 'The Empty Plains'*), and, from what both her rebellious brother, Abioye, and the young mage, Montfre, said—using a strategy that she had long been developing. She believed that she and Abioye were descendants of some long-dead High Queen Delia, and that gave her the right to do anything and everything to win her throne back... including murdering people, hiring mercenaries, twisting the laws to her own ends, and enslaving entire villages to work in her Mines, collecting ore and Earth-Light crystals to create her army of mechanical dragons. Inyene had even resurrected ancient 'Laws' of the Middle Kingdom, tying them to her offerings of loans and supplies, only to increase what the Daza owed by adding debt and forcing them to work for her.

"Sssss!" A hiss of annoyance filled my mind with a sense of reptilian outrage. It was my bond partner, Ymmen, the black dragon whom I had helped heal in the mountains of Masaka.

"Foul things. Insult to all dragon-kind." Ymmen's feelings were even stronger than mine on the subject of the mechanical dragons— and I didn't blame him, as the mechanical, clockwork, and steam innards were clad in the stolen and discarded scales of living, breathing dragons.

It must be like seeing someone wearing your friends, I thought with a shiver of horror. At least we Daza gave up prayers of respect for the animals we hunted and skinned. At least we even protected the beasts we also hunted from the wandering prides of wildcats or wolves!

All Inyene was doing was trying to build an army that would overpower any opposition. There was no respect or honor there. Just greed.

Which was why I found myself in this stupid fixed-pole tent. I grumbled as I got myself ready. I could tell from the sounds of the distant Hooping birds somewhere outside that it was before dawn. The sky would be graying and the Plains dark, perhaps with the first mists lying over the ground. I used to love this time of the day, second only to dusk, when the Plains would come alive with mournful birdsong and the calls of the distant herds of antelope, bison, gazelle, and the gigantic bull-like grazers we called the Orma.

"You could leave. Fly with me and the others," Ymmen suggested, although I could sense through our mental connection that the dragon's thoughts were tinged with wry acceptance of what he knew my answer would be.

"Ahh, Ymmen—if only…" I said with more than a twinge of regret. And I dearly wanted to see my two friends whom Ymmen was currently looking after: the mage, Montfre, who had worked for Inyene but rebelled, and my god-uncle, Tamin, who had helped me escape from the Mines. But as much as I wanted to see them, I knew that would risk what I had to do here, on this expedition. There were Daza here who needed protecting, and Montfre had already taken the blame for killing Dagan Mar. If any guard saw him or the black dragon, then they were sure to send a messenger or bird back to Inyene to summon the rest of her mechanical dragons to hunt him down!

"I know. I had to ask. Again," my dragon friend said. It was his way —he was mature even by dragon standards, but there seemed to be some part of his reptilian heart which despaired over the circles that we humans ran around in.

"Ha!" I sensed a blossom of sparks and a lizard's mirth. Which I guessed meant that I had been right.

But Ymmen knew as well as I did why I had to stay here, with Inyene's expedition across the 'Empty' Plains to find the artifact known as the Stone Crown. *I* was the one supposed to be navigating them, thanks to my Daza heritage. And I was the one who had been promised, not just my own freedom, but that of my people if I managed to help Inyene find it.

And if Inyene got a hold of the Stone Crown, then she wouldn't just have her mechanical dragons at her beck and call—she'd also be able to control all of the natural dragon-kind, too…

"Never!" the black dragon growled deep, filling my mind with frenzy and ash.

"No, never," I swore.

There was a grunt from outside the tent, and the flap of canvas was once again pulled back for the broken-faced guard to glare in at me suspiciously. "You're talking to yourself again?" I saw his hard eyes flicker across the store boxes and sacks, as he expected an accomplice to be hiding in the shadows.

"It's a Daza thing," I said contemptuously, throwing the green cloak around my shoulders, fastening it at my throat and storming towards him so fast he had to step out of the way.

"The Lord Abioye wants you anyway," the guard growled at me, hurrying to keep pace with me as I marched across our makeshift camp.

"Good." I announced as haughtily as I dared (I was still, technically, a slave to these Westerners—albeit one who 'knew' the way through the Plains). "Because I want to speak to him, too!"

Even to my own ears, my comeback sounded a little weak. *Ugh,* I sighed.

Get your copy of ***Dragon Quest***
Available January 29th 2020
AvaRichardsonBook.com

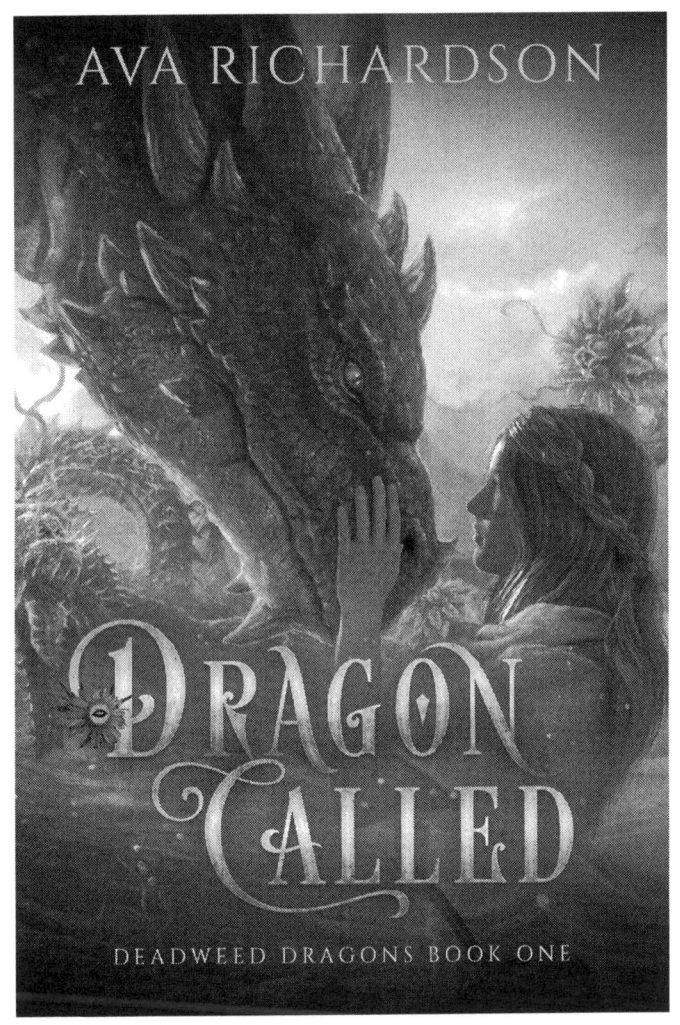

BLURB

In a kingdom that has fallen into chaos, one young woman—and her dragon—are thrust into the role of bringing balance to the land.

From the moment Dayie washed ashore as an infant, everyone in her tiny village treated her as… different. She didn't belong, no matter how hard she tried. So when a vicious, deadly scourge called Dead-weed overruns her village, she's blamed and sold to the Dragon Traders for fear of her powers and the mystery surrounding her origin.

After years of service to the ruthless Dragon Traders, Dayie wants her freedom. To repay her debt, Dayie steals a dragon egg. But she winds up with far more than she bargained for when her egg hatches before she can get it to them. Now she must hide her hotheaded young dragon Zarr or risk losing him: either to the Dragon Traders or the Deadweed that's creeping ever southward.

When the Dragon Traders travel further south to evade capture and Deadweed attacks, Dayie meets a mysterious Dragon Rider named Akeem, who tells her magic is behind the spread of the Deadweed, and that she's been bonded with Zarr—for life. With these revelations, Dayie now faces a choice: give up her dragon for her freedom or take her place with Zarr in the Training Hall of Dagban. There, she may have the chance to avenge her parents' deaths and solve the mystery of ever-spreading Deadweed.

Dayie's destiny awaits, if she's brave enough to follow it…

Get your copy of **Dragon Called** at
AvaRichardsonBooks.com

EXCERPT

Chapter 1: Dayie, where she shouldn't be

"Go, quickly now, girl!" hissed the stocky and shrouded shape of Fan Hazim; my mentor, boss – and owner. She didn't waste time on the niceties, I noticed, but then again, she never had in the eight years I'd been in her 'employment.'

Employment. That was a joke. As if cleaning pots and folding canvas and doing the thousands of other things I had to do for Fan's travelling crew was really a job. I never saw any money, all of it going to work off my 'debt' for having the misfortune to be sold at age seven to this woman.

"Well, what are you waiting for? I have to get back to the Festival, and we can't let the Torvaldites suspect what we're up to!" Fan flicked her dark hair over her shoulder and gestured to the small crevice with one tanned arm, heavy with the deep blue inks of her tribal tattoos. She called herself a Headwoman of her tribe of itinerant wanderers – but I had never seen her join in with the old Gypsy songs with the others around our caravan campfires.

Another glare from Fan and I knew that I had dawdled enough. "Fine. Just don't leave without me," I muttered, hunkering down to crawl into the crack in the rocks of Mount Hammal.

"We'll be gone before morning, child – so you'd better be back before then – unless you're already dragon meat!" Her cackle echoed behind me as I crawled and scraped my way through the stones of the sacred mountain of Torvald and into the home to their infamous dragons.

The tunnel was tight, and it smelled slightly of old mouse droppings

313

or perhaps fox. Nothing seemed to live here now though, and I wondered if the great lizards that I was climbing towards had eaten them.

No, they're far too small, aren't they? I thought glumly, remembering Fan's ghoulish words just last night, in out camp outside the walls of the citadel of Torvald. "Dragons eat sheep and cows and deer – and most of all, they like the meat of young women!"

Ha. I'd never heard that the Torvald Dragons – those noble beasts that were ridden through the sky by the Torvald Dragon Riders – ate people. The wild mountain blacks, and the Sand Dragons yes, but not the Torvald ones.

Back home in the southlands, our dragons came in just three sorts – and all of them were as mean as a hungry desert cat, or so I had been told. We had the blacks, the orange and yellow Sand Dragons, as well as the much smaller Orange drakes, whereas up here in the north they had the Sinuous Blues, the Stocky Greens, the Giant Whites and of course the Crimson Reds. I'd seen the Torvald Dragons many times as a part of Fan's surreptitious travels, but I had never been as close to them as I was about to be now.

This was a dumb idea, I thought once again as I teased out the tiny bit of earthstar crystal on its chain that Fan had given me and knocked it a few times on the rocky walls to get it to wake up. I didn't know how it worked, but I was very pleased when the little shard of blue crystal started to glow a faint blue-white light, allowing me to see a few feet ahead. The tunnel rose unevenly over rounded rocks and jagged piles of rockfall littered its course.

Please don't collapse on me, I thought as I pulled myself up over the hump of stone and squirmed under the next shelf of rock. But I was light – I wasn't stocky like the others – Fan and her husband Rahim, their only son Naz, and their small crew of other Gypsy travelers. I stood out like a string-bean in a field of potatoes with my thin body and my long, platinum-white hair. Another reason I had ended up with the Hazim family, I guess. The villagers who had adopted me had been certain that I was a witch.

A few fragments of rock scraped and moved under my grasping hands and I froze, my heart hammering even as my breath stilled in my chest. I waited for the ceiling to shift, but it never did.

"Come on, get this over and done with!" I whispered at myself, knowing that even if I failed, it would still be a long trek back down the sides of the mountain to where the Festival of Summer was in full swing.

That was the reason why Fan had driven us all the way up here – or I guess you could say that was the cover that she had used to get us here. The rest of the Hazim troupe had transformed our caravans into show booths, and, Fan Hazim was no doubt returning to one of them to dispense made-up fortunes from tea leaves and playing cards. The others would be playing instruments or performing tumbling tricks for the fat, complacent people of Torvald. We would be just one more troupe of performers in a sea of others by the outer walls of the Citadel – easily overlooked, and hopefully just as easily forgotten.

"It has to be tonight," Fan had told her husband Rahim, her husband, just last night. "The Festival offers us the only opportunity to sneak into the Dragon Enclosure and get our hands on some ACTUAL dragon eggs from Torvald stock."

Rahim, ever the avuncular, and friendly one that I had liked far more than his wife had surprised me by nodding his agreement. "And it has to be Dayie," he had said about me.

Cheers, Rahim.

I was the thinnest, and I was the only one of the troupe who looked like I might have actually grown up in Torvald (which I hadn't – I had far too many scars and bruises for that) with my fair complexion. If I was caught, I might be able to lie and say that I was just a stupid city-girl who had thought to have an adventure. I'd probably still be punished, but not as badly as a foreign emissary from the Southern Kingdom, sent to steal Torvald's most valuable asset.

The rocks moved again, but this time when they shifted a little, they let in a chink of fresher air. I was close!

"Now, where are you?" I whispered, holding up the light. This tunnel I was in continued on into the darkness, but the shifted rocks had opened up a smaller, narrower cleft in the rocks above from which was *definitely* flowing a river of fresh, cool night air.

Do I continue, or try for up? What had Fan told me – that these tunnels were ancient, and that the dragon mountain was riddled with them? I could be stuck in here for days if I didn't take the chance now!

Gritting my teeth and wiping the sweat from my already dirt and dust-smeared brow, I chose up.

"Almost…" my fingers (bound with strips of linen to stop the sweat and help me grip) searched and dug at the walls until I found a crack big enough to haul myself up from. "There!" The muscles in my back ached as I pulled and kicked until I could brace with my soft-booted feet against either side of the chimney walls and reach up a little further.

In this way I climbed up the rocky walls of Mount Hammal, following my nose.

Maybe I should have chosen the other route, I had a moment to think just as the rock I was shoving at gave way, and I burst to the surface, scrabbling quickly hand over hand, seizing at handfuls of tall, whip-like grass and panting as I collapsed. Above me, the vegetation waved in the night, the thick-leaved trees making a sighing sound as their branches shook a little – and between them they revealed the brilliant stars of the night sky.

There was the Hog, and the head of the Serpent. I recognized the stars that could be seen even down in the southlands, but the rest of them were a mystery to me. These strange northerners and their strange stars, I groaned as I flipped over, and found myself staring at a giant dragon claw.

Holy crap. I blinked, staring at the sleek black sheen of the claw. It was curled like a cat's but whose inner edge had small serrated burrs that I knew would be able to rip leather and wood and even metal. It was also about as big as my entire torso.

But thankfully, there currently wasn't a dragon attached to the other end of it. I was looking at an old talon from either a long-dead dragon or the result of a horrible injury to the Enclosure dragons. From the size of the thing, I suddenly understood why the Southern Kingdom were so keen to have another Torvald dragon.

Okay, Dayie, think... I folded myself back into a crouch, searching my travelling pouches attached to my broad belt for the little thick brown glass pot of salve that Fan had given me. She had watched as I had slavered it all over every possible bit of exposed skin just before sending me down the tunnel, but I didn't want to take any chances, and so reapplied the thick, goopy paste again.

"This will hide your scent. The dragons will think that you're another dragon," Fan had told me, which made me wonder at what under the stars she had used to make this vile stuff. Nope. Actually, I really didn't want to know.

It was only after I had managed to walk a few meters down the sort-of trail between the thick vegetation that I stopped to wonder: *Aren't dragons insanely territorial?* Had Fan meant that I would smell like one of the *Torvald* dragons, or *any* old dragons? I stopped, waiting for the shrieks and chittering of alarm from the Enclosure around me – but nothing happened.

"Phew!" I whispered, and then clamped a hand over my mouth. *And didn't dragons have the best hearing in the world?*

But no one had managed to get this far, that I knew. And so I took another few hesitant steps. The ground underfoot was damp and thick with the hummus of this strange place. It looked a little more like the oases that scattered the southlands, spiky-leafed plants or trees with strange, fibrous barks next to spreading leaves. Past the vegetation, the silhouette of the high walls of the Enclosure cut across the skyline. The Dragon Enclosure of Torvald was huge and sat inside the same mountain that the Citadel of Torvald climbed. It was here, in this ancient crater that the Torvaldites bred their dragons before sending them up to train at the famous Dragon Academy, to be their fire-full steeds, dominating the skies.

"Sussussuss-r!" The sound of the hissing whistle—close by—made my heart skip a beat. I waited for the alarm call to start, but only that strange, wheezing sort of hissing noise returned.

"Mamma-la, mamma-la…" my voice quavered on the words of the song that I used ever since I was a little girl. A song that I don't even remember learning, but one that I knew was a part of my heritage.

I had been adopted by the villagers of Happa when I was just a little girl, and even though they did not know where I had come from, (a shipwreck, they thought, because they found me on the beach there) I had arrived with just one thing to call my own: this song ingrained in my memory. My adoptive parents had said that it must be the nursery song of my real mother, and that my mind had clung onto it because of the terrible events that I must have been put through. All I knew, was that when I sang it, I felt safe, and it seemed to calm the Gypsies' horses and dogs too. I don't know whether it worked on dragons, but I was willing to try anything in order to not get eaten.

"Mamma-la, mamma-la," I sang, my voice sounding thin and stupid in the night air.

"Sussususs…" the whickering hiss eased a little, and, as I pushed aside the foliage to step forward, I saw why. I wasn't dealing with an angry, territorial dragon but with a sleeping one.

It was beautiful. The Great White was curled up around itself, nose to tail like a giant, house-sized cat. Its bulk had flattened and crushed the trees and bushes around it, making a sort of nest for it to sleep in. Its scales gleamed dully in the starlight, looking almost milky and translucent, and my heart squeezed in awe at the sight.

I had never seen a dragon this close, and I didn't think any of our retinue had seen one like this either. The dragon was massive, larger than all our caravans stacked end-to-end – but it also looked serene and comfortable; cute even in the way that it huffed and sighed in the night. Its scales were a blanket of armor that fitted naturally and perfectly, some of them burnished and smooth like mirrors, others smaller and hard like nails. I had never known that there was such variation in their skin, I thought as the Giant White went from ash-colored, to chalk, marble, milk and silver.

"Mamma-la," I whispered once more, and the Giant White's lungs sighed a deep breath. It made me feel honored and special in a way that I had never felt in all of my years with Fan Hazim.

Maybe I *can* do this, I thought, seeing where a small trail led out, behind the nest of the Giant White and up the near slopes of the Enclosure wall and to where a line of caves was bored into the rocks.

All dragons lay their eggs in caves, right? At least, that is what the wild southern dragons do... With a last, lingering look at the sleeping dragon, I picked up my pace and skipped up the slope, towards the dragon caves.

The air from the mouth of the cave was warm and tinged with a scent that I did not recognize—somehow fragrant and slightly bitter at the same time – a little soot, mixed with rose or jasmine, perhaps?

Now standing on the ledge in front of the line of caves, I could look out across most of the Torvald Dragon Enclosure to see that the entire caldera wall was marked with them. Fan had been right that this place was riddled with caves, it seemed – and from a couple I saw thin ribbons of smoke curling sluggishly into the night air. Those were the occupied ones, clearly.

But which one to choose? I regarded each of the nearest entrances in turn. None of them had smoke – but that didn't mean that they weren't occupied, right? For some reason, my steps were drawn to the last, smallest of the three caves. As I crept forward, my soft boots crunched a little on the layer of grit and sand, I noticed that the opening was smoothed as with the passage of many feet. *Claws, Dayie – they're called claws,* I reprimanded myself.

I pressed on, to the mouth of the cave, my heart in my throat as I peered in…

The starlight reached into the cave over my shoulder, illuminating a large mound of fibrous material. Hay and straw and leaves. The Dragon Riders must stock these caves with bedding material, I realized.

They're here. They're close. I knew in my heart in the same way that I would know when one of Fan's horses was slowing down because she was about to throw a shoe. I had never questioned these intuitions before, they had always just come naturally to me in a way that my adoptive parents Obasi and Wera had said was a gift, though it was a gift that other people wouldn't understand.

My feet moved closer into the murk. I didn't use the earthstar crystal this time, not wanting to accidentally wake up a mother dragon on her nest!

But there was no mother dragon here on this mound of nesting materials. The stones underfoot and the rocky walls already radiated heat, and the large eggs that I could now see were already packed down, deep into their home. There were three of them, each the size of a large melon, but egg-shaped, not round. They were each speckled with dots, some of which gleamed in the starlight.

Without thinking, I reached out a hand to the nearest egg, to find it warm underhand. This one would hatch soon, I knew without understanding how, and the egg quivered just slightly under my skin. There was a baby dragon in there – *what did they call them, newts?* – and I had never felt so elated in all of my life.

It wasn't the achieving my mission. It wasn't the joy that this would bring to Fan, or the money that it would earn, or the hope that it might eventually bring to the Southern Kingdom itself. It was just the fact that it was me, little Dayie, here with such a new life that was fragile and strong all at the same time.

I didn't need any more encouragement. I drew out the padded egg-sack that Fan had made for this purpose, and, very carefully tugged it down over the egg and lifted it up.

It was done. I was now a Dragon Thief.

Get your copy of ***Dragon Called*** at
AvaRichardsonBooks.com

WANT MORE?

WWW.AVARICHARDSONBOOKS.COM

Printed in Poland
by Amazon Fulfillment
Poland Sp. z o.o., Wrocław

55751655R00190